I0680180

Fatal Choice:

The Last Days of the U.S.A.

Charles E. Rickard

Dorfin Publishing

P.O. Box 628

Randallstown, MD 21133

*Cover designed by: Tommy Bruno Designs
Los Angeles, CA*
www.tommybruno.daportfolio.com

ISBN-13:   978-0-9834540-1-4
ISBN-10:   0-9834540-1-9

Dedications

This work is dedicated to the land I love, the United States of America. It may be old fashioned to say it, but I truly am devoted to this nation and concerned for its future. I could weep for what I see coming. It is my sincerest wish that she will survive and again flourish with honor and pride.

Acknowledgements

I could never have finished this work without the help and insight of my most ardent critic, my son, Charles. He is an absolute genius at seeing through me and my writing. It is a bit unnerving, but a wonderful gift.

I want to thank all of those people that have had a undying faith in me through the years; especially my daughter Mary, and my parents, Billy & Sara.

My wife Nikki has been a true miracle in my life. Her cooking, caring, and sheer will-power has gotten me through many arduous and tiring days, and given me the strength and determination to not only complete this but most of the other activities in my day to day efforts.

Lastly, I want to thank God for giving me the ability and insight to bring this to you.

Author's Notes

In 1979 I saw in some obscure, long forgotten article a story about Executive Orders 11490, and 11921. I could not believe what I had read. After calling then Maryland Senator Paul Sarbanes' office for copies, I received them a few weeks later in the mail. Obviously that was long before computers and the internet.

Everything I had been told in that piece was true. That was when I began my search for the reality of what was truly going on while most of us were living our lives and paying our bills, not knowing for sure what that was. As I began to learn more and more, I tried to share it with anyone I could, simultaneously boring and disturbing friends and colleagues alike.

When Alexander Haig made a run for president it hit me. With all of the progressives and liberals, or whatever they were calling themselves at the time, trying to destroy the foundations of this great country, it would take a strong military man to pound in the final nail.

I wrote the Epilogue and what is now the first half of Part 1 in 1991, but did not finish. As with the rest of the country, I admit I became somewhat complacent.

When Bill Clinton was elected, I had renewed interest. That diminished when it became apparent that he was much more a playboy and showman than an ideologue.

Always remaining in the back of my consciousness, I did not put words on paper during the Bush administration either, even though I full well knew he was a big government liberal and certainly not a savior.

After their TARP legislation and the current administration with the Congress, Senate, and Supreme Court's undeniable national socialist programs, I could no longer wait. The end result is this novel of our near future.

Let me state with as much clarity as possible. I pray to God that nothing in this writing comes to pass, that the nation wakes up and turns on those who would destroy us. However, I am saddened to say, I doubt that will happen. Deep in my heart I know that not only is everything presented here possible in one form or another, it is highly probable.

I have said thousands of times over the last thirty years, there will come a day in the near future when each of us will be called to choose a side. God grant us the strength to select the correct one and defend our legacy with valor and honor.

Take what you will from all of this, but please, be prepared.

C. Rickard

A Personal Message

My name is not relevant. I am chronicling the events of these past years as best as I can. I was deeply involved in much of what happened; however, I have no intention of revealing my identity or that of my colleagues who supplied the details that I lacked.

I also have the experiences, thoughts, and firsthand knowledge of hundreds of people I have interviewed. Many I knew personally, but most were introductions. I believe I have accumulated the best information available. A lot of it I am making available in this recounting, with much more held in reserve for future use.

I will try my best to limit my words to our experience and my research. But as anyone who has been through a devastating series of events can tell, you do form opinions. I promise to limit them as much as possible to the furtherance of the story.

I have filled a few holes with speculation, but only to help the story flow. Everything important is strictly the ascertainable facts.

Life in the United States was changed inexorably and will most likely never return to what it was just a decade before the battles began. The good fight was fought and hopefully culminated though not with an anticipated or acceptable results; only time will tell if that is the case.

The old adages "Nothing is ever what it seems." and "Follow the bucks." was never truer than during that time… and now. As in the first Civil War, brother fought brother and kin betrayed kin at all levels of society. Paraphrasing an old saying for your edification, "Don't believe anything you hear or see, it's all a lie."

Understand that I am trying to relate the facts as I know them, and on a time line that will make sense as the story unfolds.

It has been difficult for all of us. Most have lost everything they had worked their entire lives to attain and will never be able to retrieve or rebuild any of it. Many have lost loved ones, through active destruction or neglect. The change has been mind altering in every way imaginable.

Basically cynicism is all we have left. I saw at one time that a definition of a cynic was one who searches for the truth. If that is so, then I am that seeker, as I am still looking for that level of honesty and some sort of sanity. I have also concluded, it doesn't exist outside of spirituality and God... and now unless He tells me directly, I don't believe anything I see or anyone I hear.

I sincerely live in the hope that time will heal the wounds both physically and mentally of a once glorious nation filled with enthusiastic, hardworking, and compassionate people. But alas, that is most likely a dream of a land and time long gone.

Prologue

Saturday, April 15th, 2:17 pm, CDT

Limousines lined the street on the 1800 block of Davis Avenue near Hutchison Boulevard in downtown Dallas, Texas. More were double parking as law enforcement officers guided them into their spots and immediately checked their identification.

Chauffeurs mingled loosely with men and women in black suits who wore government-issue dark glasses even though the clouds in the sky blocked out the sun and threatened rain.

Two police helicopters circled tightly around the air space involved, adding an aura of importance to the entire scene. TV station copters were hovering at a distance of several blocks as evidently they were prevented from flying over the main staging area.

The concrete steps to the First Southern Baptist Church were clear between the sidewalk and the front façade of white pillars and dark wood double doors. Part of the same contingency of the suited people stood silently before those doors.

An air of expectancy was clearly evident by their demeanor, glances about, and slight calculated movements.

Local television crews milled about in a restricted area to one side of the church. They were prepared and anxious to send their version of the event out into the ethos as soon as possible.

Cordoned off behind them and on the opposite side of the church were the uninvited crowds expectantly waiting for something to occur. Anticipation was written on all of their faces. This was indeed a major event.

They didn't have long to wait. Within a few minutes four of the front doors were flung opened wildly as hordes of a wedding party emerged in a flowing stream of humanity. The typical scene developed of well-wishers, guests, and wedding party members loudly mingling and interacting.

The crowds on either side of the police barriers joined in with shouting and applause. There was pushing and prodding to the point of generating concern on the faces of those whose duty it was to prevent any problems.

All of the suits were anxiously milling about, talking to whoever was on the other end of their earpieces.

The exuberant bride and groom exited and greeted everyone. A man expensively attired in a dark blue suit followed them smiling and waving as was expected.

This was Senator Milford Keiferland of the Fort Worth Keiferlands. He was accompanied by his wife of thirty years, Nancy. Both were beaming as they watched their son move with the grace only developed through the efforts of time and training.

Another couple followed them, the parents of the bride. They were likewise thrilled at the events unfolding before them. Their clothing did not reveal their lower status on the social ladder. If one were able to see their faces up-close, the pinched skin around the eyes and mouth would clearly reveal a myriad of worried thoughts coursing through their overly active brains.

They were never convinced that the marriage would work out, but they had reluctantly kept their thoughts to themselves.

Within seconds none of the troubles felt or emotions sensed and not revealed was to count as more than a speck of minutia in the sand of time as black figures with automatic weapons emerged from the trunks and doors of five of the recently arrived limos. Before any of the government and private forces could get in more than an occasional shot, the bodies began to pile.

Only moments later two flashes were seen a few blocks away as missiles were launched almost instantly blowing the police copters from the sky. Debris from one of them rained upon the holding area of the television crews; blackened slabs from the other careened into the street behind the crowd of screaming onlookers on the opposite side killing and injuring those in the way.

Three of the hooded figures broke from the others and focused their attention on the wedding party who were frozen in their places for the mere seconds that had elapsed. Their fear turned to panic as they eventually turned to run back into the church. This was to no avail as others were behind them and blocked the way. As if lined up before a firing squad, the bodies fell and those behind them became victims only seconds later.

Neither the bride, nor the groom, nor their parents had time to change any of their thoughts or feelings that were previously foremost in their consciousness. They were some of the first to die.

Only minutes later two vans screeched into the area knocking several of the remaining onlookers back onto the sidewalks. With no resistance remaining except for the occasional shot made by a half-dead agent totally missing the mark, twelve of the attackers ran for the vans. They carried three of their fallen comrades and tossed their bodies into the vehicles and climbed in immediately afterwards.

Through the half open doors they shot anyone that was still moving as they sped away.

When the vehicles were out of sight, a few of those people still alive stood or leaned against something and surveyed the area. It was a scene of total mayhem and gore.

One reporter and a camera-operator tried to compose themselves and shoot what they saw. As she tried to speak, the tears poured from her eyes and ran over her black smudged face. Her voice cracked and she finally stopped even attempting to describe the unthinkable horror before her. The camera said it all as it broadcast every detail to a terrorized world.

PART 1:

Antebellum

1

A tall man in his early fifties walked quickly, almost running, down the hall of the White House. This was Ron Erickson, the Chief of Staff to the President of the United States. A lone bead of perspiration rolled quickly down the right side of his normally passive face, and weary eyes were lowered in their dark encircled sockets.

His slumped shoulders belied the weight of his position, even though he continuously tried to rectify his posture with little avail. Once a strapping young man and semi-pro athlete, his six foot body expressed in every way the enormous beating his psyche had taken managing his office.

Never in his wildest thoughts had he imagined the character of the man he was serving existed. He never hesitated when his party asked that he handle the affairs of their titular leader because of their innate distrust of him.

As he arrived at the President's bedroom door one of the two secret service agents on duty walked toward him anticipating his questions as they always did. It was truly quite annoying.

"Is the President still awake?" Erickson asked, breathing quickly and shallowly.

The agent nodded and said, "He just a moment ago stepped out and told us he was turning in. I'm sure he is still finishing his drink."

He caught himself smiling a little thinking of the President's predilection for detail and protocol. Many of the men and women that had frequented those rooms and halls resented the confining nature of the office, this life style, and the code of behavior; but not this man. He relished it all.

To Jake Madison everything in this experience bolstered his opinion of the one person he admired the most, himself.

Erickson tapped lightly on the door and heard, "Come in".

The voice that worked its way loudly through the door was strong, confident, and very authoritative, even with those two short words.

He turned the knob and entered to find an impressive man of amazingly average stature standing in a robe next to the bed with a drink of milk in his hand.

Looking first at Erickson and then at his milk, he smiled and said, "Join me?"

Shaking his head cautiously in the negative, he answered, "Have you seen the news?"

"No. I've been trying to do some reading and relax," he quietly responded, a look of concern crossing his now serious face.

The president reached for a remote on his nightstand and clicked it. A rather small screen above the fireplace came to life. There was a young male reporter grasping his ever-present microphone and fairly shouting into it as various rescue personnel scurried around behind him.

"Yes, Steve. That's all we know." He almost couldn't get the words out and appeared to be authentically shaken. There was no typical television news emoting present in his tone or words.

A voice responded and the picture went to a two shot with the reporter on the right and the well coifed gray haired studio anchor on the left.

"Do we have any evidence that this attack was orchestrated by the same group as the assault on the Keiferland wedding party two

9

days ago in Dallas?" The anchor weighed in with real concern in his demeanor also.

A Chyron ran across the bottom of the screen, "Steve Hanlon, at the scene of the midtown Chicago subway bombing"

"It is too early to tell as events are still unfolding here..." He glanced over his shoulder, "... and as far as we can tell no one has come forward to claim responsibility... and the police, FBI, and fire department have only begun searching through the debris."

The anchor broke in at that point. "For those of you just tuning in, bombers attacked two CTA subway trains just a few minutes ago at ten fifty-six Chicago time. The detonations were almost simultaneous indicating, I would think, extensive planning.

Normally the trains would not be very crowded, but one was full of folks leaving a baseball pre-season game and the other a major concert. The cars were all packed and there were more of them than usual because of the anticipated crowds. We have no numbers on the casualties or injured, but it could be in the hundreds, maybe thousands."

The picture disappeared and the room was silent.

Neither of the men spoke for a long while.

The President walked to the large window to his right and looked outside deep in thought. It was obvious that the gears of his mind were interlocking at an increased pace. His knuckles were wrapped around the remote so fiercely one could fear if it would be crushed.

Erickson stood there in anticipation not knowing if this were show or reality. After a while he couldn't constrain himself any further, he asked, "How do we respond?"

The President continued to stare into the dimly lit Washington night.

Knowing he presented a grand target in his present position, he said, "Do you think it is wise to expose yourself like that? Someone could..." He never got to finish his question.

"Do you really think I give a shit about that? If they're going to try it, they will. I'm not going to hide." Madison had walked towards

10

him, and moved back to the window in utter defiance of the suggestion.

"But Mr. President..." He stopped and reconsidered his line of questioning. "What are we going to do? We have to at least..."

The President interrupted him again.

"I want a meeting with Curtis, Sonfeld, Wilkins, and Murdock in one hour."

"What about the cabinet, or the military?"

He glared at Erickson and said, "What good are any of them? The cabinet is a bunch of pussies and even if I declared martial law, the army is still handcuffed by the vestiges of the Posse Comitatus Act Bush left me. We have to finally get rid of that piece of shit!" This expressed his utter distain for any law that controlled his power.

When he was in the public eye President Jake Madison was a class act in dress, manner, and style; however, in his private quarters and behind the scenes he reverted to the salty language and stature he learned in thirty-five years of military life.

"Damn it, just do it!" was his final order. "The security and future our country is on the edge of a precipice."

Erickson quickly left the room knowing that the President would be in the strategy room in fifty-nine minutes and everything and everyone had better be there waiting for him.

After he had gone, Madison walked to his dresser and opened a drawer. He picked up a cell phone and opened the cover.

Pressing a couple buttons he activated an autodial number and then placed it to his ear. Soon he heard it ring and a voice answered, "Yes?"

"Now it's our turn," was all he said.

He closed the case, placed it back in the drawer, and began to get ready for the meeting.

2

The Hancock Inn in Georgetown had its usual group of diners. Its modest interior and small crowd reflected its age and local clientele. In the quietest section on the right side sat two men facing each other across an antique looking table. Only one other person was near them, eating about three tables away.

The menu was upscale bar food, and was a major late night attraction to the private and government employees that worked late into the evening or night, and lived nearby. At this hour, they had not yet begun to fill the small rooms.

The two men at the far table watched a television screen across from them playing out the same scenes as the President and his Chief of Staff were watching concurrently.

When the channel went to a commercial, one of them spoke quietly.

"How do you think he'll react?"

This was Leonard Childress, the Senator from South Carolina and the Chairman of the Finance Committee, one of the most powerful men in Washington. With his decades old apparel that was high style in its day, he was everything a southern gentleman once represented. Their loose fit belied his constant battle with food consumption.

His modestly long gray hair made the necessary statement of contempt for anyone's opinion other than his own. It was all for show as he was truly a gentleman. Though, never one to hide from a conflict, he still quietly acquired any and all information necessary to win political conquests into which he might become embroiled whether of his own making or not.

"God knows," responded the other man. Carl Higgins was a former Four Star General in the Army. "When I served with him he was basically an unknown quantity. You never knew what he would do. He did follow orders to the letter if he disagreed with them and to the nth power if he thought they were appropriate.

In his heart he probably feels he is a patriot and a true-blue citizen. But in the long run he's going to do what is best for him, not the country. Jake doesn't give a shit about anything or anyone other than his own goal and himself," he offered. "They're usually one in the same."

"Then it is all a crap shoot," Childress responded.

"Yes," Higgins said sullenly. They were silent again.

The General was cast in the same mold as Childress though it was difficult to imagine their extremely close relationship by appearances alone. He was about the same stature and age as the Senator; however, he had retained a musculature and grace of movement only possible by years of training and use in the field. He had not gotten his stars from administration but in all forms of combat, both overt and covert.

Though the years were mounting his past stallion like frame, the flab was just now beginning to manifest itself. He was always thinking that he should get back to an exercise regimen, but it never came about. He knew he deluded himself into thinking his constant activity was in some fashion an equivalent of it. Either way he didn't quite accept the concept of getting older, but its inevitability was sinking into his consciousness further each day.

Right at this moment his chiseled and cracked face was showing the deeper crevassed lines of concern and trepidation.

The commercials concluded and the place became silent again as most eyes were glued to the video feed of mayhem and frenzy. No one noticed or paid any great attention to the two older men talking quietly.

Carl leaned into his friend's face and said in a low voice, "After the idiocy of the Bush and Obama administrations and all that came before them, you can bet your ass, he will be able to do what ever he wants and get away with it."

Childress sighed and drank some more of his coffee, and shortly stated, "I thought when we took control of the House in 2010, all of that bullshit would end, but they had already established too much internal control. Too much money entrenched in too many pockets, and political parties no longer mattered. I hate to say it but we all dropped the ball, and it may be too late."

"I believe we have to start planning a counter-strategy, just as you implied six months ago," Carl replied. His training was to try and operate several moves in advance.

He referenced their brief meeting in Atlanta in October before travel had been further curtailed. It was difficult for them to sit down together without drawing a lot of attention, which they didn't really want.

The mood of the nation had changed, and there was so much fearfulness and suspicion that eyes and ears were everywhere, waiting for something to happen.

Of course there were the ever present idiots that would rat out their own grandmother, if they thought it would curry favor with the right people. Both of them held these flawed individuals in utter contempt.

"You speak with your people, and I'll contact mine and let's do this again next week. I know it's taking a chance but we are probably going to be risking a lot more before this is over," he continued. "However, it is time we stopped meeting in public. It's no longer beneficial or prudent."

Childress nodded and walked to the rest room.

While he was gone, Higgins paid their bill in cash and left before his friend returned. It was just their method and was carried out flawlessly, as to not attract any undo attention.

Upon his arrival at the table, the senator sat down, fidgeted with some notes, waited a few minutes and then he too left by a second door.

The other diner sitting behind them watched both men, covered his check, and left through the door the general had exited.

He looked around trying to get a focus on either of the men. When he couldn't, he walked toward a parked car at the left of the building.

As he entered the shadows he paused and again studied the streets in all directions. Seemingly satisfied that the effort was futile he renewed his move to his car.

As he reached for the door handle, he felt a gun poking at his ribs. His immediate response was to start to raise his hands.

"Back up slowly and don't make a sound," a voice commanded with a menacing tone, "and lower your damn mitts."

He did what he was told and they moved into the darkness of an alley. The sound of a brief scuffle could be heard and then the slamming of a door, then another.

A car engine came to life and the noise of its motor sped away into the night.

3

Ron Erickson paced around the strategy room with his head down as four other men sat at the table with their hands identically placed on the surface in front of them.

His constant movement was beginning to get on their nerves. Three of them were fidgeting wanting desperately to say something, but they all grimaced with the absolute knowledge that was not going to happen. For the most part they never spoke unless spoken to first.

Erickson stopped walking and looked up when Madison entered the room. He was about to speak but caught himself as the President looked at him sternly.

He said off-handedly, "Thanks Ron, I'm going to be a while. I'll call you when I'm finished."

Trying not to show his feelings about being summarily dismissed, he left the five men and closed the door behind him. He told himself that he was used to being on the outside, but it wasn't true. A chief of Staff was to be just that the President's right-hand, but in the past few months all of that had disappeared. He wasn't going to leave the position, but he had to make some serious decisions, and soon.

Even though he had not wanted this assignment, he was totally conflicted because he was one of his most ardent supporters in the beginning, and truth be told he didn't want to admit to a misjudgment. His mind was presently in a state of utter confusion.

After they were alone, the President walked to the table and for a short while looked down at the four men sitting there without making a sound. It was just long enough to establish who was boss, as if that needed to be done. Madison enjoyed every second of it without revealing an iota of those feelings to them. It was always thus and would forever be that way. He glanced at each in turn.

Immediately to his right was Chaz Sonfeld, his National Advisor. He was a squirrelly little man with a complex ego and very competent brain; some even called him a genius. Though not a Mensa candidate by any stretch, he was persistent and hard working.

Normally these would have been admirable traits but the convoluted and heinous nature of his thoughts and writings were horrifying to anyone that paid attention to them.

The ideas he promoted included medical determinations of who was worthy of saving and who should be left to die. His blunt statements and theories in this regard were welcomed by the progressive left as it encapsulated one of their mainstay arguments almost to the letter.

In the early twentieth century they had gone so far as to promote euthanasia as a method of cleansing the human gene pool. They were never successful in that point but did get sterilization laws passed in many states, as well as the practice of frontal lobotomies to control what was to them unacceptable behavior.

In the fifties and sixties "troubled" family members were dealt with in this manner. Even the self-righteous Kennedy clan used it on one of their children and was never questioned as to its need or efficacy.

Unless you count the total loss of personality and feeling as an asset, there really was no need for it. Thankfully the practice had all but disappeared. Sonfeld would love nothing more than to reinstate it.

Why anyone could respect or even want his council was outside of any sane person's ability to understand. However, he had been with Madison from the moment he had been driven from the Obama White House by the noisy right wing that hated his point of view on everything. He worked diligently behind the scenes until after Madison's election.

Tongues wagged full time when his position was announced, but by that time the talk show hosts that helped bring him down earlier were gone themselves and could no longer be a threat. Even though a couple of them had relocated to Canada and Mexico and now broadcasted from there, the radio signals could not reach the huge audiences they once had. Their voices had been silenced on the mainstream airways, television, and even satellite radio after constantly being harassed by friends of the past and current administrations.

Though it all may have appeared disconnected, Sonfeld and Madison had been close, even though clandestinely so, for years. They were actually distant relatives who had met at a family reunion and stayed in contact.

As in most meetings he kept his arms wrapped around his diminutive body as a shield, always expecting the worst. This was probably a defense mechanism based on the knowledge he was in actuality a disposable moron and a very evil person.

The second on the right was Paul Wilkins, another advisor, a man more powerful than his minor title indicated. They had met in boot camp and served together most of their military years. He was his Chief of Staff for over fifteen years, and was basically in that position now; Erickson was simply a figurehead.

Wilkins was born into the military. His roots there went back to before the first Civil War. Being an army brat, he was continuously moved from one part of the world to another.

His physical body matured into that of a strong motivated warrior. Though not as tall as he would have liked, he molded his five foot six body into what should have been an object of pride, but to him it was simply adequate. That was his mental state, a person of competence needing a leader to guide him. He was a follower and to a certain extent accepting if not proud of it.

Losing his father when he was fourteen was not only a devastating blow, but somehow altered his very nature and thinking processes. Instead of just helping to take care of the family when they were forced to leave the shelter of a military base, he immediately began to plot when and how he would enlist. When he finally did, he sent monies home for a while until his sister was old enough to take over.

Seldom visiting his family, he had no contact with them and was in Iraq when he received word that his mother had died. He hadn't attended the funeral even though his commanding officer had arranged it, and his sister had not spoken to him since. He really didn't give a shit.

About that time he had been able to get transferred to Madison's unit. It did not take him long to learn the man inside and out. In fact, there was very little about Madison that he was not aware. He knew that was valuable information and he back-logged it all.

He like Madison was a proud American and believed that they knew exactly what the country needed to survive and prosper.

When he decided to run for President, Wilkins was there, verifying that decision and most others after that. He ran the campaign behind the scenes just as he had operated a regiment, and you can believe no one disobeyed.

He had myriad contacts in business, finance, Wall Street, and the media and used each as needed. These were based on an uncle who had owned a conglomerate of radio and television stations and major interests in the munitions industry.

His uncle and father were estranged most of their lives, probably because he did not respect his brother's ability to make money, and more importantly he objected that it came from questionable sources. Wilkins had no such qualms and threw a lot of business to his uncle and was rewarded with massive amounts of business and political intelligence, and a nice bank account in Belize. Payoffs and mutual back-scratching was always the order of the day.

He was a force with which to reckon, and that was an understatement. His preference was to be in second chair with the discreet power. It was indeed his comfort zone.

On the left was Paul Curtis, the National Security Czar. Even though former administration detractors had disliked the title "Czar", the name stuck. The positions were now fixed if not universally accepted, especially after the last White House eventually had fifty-six of them.

Madison only had appointed five. He was a control master and wanted that power consolidated, solidified, and close; therefore, he had placed all of the previous areas under these few people.

Curtis ran the former Homeland Security, FEMA, FBI, and other agencies Madison had rolled into what was now known as the National Security Forces.

The latter was originally the national police force that had been established ostensibly for stateside law enforcement and protection under the Obama administration. He had spoken of it in his campaign, but few saw it as a problem. In fact, it was nothing less than a federal law enforcement agency entirely at the command and whim of the President.

After its formation by one of the many executive orders written in his second term, it grew into a massive organization that was a power in itself. Robbing other departments of their top leaders and supervisors diminished their ability to perform their assigned duties. This was another way to consolidate control. Madison simply continued that approach.

Now FEMA and the FBI existed in name only so that the enactments, laws, and executive orders previously authorizing them would not be violated. For all intents they were no longer autonomous, or effectual.

He ran these agencies with a proverbial iron fist and no one objected, unless they wanted a call from the President and a visit from the IRS.

Curtis was one of the few non-southern boys in the circle. His history was indeed the antithesis of the others.

His parents were hippies straight out of the sixties, free love, drugs, and rock 'n roll. They had lived in communes and practiced what they had preached, walked the walk, and talked the talk as it became known.

The genetics went totally awry when he was born. His contempt for them and their lifestyle developed at an early age and never waned. Free-love, or free-will were not in his vocabulary. He lived for the day that the government would control all this bullshit, and he wanted desperately to be the one to shut it all down.

Back in the eighties a study was done that seventy percent of the people in any line of work were not fit psychologically for their position. This was particularly important to police departments. Many of their officers were not only unfit, but many were sociopaths who just liked ordering people around and beating them up. That changed until some jurisdictions were so desperate they even hired felons. Curtis was in this deviant group to the nth degree.

He was patiently waiting for the day when his fondest wishes would materialize and the sheep would be at the total beck and call of the shepherds. They simply could not function effectively on there own, a potent chief was an absolute necessity.

The final attendant seated second from the left was Sid Murdock, the Communications Czar, possibly the fourth most powerful person in Washington another holdover from the military, and a close ally of Madison. He too had worked with the previous administration, but also behind the scenes, waiting, learning, and whispering in appreciative ears.

The takeover of the media began long before, but he had been at the FCC for more than ten years and had the dirt on everyone there and many on capital hill. If he wanted someone silenced, it took little effort to accomplish.

He was a large corpulent man, with a common everyman face, but he was not to be underestimated or taken for granted. As pedophiles are many times described as the kind old man down the street who no one suspected of being able to harm a fly, so was his

21

appearance conveniently deceiving. It was a good idea to not turn one's back on him, unless one wanted to face a time of deep regret.

For a large man he seldom perspired. The inward calm he possessed belied the constant thought processes that churned through his more than adequate brain. His purpose in life was to further the ambitions of his betters and control the minds of the weak populace at large. He did his job very well.

If someone viewed this room and the meeting that was to commence, one observation had to be made. The five most powerful people in Washington were male and white. Life came full circle once again. The legions that fought tooth and nail for the progressive liberal agenda gave these men the tools they needed to conquer and rule. Their efforts were truly appreciated by each of them.

Their combined influence, internal angst, and pent up energies could easily burst forth as rage, control, and potential devastation.

It was not by error or chance that they formed their alliance or that Madison was the leader, now and for the foreseeable future.

4

John Enman crossed the floor of his bedroom to his waiting wife. They were both exhausted from attending two dinners in one evening. He would have to speak to his assistant again about that scheduling mistake, but he knew she would simply ignore him as she had done for thirty years and tell him to "man up". She just didn't get the fact he was tired of the constant hassle of the hustle. Maybe he was just realizing it himself.

Just as he was pulling down the covers of his luxurious bed, the phone rang. As he reached for it he did find solace in the comfort he could afford. He was not born to wealth but he surely found consolation in it.

He picked up a cell phone as it rang for a second time. He looked at the display. It read "23". He hit the end button and reached for his robe. After tying the strap, he told his wife "good night".

She knew better than ask what the call was about, as she had long ago learned two things. One, it was probably business as usual and two, he wouldn't tell her anyway. Pulling the covers to her neck and she rolled on to her side.

He had a flash of feeling for his wife as he moved to a door on the opposite side of the room. One day he should try to tell her more

23

how much he loved her, but time had not only sealed a relationship between them, but also had installed a gulf that was hard to bridge. The day must come soon when he would span it before it became an abyss. His thoughts by necessity were on hold with this because the phone rang again.

As he placed his palm in front of what appeared to be a Greek statue, a beam from a hidden laser reader scanned it and the door opened silently.

He walked into a secure soundproof room that no one except him and one of his repairman with a high security clearance had entered since it was completed. It was a simple but highly sophisticated electronics center with every type of communication and techno-security equipment money could buy.

From here he could have meetings with any of dozens of his minions, allies, benefactors and even his "enemies" if that was necessary on the most advanced encrypted networks available. He had done all of this many times before, and moved mechanically as he began.

This particular "ally" was never to his liking. It was Gregor Saranoff. He had worked with him for more than a decade now. It had seemed like a prudent venture at the time, but had proven to be a curse almost immediately.

To most of the world Saranoff was the ultimate philanthropist, giving hundreds of millions of dollars a year to non-profit organizations in several countries. There appeared to be no hidden agendas; however, if he called in a favor, he expected it to be granted post haste without reservation.

That was how he had originally met him. His wife's favorite charity had received a half million-dollar donation and of course he had to attend the presentation and agree to meet with Saranoff. At the time, he felt it was an honor.

Initially he seemed to be what his advanced publicity indicated, a real rags-to-riches poster boy. Born in the Ukraine during the Cold War, he was able to grow to be a wealthy man by his twenties even inside the communist states. After the dissolution of the Soviet

24

Union, he schemed his way to a large fortune which he "risked" in shorting the world currency markets at various times and amassed a huge fortune of tens of billions of dollars and untold numbers of enemies.

Generally speaking most traders despise market short sellers, even if on the up-and-up; however, there was constant speculation he had in some way manipulated the trading, but no proof was ever established. The occasional witness came forward, but disappeared almost as quickly. Few were brave enough to ask why.

John knew now how it was accomplished. He had probably befriended hundreds of people like himself and later made the calls that had to be answered.

Saranoff had offered to assist him with several of his mergers at a very modest fee, which he normally sent to some of his "charities". An aggressive nature made him agree without a second's consideration.

His company had grown into one of the largest technology and media companies in the world, and without investing one cent Gregor had him in his back pocket.

The knowledge that others had tried to leave his clutches, only to lose everything within months or worse, gave him cause not to even try that action. Obviously, he would not make the attempt, not only because he liked his life style, but also because he was simply tired.

A light flashed atop one of his screens. He pressed the enter button and the face of a man in his late eighties immediately appeared.

"My friend," Saranoff began, "how are you today?"

It was always the same bullshit opening.

"I am fine my friend", his horseshit response. "How may I help you tonight?"

It was too damn late for this, but there was no way he would even make reference to the hour.

"I am becoming concerned with our friend," Saranoff continued.

This "friend" was Jake Madison, the President. John had been prominent in politics for a while, mostly with the Democrats. Early on he had given money to both parties as most large businesses did, but upon realizing he could get more in return with the DNC, he ultimately gave them the most.

He helped considerably with bringing in key support for the Obama campaign, both financially and major endorsements. His business flourished after the election, and he received multiple appointments in the government and the financial community. He should have again seen what this would eventually cost him, but it was a hell of a ride while it lasted.

His mistake was getting Saranoff involved. Directly and indirectly, he was able to get over sixty million dollars into the 2008 campaign, and another hundred and twenty million into the 2012 run, with inflation about the same money.

When Jake decided to run, Saranoff didn't care that his purported views were only slightly left of center; he put a several hundred million into the fray. Again adjusted for inflation, this was a just a little less than he had given to the Obama campaign. The spending of the Obama administration and his first Congress, and the inability of the Republican congress to curtail it, had debased the dollar to a fraction of its former value.

Jake wasn't as liberal as Gregor would have liked, but the country was not going to elect another leftist, and he wasn't about to have a right-wing Republican in the White House. His money made the difference in a close election. Jake won with 49.5% to Mitch Reynolds 48.5%.

The other 2% went to the far right third party, and of course to all those who voted none-of-the-above and Mickey Mouse. As is the usual case, the third party screwed the country over, as most of the votes would have gone to Reynolds and Madison would have been out.

"Are you with me my friend?" Gregor asked.

"Yes, I'm just tired," he said before he caught himself.

"What is wrong?" Saranoff asked, feigning concern.

"Oh, nothing my friend. Please, accept my apologies."

"As I said, we may have a predicament," Saranoff continued. "I have heard whispers that these terrorist attacks are being funded and orchestrated by your own people."

"I sincerely doubt that Gregor." John was taken aback. "Americans don't kill Americans!" Deep inside he wasn't really certain what some of them were capable of doing.

"Maybe, but my sources say it is not Jihadists," he rebutted.

"You're wrong! Madison is a megalomaniac. I am convinced of that, but he is not a traitor." John was furious, and yet something else in his mind just blinked on. However, he was not about to voice this at this time, and to not to this man.

"Regardless, he needs to be watched." He remained calm.

"I'm sure you have someone doing that continuously," John replied.

"Yes, but only at the cabinet level, not in his inner circle." Saranoff was becoming agitated.

"I'll look into it as best I can," John offered. "But I don't have much pull in DC any more."

"I know you will," Saranoff said a bit threateningly. "Now go back to that pretty wife of yours, it is late."

"Good night Gregor," John said trying to control his anxiety and anger.

The screen went black, and the computer turned itself off. "Green shit" John thought to himself as he exited the room, his mind racing. Even though he had made billions on the "Green Economy", the whole scam pissed him off, and if he were honest with himself, the guilt of his initial involvement probably caused much of the stress he now felt. So many assholes had raped the public with their climate change and other phony bullshit, he was truly regretful and embarrassed at the very little he had done.

The door clicked shut behind him, as he got into bed. His wife was already asleep. There would be no rest for his troubled mind that night.

5

Jake listened as Chaz Sonfeld ran on. Wondering how Obama had put up with this ideological drivel for all those years, he couldn't believe how anyone could buy into this crap. It seemed like an hour, but he had only been talking for two minutes. "My god..." he thought, "could even his mother have tolerated this?"

"Enough Sonfeld," he gasped thoroughly fed up.

"Hitler would have loved this guy," he thought, "but not for long".

As he looked down the length of the table at no one in particular, he began, "All of that happy horseshit is fine, but we have a situation here. If you think poverty, deprivation, and any other crap is the cause of these attacks, you're simply an idiot."

As usual he felt better putting Sonfeld in his place. He was a good loyal man, had many friends that were vital contacts, and so he had to be tolerated, at least for the time being.

He looked directly at Paul Curtis and asked forcefully, "Do we have any evidence where these assholes are from? I need names... places."

Curtis answered bravely, "We have had twenty-one labs working continuously since the attack in Dallas. With over thirty-thousand

28

blood samples alone, it is a formidable task, and so far none have been matched to anyone who wasn't there for the wedding."

He continued, "The only possible items of value were the recordings we retrieved. The killers were using Russian AK-47's."

"That narrows it down to about... oh... most of the world!" Madison was agitated.

Jim Wilkins interrupted, "I have heard speculation these were home grown terrorists, maybe even sanctioned at high levels of the government." He was obviously comfortable in saying whatever he pleased.

"Bullshit again!" Madison roared. "Where is this shit originating?" His fecal references were his back stage persona and by now made no impact whatsoever on anyone, especially those present. Frequency inured them as to any affect, and it was when he became silent that the true angst began.

"I'm not sure," Wilkins answered.

"We've heard the same rumblings over several channels in and out of country," Curtis stated in a low voice.

"Just damn great," Madison said almost sadly. No matter what, he loved his nation and did not want to see it besmirched.

"Too bad we don't have the old talk show hosts to blame it on," Sid Murdock interjected.

"We need something to feed the public, anything," Sonfeld lamely presented. "All they want is something to hold onto, someone to hate."

"He's right," the President said almost in disgust. "Find something and get Gibson and Hayworth out on any of those stupid news shows, and send talking points to all of the networks, it's time they earn their keep."

Ron Gibson was the White House Press Secretary and a very competent spin-meister. He too was a hold-over distraction from the previous administration. Coming across as a big likeable bear was an asset. Of course, behind his back he was and had always been the laughing stock of DC. Only the memory of Dee Dee Meyers gave this perception any relief.

Carson Hayworth was the current Speaker of the House. He had held the office since the democrats had taken it back in 2014, and was an ass-licking sycophant, a real "tool", but a very useful one.

"Find what we need," Madison said menacingly in a surprisingly flat tone. "Now get to work. You all can sleep next year."

They all began to leave. Gazing at his hands as if he would ever have dirty finger nails, he directed, "Jim stay."

The other three immediately left and closed the door. Wilkins sat back down in his seat.

"Jim, we need something to tie them to somewhere in the Middle East regardless of their origin."

"I'm working on it as we speak Mr. President." Wilkins always observed protocol in the White House and in public, which was the way it he felt it should be. Madison liked it and quite frankly his military background demanded it. He would let his guard down when they were hunting or fishing together, but even then most of the time the secret service was near by. Blundering simply wasn't an option.

"And?" Madison asked.

"I will have something shortly."

Madison nodded. He knew Jim would obtain what they needed, whatever the cost. He always did.

6

Carl Higgins had driven to Richmond Monday morning after his meeting with Senator Childress, with the man from the Hancock Inn in his trunk. He turned him over to the local cell and prepared for his meeting.

As with any good counterinsurgency group no one knew with whom they were working. Only select leaders were aware of their counterparts, and then seldom did that exceed five to six others. Most had fewer than a dozen operatives under them who were totally unknown to the other heads. That way the network was immune to mass recognition and minimal chances of being compromised. Terrorists had used this method for centuries. It worked well for them, so why not the patriot underground.

Higgins and a couple close friends had begun to organize only two years before and now had over two hundred thousand compatriots involved, sworn to defend the United States at any cost. Many were ex-military thoroughly disgusted with the Mid-east pullouts during the Obama administration. Most had lost buddies and felt betrayed by their Commander-In-Chief, the Congress, and the Senate.

Scared and fed up, hundreds of others joined swearing allegiance, their life, property, and honor just as their counterparts had two hundred and forty years earlier.

If the general public were made aware of their existence, the media would blast them as a militia as they did the crazies back in the eighties and nineties. The government wasn't about to give them any publicity and really wasn't aware of their total strength or depth. If it ever did, the pace of change would have escalated even more quickly than it had.

What amazed Higgins was the diversity involved, every race, religion, and ethnic group was represented. He had heard many stories from all of the states about this; it pleased him and gave him a real sense of pride. Of course he knew none of them. Hopefully there would be a day when all of that would be unnecessary and they would all receive the recognition they so deserved.

The door to the room in which he was staying had a patterned knock. He reached for his 9mm and waited and another pattern followed. Then he walked to the door and stood to one side and opened it. He never looked through the peephole as many had died with a bullet in their eye doing that very thing.

A woman entered. She was a brunette in her late thirties and strode with confidence into the room. Gloria Martin knew who she was and what she was doing, as to that there was immediately no doubt.

A statuesque five foot ten inches, and every bit of it muscled, her ability to handle herself would never be in question. As a marine she had seen combat from every view point and always stood ready to serve.

Her relationship with the General went back years, and as one of the cofounders of the group, her loyalty was a forgone conclusion. She was the leader of the Richmond cell.

Gloria and Higgins had to attend to some business before the general meeting in the evening.

"Did he give up any information?" Higgins began, referring to the man from his trunk.

"Not at first," she answered matter-of-factly.

"Did it take much work?"

"Not really, "she continued. "They are all street thugs at heart. Brave as hell in groups and weak as shit alone."

"Part of the Federal Constabulary?", he asked, not knowing why; but he liked saying that occasionally, probably harkening back to his wasted youth in front of the TV watching old British movies.

"Of course, he was undercover. God is that a laugh. These assholes have so little training; they couldn't stakeout a blind man without being seen."

Most of the National Security Forces now were ex-neighborhood organizers, union members, or petty criminals who were paroled if they joined. The politicians knew the military would never fire on U.S. citizens, but a paid lowlife would have no such qualms, and most proved the theory accurate.

The Louisville riots three years before were the testing grounds. Five thousand of the Feds were sent there to quell the "rampaging mobs" that had "stormed" the local government food centers. After the economy had tanked in 2008, matters had gone from really bad to horrendous by 2012 in many select, or chosen, areas of the country. These were mostly ideological conservative strongholds, or at least that was what the elected elite thought, and that was all that mattered.

This was the story the government-backed media reported. In actuality, it was about a thousand hungry people wanting something to eat and a place to sleep and trying to have their plaintive voices heard. Four hundred and thirty-six of them were killed, and most of the others hospitalized.

The real untold story was that even some of the Federal thugs couldn't abide by that action, and most of them were disciplined, or never heard from again. The ranks diminished a little afterwards, but those who remained were mentally hardened for the tasks ahead.

A few left the force and were now part of Higgins and Martin's movement.

"Was he ordered to watch us?" Higgins asked.

"I don't think so. He was on a fishing expedition. I believe he just recognized you two, or just was nosy and wanted to see if there was anything to your meeting," she offered.

The troops were encouraged to rat out anyone they could as it helped with promotions, and carried monetary bonuses. There were several cases in which family members had turned in their own kin for a few bucks. Judas would have been proud.

"I don't think he had a chance to report anything," he stated.

"He swore he didn't," she said flatly.

"He had better disappear."

"He already has." There was no ambiguity or emotion whatsoever in her voice or demeanor. She had lost three close relatives in Louisville, her two small nieces, and her sister.

Higgins knew all traces of the body were gone as was his car. A DC cleaning crew took care of it before he had gotten onto Rt. 95 South.

"We have to prepare for the meeting."

She nodded in agreement and sat down.

7

The President's cabinet was seated in the master conference room. All of the members were present and whispering audibly. Something was obviously happening. They knew that he would show at any time, and there was no way any of them wanted to be saying anything that would place them in a compromising position, or draw attention to him or herself. Therefore, they only spoke of cursory topics so that if the conversations were actually heard, or recorded, they were completely innocuous.

They all knew their positions and that they themselves were superfluous, but to a person each lived in hope that would change. This was the continuing liberal dream most of them shared... fruitlessly.

Of course the President entered exactly on time at quarter past the hour. Without looking at any of them, he began, "As all of you know, the attack in Seattle a few minutes ago was partially thwarted. The bomb that was detonated in the downtown area has done considerable damage in life and property. No estimates are obviously available yet."

The explosion occurred in the middle of downtown Seattle about a half mile from the Space Needle. Buildings were toppled in a half mile radius of the blast. Windows were broken up to five miles away.

The loss of live was staggering. Over forty-five thousand died that morning, though it was more than a month before anything like an accurate total could be reached. Thousands more died in the ensuing weeks.

He stopped for a moment then continued. "What was not known at that time, by anyone other a few agents and myself, is that a second bomb was intercepted at the port in Long Beach in California, and was disarmed. The assumption now is that they both were delivered at different ports to be detonated simultaneously.

The Customs Service received an anonymous tip early this morning and was able to act on it immediately."

Madison was about to continue when one of his staff came into the room and went directly to him, whispered to him, and handed him a sheet of paper.

All eyes were on him as he read it.

Finally he looked up and spoke. "It appears that we have finally attained evidence as to who is behind these attacks. I will keep you informed when and if it is confirmed."

He rose to leave when a voice rang out from a woman seated at the end of the table. Marsha Willard, the Secretary of Housing called out. "Mr. President."

He stopped in his tracks and shot her an intense glance.

"Yes, Ms. Willard," he voiced his disapproving response through his teeth in a barely audible tone.

The room instantly became silent. Some of them were afraid to breathe.

"Mr. President, there have been rumblings of government participation in these attacks. I have to in all good conscience ask if there has been an investigation into this matter."

His eyes blazed in response to her insolence. She was not one of his chosen lot, but an annoyance he had to tolerate. Her position in the cabinet had been a payback for an enormous amount of Chicago support and he was stuck with the results, at least for now.

"Thankfully you are asking me this now and not in front of the cameras as is your usual M.O."

All of the room knew she might have finally crossed the line. Half of them respected her courage, but sincerely feared for her future. The other half simply wished they were anywhere else at that time.

"I have heard those idiotic and irrational ideas also. Rest assured I will take care of that as well as these terrorists."

His departure left a void easily palpable by all present. No one was willing to make any further comments. They silently filed out into the hall, knowing that they were always being watched.

Secretary Willard realized she had hit a nerve. She also felt good that she had spoken out. Foolishly, she thought she was immune from any recourse in her actions.

8

Higgins and Martin were pouring over several binders of paperwork and reports that had been forwarded up channel over the past week. The notes were written in a code they had developed and only held non-personnel information so that if intercepted they were useless to anyone else.

He was about to ask her a question when her phone rang.

They looked at each as she reached for it. She peered down at it and her face drained. She answered.

"Yes? When?" She listened intently.

Higgins waited on edge as he recognized the tone in her voice.

"Of course." She stated bluntly, and closed the case.

She sat silent for a second then began. As she related the attack on Seattle, he sat staring at his hands. His brother worked in the downtown area and his attention went immediately to him and his family. He could not call there directly and give away his position. Martin's cell was acceptable to be used in Richmond, but if he turned his on, the GPS would instantly trigger a violation and begin an investigation. The necessary paperwork not filed for this trip. He was supposed to be in Georgetown, and his other cell was on in the hotel room there for that purpose.

There had been some talk about injecting every citizen with a GPS transmitter but that had not happened yet. It was just a matter of time.

It had been known for several years that after 2010 all cars had been fitted with tracking systems that could be activated at anytime if necessary. When it had been initially discovered, the story was that they had been installed for improved theft and personal safety. Anyone in the know was well aware immediately of the true purpose.

In the beginning to avoid the system, most of them drove older models, but even that method became worthless, as most vehicles were retrofitted at state inspection stations, again without any publicity, or the knowledge of their owners.

After two years, the devices were almost universal. Four years later the system was activated and integrated with Homeland Security.

The usual techies were able to devise a jamming system which was sold on the Internet, but that immediately was declared illegal, just before the Internet was fully compromised by regulations.

The underground modified the systems and used them for a time, but after several were caught, they had to go back to their short haul methods of switching drivers. A trip to Richmond from Washington took eight hours and twenty or so transfers from one car to another.

Six months ago, the jamming devises were updated by scanning other cars in the area and then emitted a changing ghost signal that mimicked it. The signal altered every fifteen minutes just ahead of the tracking pattern the computers monitored.

No one knew how long this would be effective, but at least it was something. Since this technology was extremely expensive, it was reserved for cell coordinators.

Local members never operated outside of their area, mainly to not draw attention to themselves.

For the past two years, any travel over twenty or thirty miles was suspect, and a travel plan needed to be filed. Obviously that put a crimp in the vacation business and it quickly became non-existent, as was any form of air travel for the average citizen. You had to have a damn good reason to fly or know someone who could get you a permit.

Because of all of this, many people simply dropped out of regular society. Since unemployment had gone over twenty-five percent, and more than thirty percent of the private sector businesses had closed, there was no compelling reason to stay above ground.

More than eighty percent of the employed in the country now worked for the government. Their salaries had been frozen for the past four years: therefore, with the raging inflation their slavery went from virtual to actual.

"I think we're ready," Higgins said.

She nodded.

They packed their papers, got up, and then straightened the room as if no one had ever been there, wiping everything clean of fingerprints and hopefully DNA.

She walked to the door, opened it and simply walked out, closing it behind her.

He walked to the other side of the main area and opened a connecting door that led him to another room and number. After sitting there for several minutes, he left through that room's door and turned in the opposite direction.

9

The Oval Office was filled with a camera and a small crew. Except for the multitude of Secret Service present, it appeared as any Presidential broadcast would.

Madison sat behind his desk as make-up did a few last minute touch-ups. This was certainly not one of his favorite ordeals.

One would think with this many people milling around that the noise level would be intense; however, the silence was extraordinary.

The President appeared to be studying some notes even though the teleprompter had been declared ready after the operator checked it over and over for the last fifteen minutes. The last person who had made a mistake running it was still in the unemployment line.

The director came from behind his table and approached Madison.

"Mr. President," he stated as calmly as he could, "we will go live in thirty seconds."

He just nodded his head to him.

"Quiet everyone," he said knowing it was unnecessary.

"We're on in five, four…" He counted down using his fingers for three, two, and one, pointed to Madison, and the President began.

41

"My fellow Americans, these past few days have been truly sad for all of us. The attack in Dallas and Chicago, and now in Seattle, has shaken the nation to its core. But I am here to tell you not to give into fear, as it will simply strengthen our enemies.

As you all know, I am a person of very few words, and I will get directly to the point. We now have evidence as to who is behind these egregious and horrendous events.

Through the discovery of evidence in Long Beach, and information from intelligence sources, we now know that these acts of war were orchestrated in," he paused for effect, "Iran."

All present looked at each other, knowing that every American had gasped at that very moment.

Madison continued, "Our fondest hope has been that the leaders of Iran had learned their lesson after Israel attacked their nuclear facilities in 2012, but evidently that was not the case. Even though their hands were extended to us supposedly in peace, their intense hatred of everything this country stands for must be the basis for their lack of civility and their strength of aggression." Again he paused for effect.

"I have ordered a massive bombing run on Teheran and several other major cities. These many years of terrorism must come to an end.

I know full well that this is not the only stronghold for the Jihadists, but if any of their allies want a taste of this, I am prepared to serve them a heaping portion."

He loved to drop into this type of colloquialism when possible. It was his "good buddy next door" routine.

"I am putting Yemen, Afghanistan, Iraq, Pakistan, and Saudi Arabia on notice. If you want all out war, I am prepared to fulfill your wishes."

He hesitated again to let that sink in. Knowing full well that the liberals that had put him in office were fainting where they stood, he smiled on the inside while looking as stern as he knew how for the camera. The country would finally be put back on the right course; he would save it from its enemies if it killed him.

"I have called up every unit of the military for immediate departure for the mid-east. Several additional aircraft carriers and destroyers will join the Third Fleet in the Mediterranean.

As my predecessors set out to free us from the tyranny of fossil fuels, my friends we are setting ourselves on a course of independence from the cults of terror that have developed in the past decades in the middle-east.

I know I will make enemies by doing this, but it is a necessity and must be done."

He paused again and tried to look sincere.

"I want each and every one of you to pray and think positively about our future as a nation and a united people. God bless all of you and may God bless America."

10

General Higgins had driven west on route 84 out of Richmond for about thirty miles. Shortly after that he exited and continued southwest on a two-lane road that soon left the suburban area and entered countryside. Not long afterwards he turned onto a dirt road that ended a quarter of a mile later at an old cabin. Apparently the new device that had been installed in his car worked. Those tech guys were fantastic.

He parked his car and walked past the rundown structure and over a small knoll. There was no trail but he walked with the confidence that this was not his first time.

As he continued on he realized he was starting to feel his age. Since he was in his late fifties this was to be expected. His years of military life and limited exercise helped, but the old muscles got tired, especially with his long hours of the past few months.

He had worked most of his life for the country he loved and he wasn't about to quit now, especially when she needed him the most. Even though he had been married twice, she had been his constant and presently only mistress.

After traveling another quarter of a mile, he saw a tent exactly where he expected it in a small grove of trees so that it couldn't be seen from the air.

He knew that at least three guards were constantly watching the area ready to protect the operation with their lives.

As he approached he heard the muffled voices emanating from inside.

"Get in here," Gloria's voice called out softly but with intensity.

His hand reached for the door flap just as she pulled it back. As he entered he saw four familiar faces, hers and three others.

"Where's number 3?" he asked.

They only knew each other as number 1 through 5. The exception to this was he and Martin, and the others didn't even know their names. He was number 1, and she was number 5.

"Did something happen?" he asked again.

"As far as we know, nothing; but who knows. 4 will find out later and get back to me," she responded.

"Did you hear the President's speech?" This was 2 asking.

"No I didn't want to be bothered with the radio," he responded.

"He dumped all of the blame on Iran."

"Do you believe him?" Higgins asked.

"Don't know. He's such a crock of shit."

"I've heard he may be trying to cast the culpability anywhere he could, just to save face," offered number 4.

"We've heard it might be someone in our own government," she added. "I find it hard to believe, but these are strange times, and who knows what is real?"

"I can't believe that anymore than Iran being responsible. The last I heard from my contacts was that the middle-east had cooled considerably since the European riots," voiced 4 again.

The "riots" as he mentioned were more like mini-civil wars. It began in France expanded to the Netherlands, Great Britain, and Italy. There had been so much unbridled immigration of Moslems into Europe in the previous thirty years that it was a powder keg just waiting to explode.

Though initially the European Socialist governments of that time had pretty much welcomed them with open arms, a good portion of the citizenry did not. It was just a matter of time before the opposing cultures clashed.

It began with the firestorms that erupted in France, as many towns and cities burned to the ground. Thousands died and the property damage was in the billions of euros. That was back when there was a euro currency.

The French government could not or was not willing in the beginning to take a stand against it. In the end it was too late. Forces from the surrounding European Union countries had to intervene and quell the bloodshed.

Great Britain stopped the rebellions much more quickly as did the Netherlands, which surprised everyone. The Dutch were the most liberal in their laws, but when the shoving started, they kicked ass.

Italy did not fare as badly as France, but the loss of life and property was extensive, as they did not expect anything like what occurred. Many believe the events there were instigated so as to widen the original arena, and it was closer to the source, the Arab world.

This and all of the continued economic turmoil that had preceded it led to the downfall and termination of the European Union. The EU had been a grand scheme to solidify the continent under a gloriously socialized compact controlled by the same businesses and families as the Third Reich. The Fourth Reich as some called it came to the same end as its predecessors.

It all happened so quickly that the United States was not drawn into the conflict. Many believed that the powers to be in DC wanted their smug European "allies" to learn a very difficult lesson. Regardless of the truth of this idea, it was indeed a fact.

"Probably the calm before the storm," 4 offered.

"Maybe," said Higgins, "but I'm more inclined to believe that they are most likely scapegoats. For whatever reason, he wants attention diverted from something here. If this is so, what does he plan to do in retaliation?"

He knew damn well that Madison would not just let things go, and he also knew that he wouldn't ask what was left of the United Nations to help.

"Going to bomb the hell out of them! He's sending every available uniform to the region," 4 chimed in.

"He threatened the Saudis and three others directly," 2 said.

"Oh shit!" Higgins muttered. "That can't be good. He's up to something."

"To other business," Martin interjected. "Have we heard anything further from the organization in the Miami area?"

"After Madison's remarks last week, recruitments are through the roof."

The President had made an off-the-cuff comment about Raul Diaz, one of the local politicos in that area. It had been interpreted as anti-Latino, and most likely was. He was determined to get Anthony Crest elected in a Senate run-off election, even if that meant alienating that large voting pool. They hated Crest for what he was, a gutless sycophant of his that couldn't care less about them.

"Get the word out to go slow," Higgins said. "The last thing we need is some new recruit getting drunk and shooting his mouth off in the wrong bar, or enrolling an undercover NSF."

They had been careful in organizing and he surely didn't want that to change with the exuberance of rapid growth.

The meeting continued for three more hours. When they departed, all shook hands and walked into the night.

Martin moved over to Higgins and whispered to him. "I got word on the way over that your brother and his family are safe. You might want to convince him to take them to Montana or some other state."

"I'll try again as soon as I can, but he can be bull-headed as hell."

"Why do I find that not hard to believe?" She almost smiled.

They too left, in opposite directions, both returning by way of the paths they had arrived.

Higgins was trying to assimilate all of the information when his training kicked in and the hair stood on the back of his neck. He stopped and knelt down.

"What had attracted his attention?" he thought.

He knelt on one knee and looked in every direction. Then he saw it again, a little glint from the window of the cabin, probably a reflection from the moon which was full enough to make night travel possible without a light, but not bright enough to make visibility complete.

Higgins had chosen this route because most of the time he was hidden by shrub-brush in lines of sight in all directions. The path had been winding and this was the reason his precautions were taken.

Moving slowly and quietly to one side, he circled around the cabin to get a better feel for what was in it. It was probably nothing but in his world you always anticipated the worst for survival.

He had reason to worry for there were indeed four sets of eyes watching all approaches to the cabin. Each looked out through a small dirty window. They had followed him to this point but lost him a short distance from the cabin. Instead of taking positions outside surrounding his car, they had opted for the inside of the cabin. This was mostly because of their lack of training, knowledge, and skill. It was also to be their undoing.

Higgins threw a rock through one of the windows; they fired frantically all at once, even hitting one of their own. Taking his time, he picked them off one at a time. When he finally broke through the front door, there was little resistance. He finished them with one shot each.

He gathered their weapons and identification before tossing their bodies into a ravine nearby and covering them with branches. They could stay there for months without detection. "Hopefully" he mused, "their car was nearby."

It was a short distance from the clearing sitting in the middle of the dirt road. He drove it over the edge into another deep ravine where it disappeared into the thick brush covering, preventing detection from the air.

Now he had to worry why they had followed him, and how much they had relayed up their channels. It was certainly getting stickier; something big was about to occur of that he was certain.

11

The Morning Show began on millions of televisions throughout the nation with Harry Reeves usually warm appearance replaced with a rather haggard look.

"Good morning everyone. Most of us were up all night waiting for the news out of Iran, expecting the bombing to commence at any moment. We received word a few minutes ago that Ron Gibson is going to have a news conference shortly and bring us up date as to what is going on.

We have had a virtual news blackout. Information agencies all of the world are reporting the same. No government that would have any knowledge of what is happening is talking. They all appear to be waiting for the president to speak first."

He stopped and listened to his earpiece, and then began, "We are going live to the White House immediately."

The picture switched to the pressroom and an empty podium. As if on cue, Gibson entered carrying his rather rotund body quickly and smoothly to the dais.

He started as soon as he was in place.

"I have some general announcements, and then I will take questions for a few minutes."

50

The normally ebullient press corps was completely silent.

"I know all of you are wondering why there has been no news from the middle-east. President Madison decided after his talk with the nation yesterday to delay the bombing runs on Iran for forty-eight hours. After speaking with several world leaders, he felt it was the humane approach.

We must show that we are more a more civilized nation than the others. This will give innocent civilians time to leave government and military complexes. We urge the officials and religious leaders not to use civilians as shields, as we will not hesitate to pursue our objectives."

Some quiet muttering was heard, but silenced with a Gibson glare.

"It has been reported to us that many of the dissidents who object to the current government have been fighting in the streets with a very demoralized military."

He stopped, looked across the room, and stated, "I'll take three questions."

Pointing to a reporter in the front row, one of the media sycophants, he called out, "Sam." It was Sam Reynolds of the Post.

"Is there any possibility the pause will be extended?" he asked.

"None whatsoever," Gibson responded succinctly. Then he pointed to the reporter three seats to Sam's right.

"Why the sudden change of heart? Isn't he afraid it will be seen as a sign of weakness?"

That obviously planted question was delivered by Susan Meyers of the Times.

"As I said it was a response to several requests from leaders in the area, and the United Nations. The last question goes to… Fred Gleason." He indicated a man in the third row.

Before Gleason could ask his question, Bart Sawyer cut in and shouted, "Ron, are we going to be given any more information or proof that these attacks were indeed orchestrated by Teheran?"

Gibson showed no sign of being distracted by the unsolicited query.

"Bart, you know the rules of order here as well as anyone, but I will answer your question this way. As soon as the National Security issues are dealt with, any pertinent evidence will be released to all of you. Thank you."

He picked up his notes and walked out of the room without another word.

The camera switched back to Harry.

"That was Ron Gibson, the White House Press Secretary clarifying what has happened since yesterday. We now have Carson Hayworth, the Speaker of the House of Representatives with us."

The screen split with Harry on the left and Hayworth standing near the Capital dome area.

"Speaker Hayworth, what is your appraisal of this latest development?"

"Well, Harry, I believe it is a sure sign of the compassion of our President. People are pouring out of the Iranian cities hoping to escape the coming firestorm that I am convinced will occur. We, the American people, are simply tired of being the target of these crazy zealots."

"Where are these people fleeing to? Are their neighbors helping?" Harry asked.

"That is the real problem. Most of them are being stopped at all of the borders and only the non-Iranians are being permitted to leave," Hayworth added.

"Why is that?"

He continued, "My guess is that there is a long history of antagonism between Iran and the other mid-eastern nations. Remember they are not Arabs and that is a huge cultural difference. The fact they are Moslem does not always matter. They have had several wars with them and I don't think they will immediately come to their defense, if at all."

"Thanks. That was Speaker of the House Carson Hayworth bringing more information to us. We'll return after this break."

As they began the commercial, the screen went blank.

President Madison held the remote in his hand, and thought, "Good work guys!"

12

John Enman parked his car below the highway off-ramp about thirty miles east of his office. He did not drive his BMW he loved so much and was not dressed in his typical expensive attire, but instead was wearing jeans, a t-shirt, and a faded blue ball cap.

He drove a rented gray Allure, one of the few cars still made in America. It was a piece of electric crap that got three hundred miles per charge but maxxed out at 35 mph. Enman absolutely detested it.

Walking about two hundred feet past the last road pillar, he moved into a group of bushes. For any eyes that saw him, he was probably going there to urinate.

"Looking good, my brother," a voice spoke softly behind him. He turned to face the man who seemed to appear out of nowhere.

The glared at each other then embraced in a hug and back pounding.

"I never thought I would ever see the day you'd be seen in a heap like that or in these duds," the man continued, pointing at the car and then at him.

"Me either Mitch," Enman replied. He grabbed his friend again as if he would never see him.

"Hold on there," he replied. "I love you like a brother, but this is way beyond even my style."

This was Mitchell Grayson, a tall rugged black man, Enman's oldest and closest friend, and a damn good private detective. By that period in our nation, he didn't advertise his involvement in the profession because licenses were no longer attainable and for his own security he had to work off the grid. As in this case, anytime you want to hide your true vocation, open a consulting company.

He was well known in all circles as the man to go to for information or problem solving. In the old days, he was the best money could buy. Because of that he was still able to get through to old contacts, especially with his client's or friend's cash. It still had the ability to get people to talk, maybe even more so under the current circumstances.

Enman knew Mitch from their college days. They lost track of each other when he went to grad school and Grayson went to the military. After several tours of duty outside the states, and serving them as an MP, he worked for the FBI for a few years, and then went private. His connections seemed to be everywhere, but he never asked his friend about them, and Mitch never offered any names. Using him for corporate espionage had always been distasteful for Enman but it never appeared to bother his buddy.

"Yeah, I'll watch it," Enman smiling weakly. "Friends for me are too few and far between."

"John, what the hell is going on?" he said.

"I don't know, guilt maybe," he answered. "Too much, too long…" his voice trailed off.

Grayson left him stew for a while.

"Did you get any feedback on what I asked?" Enman inquired.

"From what my people know, Madison has been holed up with his cronies a lot lately. Most of his cabinet has no idea what is going on."

"Do you think he had anything to do with the attacks?"

"Not that anyone could prove. " He started to pace a little. This would have seemed strange to anyone who knew him, as he was normally a strong confident individual.

"Why would anyone even suggest it?" Enman continued.

"Probably because none of this makes any sense. I'll tell you one thing though, there are a lot of pissed off people in his camp."

"I would think so."

"They feel totally betrayed," Grayson offered.

The Democratic liberal base had worked their collective asses off for Madison. Yes, he was ex-military, but he sold them on his desire to continue the programs that had lost momentum during the later Obama years. They hadn't been axed but had to be pulled back until the country got over its hissy-fit that had been stirred up by all of the conservative media before.

The plan of attack became more underground and insidious than before the election. Slowly but surely things happened. When the Israelis attacked Iran, and fear swept the country, the conservative segment of both parties almost got control back, at least that was what everyone thought would happen. The problem was that one of the side effects of Israel's incursion was gasoline reaching eight dollars a gallon. For a time the country almost came to a standstill. That was a crisis for change.

The "green" voice became louder and with all of the discontent, Obama got a second term. The freedom of movement in congress wasn't what it was before, but slowly they reached some of their more mighty goals.

The Federal Communications Commission got their regulatory rules adopted and Public Broadcasting taxes installed, and overnight all of those annoying voices on the airways were silenced, since no station could afford to have any dissention as part of their schedule. It even overflowed onto the cable-broadcasting arena. Fox News Network and even ABC Cable Network that had joined in late in game were gone or back to their government approved programming.

The stars of talk radio had either fled the country to do pirate radio, gone underground, or simply gave up.

The Internet was shortly thereafter subdued and fell under government control and was now virtually worthless unless you wanted to play games all day long, government approved games at that.

Every so often some fool would try to start something such as a free-thinking blog, but was quickly indicted on one charge or the other and silenced in jail. The prisons that were once full of drug users, now housed mostly political dissenters. America as our parents and grand parents knew it was gone.

All of the progressive politicians finally had achieved what that had worked toward for over a hundred years. To accomplish this, they had to sell out to big business and the big government they thought was the messenger of the gods.

Madison was to be their savior. In place of the cries of the citizenry that once wanted an uncontrollable big bureaucracy, there now were howls of agony about unbearable taxation, regulations, and destruction of privacy and the expectation to continue to pay for it all in worthless dollars.

However, they had created a large dependent group of voters that felt the beast could be handled and by god they wanted it to continue.

John Enman had been one of the stars of the move into bed with the government. His company thrived in all aspects, and he became one of the wealthiest men on the planet. Now the guilt was setting in, and the realization of his part in all of it was starting to eat him up. My god, he was even considering going to church.

He explained some of his feelings to his friend who listened intently. After a time Grayson spoke, "It seems to me you have a serious problem mi amigo."

Enman nodded slowly.

"What are you going to tell S.?" He was not about to even speak the name of Saranoff. As unlikely as it was anyone was listening, he wasn't about to take the chance. Not only did he not trust him, he feared Enman's benefactor, and that was a fact. The thought of his reach, capabilities, and ruthlessness sent a shiver down his normally unwavering back.

"I'll take care of him. I know what he wants to hear. Actually, he has trained me well over these years."

"John, listen to me carefully. I will only ask this once, and think long and hard about your answer. How far do you want to take this atonement thing you're contemplating?"

"I'm not sure what I want to do," Enman responded honestly.

"When you figure that out, let me know." Grayson gave his friend another hug and disappeared as quickly and quietly as he arrived.

"My god, what am I going to do," he asked himself as he turned and slowly walked back to his piece-of-garbage car. After he sat down, he opened his cell so the computer would have something to register next cycle. He was supposedly exempt from all surveillance, but nothing was a certainty. When he rented the car he even filed a trip plan, just to be sure.

"Yes, he had a lot to ponder," he told himself as he drove off.

13

Marsha Willard scurried through the halls to her office. Without speaking to any of her staff, she entered and closed the door. Her petite body leaned against it trembling. She was totally unnerved.

When she had gone into the small restroom reserved for female cabinet members of which there were only two, and began to get out some powder to brush on her fading moist face, a hand covered her mouth and a male voice with a strange thick accent said, "For your own health, go back home, now!"

She was so startled and terrified she was stunned into temporary immobility and made no attempt to move until long after the hand was removed. When she did finally turn around slowly and timidly, she was alone. She quickly walked into the hall and didn't stop until she arrived in her office.

As she moved to the desk and her body refused to stop trembling, her attention was drawn to a folded piece of white paper. Picking it up and reading she immediately turned even a paler shade of white.

Written clearly in the middle was "Go home, now!"

She had no idea who wrote it or who the man in the bathroom was.

59

As she was sinking into deep concentration, there was a knock on the door.

"Not now," she yelled.

It was opened even against her protest.

Her Chief of Staff, Wanda Peters, entered and asked, "Are you okay?"

"Yes, fine," she answered. When Wanda began to back out she commanded, "Who was in my office?"

"No one," Wanda lowered her head and responded quietly. Not being the bravest heart in the world, she was still a dependable and loyal assistant, and Marsha trusted and valued her immensely.

"Have you been here all day?" Willard demanded.

"Yes, I haven't even had a chance to get lunch yet." All she could do was stare at the obviously possessed woman.

"Fine. Alright." She almost babbled.

"May I go now," Wanda asked with a tone of wonder and worry.

"Yes. Go... but not far. I have to make a change of plans for later. I'll call you in a bit."

Wanda backed out and closed the door fighting the urge to run.

Marsha Willard, Secretary of Housing of the United States, was scared shitless, and all she could do was rest her head in her hands.

When her husband died eight years ago, she had thought her life was over, but to her surprise, but no one else's, she recovered quickly and wanted something more to do than sit around the house, or go to untold numbers of charity events. That was when she pondered the idea of running for congress. She had moved to Chicago with her husband twenty-one years earlier, so that was the logical district she would represent.

Her family lived in other parts of the country, but being her strong-minded stubborn self, she could not be persuaded to do otherwise.

She went to visit her father in Texas and finally convinced him it was a reasonable notion to pursue. He promised to help even though they were in diametrically opposite political camps.

When she returned to her home, she found that her father had already made calls to people who owed him favors, and in turn they made calls, and so on. Within two weeks all of the Democratic organizations in her area, and all of the Unions were backing her run. That November she became the Congresswoman representing the third congressional district of Illinois. That's how things are done there, quickly, efficiently, and totally controlled.

She was never once asked for favors, because she knew they were being arranged through her father, but she also understood that if called upon in the future, she would have to comply. That was taken for granted.

That favor came due when Madison was elected President. They wanted someone to sit in his cabinet and be their eyes and ears. Up to now she knew that was exactly her purpose.

What had just happened was a total shock, and a mystery. She did not understand if it was a threat or a warning, but that was entirely irrelevant, her tenure here was over.

There was no way she was returning to Chicago and the uncertainties that would present. She picked up her phone.

"Wanda, book me the next available flight to Houston." She hung up, feeling a bit better. She was going home,,, to Papa.

14

Wednesday, April 19th, 7:34, EDT

General Higgins had sent word to Senator Childress that a meeting was absolutely necessary, and to suggest an area. Since neither wanted to show up on any records as out of the town, they were going to meet at the National Cathedral. Both were ardent churchgoers, but arriving at the same time could throw up a flag. However, there was a special service being held in the evening; therefore, if seen, no one should think anything of it.

Higgins decided to enter early and leave his phone in the deacon's office and Childress would place his under a pew about a half hour later. Although there were several members of their group working at the cathedral, only one was known to both of them. She would be their sentry and prepare a meeting area.

After he arrived and made his appearance in the sanctuary he took a seat in one of the back pews. He knelt to pray. Though it was ostensibly for show, he indeed asked God to watch over the country and all of his people. The prayer was earnest and rather desperate.

In a short while, he moved to the vestibule and joined up with his host, a woman in her early fifties. She showed him to a small room behind the main pipe organ. He sat and waited.

Right on schedule Childress arrived twenty-two minutes later and she let him in. Shutting the door behind her, she moved to a station where she could see almost every section of that part of the church, and every approach to the room. Hidden under her attire was a 9mm automatic at the ready.

Higgins shook his friend's hand tightly.

"Something wrong?" the Senator asked.

He explained what had happened outside of the restaurant at the last meeting and the incident at the cabin. Of course, he gave no names or details.

"Have there been any other indications that they might be onto us?" Childress wanted to know.

"I don't think that is the case. Both incidents were probably happenstance; however, we must now be even more vigilant," his friend answered.

"Have you been able to find if any of that bullshit Madison spewed was true?" Higgins went on.

"There is a total vacuum. No one knows anything." He looked directly at Higgins and continued, "What was so important that we had to meet like this?"

"Recruiting is proceeding way ahead of schedule, if fact I sent word to slow it down a bit."

"I wouldn't do that if I were you," Childress offered.

"Why?"

"Do you realize that when this order is fully operational and the troops are completely deployed, there will be only a skeleton group of maybe two thousand active ground forces and maybe twenty thousand support staff left in the country, and, they are mostly civilian." Childress was pointedly precise with his words.

"Damn, with everything that has happened, I let that one slip by. I must really be getting old." Higgins was a little down.

Childress reached over and touched his arm and said, "We both are... and tired."

He nodded.

"That brings to me to another problem, our finances," Higgins was almost back to himself. "He had to hold it together," was the thought running through his mind. "We need money for the South and New England. I know we spoke about writing everything north of Maryland off; however, I think we need at least a few units in abeyance there."

"I'm almost certain that I'll have funding next week, and possibly a large amount," the senator tried to give him some reassurance.

As usual no further questions as to the source was asked and no details were proffered.

They exchanged a few pleasantries, shook hands, and tapped lightly on the door. Their compatriot quietly opened it and escorted Higgins out. Senator Childress sat back on the chair and patiently waited his departure time.

15

John Enman wasn't looking forward to making this call. He knew what he had to say, and more importantly what he must do, but that didn't make this task any easier.

He had received Saranoff's signal at least three times and hadn't responded.

Not wanting to delay the inevitable any longer, he turned on his computer and the encryption software.

Shortly the screen brightened and Saranoff was there.

"John, are we not friends?" he asked a little threateningly.

"Of course we are," he answered.

"Then why have you avoided calling me?"

"That was not my intention," he lied.

"Where were you?" Saranoff continued pushing.

"Doing what you ask. Trying to get information."

"Was Mitchell able to discover anything?" Saranoff asked bluntly.

"How in the hell did he know about Grayson," Enman asked himself, knowing full well Saranoff had the best intelligence system in the world. He was playing with him and that increased his anger exponentially.

"My sources have little to add to what is available on the television…" he paused, "except that he is being quiet with his own cabinet and meeting regularly with his four comrades."

"I knew that already," Saranoff testily interjected. "Tell me something I don't know."

Now Enman knew what he had always suspected, Saranoff had contacts in the cabinet. Hell, he probably owned a couple of them. No wonder Madison kept them at a distance.

"Maybe you should start selling oil short, like you did those currencies," he changed the subject.

"Why would I do that my friend?"

Again with that "friend" shit, he would be so glad when he no longer had to endure that.

"The price of oil dropped nearly eighty dollars today and closed at three hundred and ninety two. Gasoline was down two dollars and ten cents. It seems the markets are calming after the delayed response and the reaction of the other countries," Enman stated.

"Let me give you a lesson my friend."

"I'm truly not your friend" he imagined himself telling him.

"Before this is over there will be major conflicts maybe a war, if not with the United States, then one or more of the other western nations," Saranoff said very authoritatively.

"So you are buying then. I don't think I would invest much in that…"

He must hit a nerve. His statement was probably interpreted as questioning Saranoff's acumen in finance.

"Not only did I buy more today on that drop, but I have accumulated oil for the past two years."

"I hope not too much," he was testing his new found feeling of strength.

"More than one hundred billion dollars," he literally boomed.

"That's not small change for anyone, even Saranoff," Enman thought. He said out loud, "How can you trust any futures market continued existence, especially ours?"

66

"I don't, not entirely. Yes, I bought a considerable amount on margin, but privately more than in the market. Mostly I bought physicals, taking delivery, all over the world. I even have over five hundred tankers loaded to capacity," he was nearly shouting. "And I bought three refineries."

Suddenly he stopped, hesitated, and began again in his typical controlled manner. He never thought he would ever witness that from him, and doubted he ever would again.

"John," he started slowly, "I am disappointed in you. I believe I am discerning weakness, and you know how I detest that."

"You are wrong, my friend," he said, inwardly smiling. He could lay on that shit too. "Believe me, I will work on this problem and many others, and I will find the truth."

"I couldn't care less about the truth as most people know it, I want answers. I can only make decisions with good information. You are not my only source, but you must come through for me... for obvious reasons."

He was more than just implying. It was as close to a threat as he had ever heard from him. Something big was brewing and now he knew he must prepare for it.

"I will get back to you, hopefully soon'" he told him.

"Sooner my dear friend, sooner," hissed, and the feed was gone.

Enman leaned back in his chair and felt the tension leave his body. It wasn't he didn't fear for the future. He did. The relief from indecision was overwhelming. Tears almost formed in his eyes with the realization of what he had just emotionally accomplished.

He was extremely concerned for his family; however, there was not much reason to do anything rash. There was probably plenty of time, and besides he could not think of a place where they would be safe from Saranoff.

After leaving his room and he joined his wife in bed, where she was reading. When he leaned over and kissed her, she was a little startled.

"Is there something wrong?" she said with a little worry in her voice.

67

"No," he answered calmly, "all is well, for once."

He nestled his head against her shoulder and fell asleep quickly for the first time in years, and slept very well.

16

The Evening News with Joyce Hastings was preparing to broadcast in eight minutes. Normally she was a cool professional, totally dedicated to her work. Well, loyal to her paycheck was more like it. Journalism as our parents knew it had died years before. Now they received their talking points from the powers to be, just as they did any other instructions.

She, as everyone else in the surviving media, read the teleprompter that was not only scripted, but also reviewed by the federal censors up until the time they aired. This was supposedly unknown by the public, but anyone with a bit of sense could see right through it. She had no qualms about any of it. Hell it was fun; at least it had been in the beginning. Now, it was just easy work, and a fairly big salary. It was nothing like the old days, but a hell of a lot better than waiting tables. That was exactly what she was doing three years ago.

A good-looking guy had left her a big tip and a phone number. When she finally called him, one thing led to another as they say. He produced the news, and when he got pissed with the last anchor, he was abruptly fired. She had literally slept her way to the top, instantly. It helped that she was a natural at it.

The fact she was a sexy old Hollywood type beauty aided her not only with bedding the producer but with her male audience. It didn't take long before she had captured the largest audience of the three remaining networks.

The old anchor had no recourse but to leave. He knew the fates before he started. The major unions had crumbled with the FCC changes, and no longer protected any of the television people, or film productions for that matter. The guilds were collateral damage to the takeover by the Obama government in its last years. That was a fitting end for the very people that had helped the left take power in the first place.

The set was buzzing and Hastings was not certain why.

"What's going on?" she asked.

She got a couple shoulder shrugs, and not much more.

Shortly a little man with a slight build ran up to her and handed her a piece of paper.

"Read this at the end of the show, not the teleprompter." He left as quickly as he had arrived.

She almost gasped. Instantly she got a twinge in her stomach and felt a cold sweat coming on. "Buck up," she told herself.

The make-up person came over and touched up her face, which by now she needed.

The stage director gave her the countdown and they began.

"Tonight, we bring you the latest in news from Iran. About fifteen minutes ago bombing began in Teheran and ten other cities. It is set to continue for one to two hours.

As far as can be ascertained, approximately fifty thousand non-Iranians have been able to leave the country. Another four to six million more people are literally sitting on the borders not knowing what lies in their future.

They have received no aide from their own government and see little coming as the bombing will destroy most of the leaders of the functioning theocracy who were determined not to abandon their homes and offices.

Though not allowing them admittance, the surrounding nations have sent supplies and food to the camps, as has the United Nations."

She continued on as if it were a normal evening. Emotion was entirely forbidden. Just read the news and take commercial breaks.

Finally the last moments arrived. She picked up the paper that had been handed to her.

"Finally I have a rather startling announcement to make." Those words were not written on her notes. They were the first and last she would ever say of her own.

The teleprompter operator became hysterical. There was nothing like that on the screen. He almost fainted.

"This will be the last telecast of our network. Not just the news, but the entire network. We will go off air and remain so indefinitely. Thank you, and good night."

17

Thursday, April 20th, 9:30 PM, EDT

Jim Wilkins had been preparing his notes for most of the day, and was ready to proceed as soon as the President arrived. That he did at precisely nine thirty as scheduled.

Madison strode into the room and sat down. The secret service that were with him stationed themselves outside and closed the door.

His muscular body and chiseled face had taken him far in the military and now in politics. It was difficult for those who did not know him intimately to dismiss or ignore him, and since he had no one close to him, this included almost everyone in the country.

He had never been married mainly for the reason he preferred fighting and intrigue to sex. When the latter was needed he either paid for it or had someone summoned, very much like John Kennedy.

"Bring me up to date," he directed.

Wilkins as always was very methodical in his approach.

"First, you probably heard that Central Broadcasting shut down this evening," he began.

"Do you know why and who ordered it?" he asked.

"No. It wasn't one of our people. I doubt if John Enman did it. He's not really involved in anything day to day."

72

"Maybe that piece of shit, Saranoff," Madison suggested.

It was no secret as to what and how much he owned. The Feds had a room full of files and records, and enormous computer databases on him and they were certain that was not everything.

It wasn't, and most of what they had accumulated was information on corporation facades or misdirections; several key government employees on his payroll saw to that.

Hell, he guessed even he owed him his office, but he didn't consider it a debt that would ever be paid.

"Who knows, but I doubt it. How would that benefit him?" Wilkins wondered.

"Put someone on it, but in reality, who cares? The two networks that remain are more than enough. I doubt very many people watch them, and really I don't give a shit," the president responded nonchalantly.

Wilkins looked at his papers and continued, "Next, the troops will all be deployed by next Monday."

"Good. How has recruitment and training been going with the Security Forces?" Madison asked.

"We had three thousand new enrollments last week. With unemployment at thirty-two percent you would think they would enlist in droves," Wilkins bemoaned.

"You would think that," the Chief said.

Wilkins almost hesitated, and then he continued.

"I guess we should be happy with that. They are not the most popular police force out there."

"I still believe we should conscript them from the local cops. Besides most of our people are fairly worthless, ruthless maybe, but not very effective," Madison interjected.

"The initial group Obama started with was pretty good, but those that joined the past two years are lacking in almost every way, and training doesn't help much."

It was difficult to ask Americans to kill or even hurt other Americans and that was exactly what was required at times. If the United States were to be saved from the tyranny of Wall Street and order restored, sacrifices were going to have to be made. If there was anything else in his heart, it was his desire to go down in history as its savior.

"Riot" control and patrols were most of their duties. The problem was that standards were so low that the majority of them were only marginally intelligent and were basically psychologically unfit for the job, at least in a civilized society. But these days their deficiencies were not only acceptable, but also vitally necessary.

"How are we doing with the Intelligence Division?" Madison asked.

"As good as can be expected. They are the best we have."

Wilkins knew that was not saying much. They did use what resources were left at the NSA, DOD, and the CIA. Since they were shadows of their former selves, little was useable, and not that trustworthy, the former administration had seen to that.

"That brings me to something else, it may just be an aberration, but our AWOL's and desertions seem to be up, not dramatically but still noticeably."

"Is that underground pissing with us again?" the President asked.

He refused to call them "the Patriots" as most of those who knew of their existence did. Madison considered them anything but that. He believed them to be a cancer eating at the fragile fabric of society.

"I don't believe they are a large organization. We have had a difficult time assessing their relevance or accumulating any real information on them, and something else," he shuffled some papers then continued, "we did apprehend a car with a new, hopefully unique, counter-surveillance device. It seems to pick up signals from vehicles near it and use their signals for a short time to avoid detection. I assume it is for mobility."

"What of the driver? Madison asked.

"He claimed he knew nothing about it and said maybe it was installed by someone when he had it parked."

"You believe that?"

"Of course not, but he said that until the end." Wilkins offered.

The liberals had decried torture under the Bush administration from every dais in the country, but had secretly developed their own covert system in its place for use in country, which this administration used quite effectively. They had none of the compassion they voiced in public when the information needed was for them.

"We have people working on it. It should not be too long before our network can correct its effect. Hopefully it's just one of those diehard hacker types."

"After next week, I want you to dig into all of this deeper. I know they will be a thorn in our sides, and eventually we will have to weed them out," the President stated bluntly. "We will need to know precisely what we are dealing with."

Wilkins knew that he wanted to cover all bases no matter how improbable. They really did not know the extent of the "underground" and they both found that entirely unacceptable.

They continued with other business for several more hours, neither needed a lot of sleep, and after all, this work was their entire existence. They always felt they were doing what was best for the country, as deluded as that might seem now.

18

"Why are you calling like this?" Mitchell Grayson asked.

John Enman was sitting in front of his computer, knowing full well that he and his friend were safe in their discussion.

"I felt this was the best way to communicate now. I'm certain that I am being watched," Enman began.

"By whom?"

"I'm not sure, but S. seems to know everything I do and everyone I talk to."

"Everyone?" Grayson asked very seriously.

Enman nodded, and then asked, "Did you get the package?"

"Yes," he answered. "But I haven't opened it yet."

"Get it."

Grayson reached behind his desk and retrieved a small package and quickly removed an old-style flash memory. That was their way of exchanging information. It was considered safe, as most people and businesses hadn't used them in almost five years.

When he read what was on his screen, he looked up in astonishment.

"Is this what I think it is?" he asked.

"Yes."

"How much?" the detective questioned.

"Everything," Enman responded.

What his friend was reading was a list of the locations, passwords, and necessary information for him to access all of his "hidden" assets. Mitchell's name or their alternate ID's were on all of the accounts. He had seen to it as he processed the deposits over the years. In his heart he knew that one day it would come down to this and he was the only human other than his wife that he trusted.

He had been buying diamonds, gold, and other precious metals for quite a long time. With the inflation of the past decade it was now probably worth nearly fifty billion dollars. Obviously that didn't buy what it used to, considering the national debt was over a hundred trillion dollars and rapidly growing, and a hamburger was about twenty-five dollars, but it would help the cause.

Before his friend could ask, he simply stated, "Penance."

"How did you know?" Grayson asked.

"I guessed a year or so ago."

Enman had learned or suspected his friend was involved in the movement, and as usual he was right.

"Use it well," he stated earnestly. "I don't know if I can do more. This was all done off the books. That was hard then, it is almost impossible now."

He had also closed businesses that were nonfunctional or a drain instead of profit-producing. It had killed him to lay off the hundreds of employees involved, but he felt that in the long run it was better for everyone, including them.

He had also set in place the process of combining and restructuring many that he deemed absolutely vital for the future.

"Is there anything we can do for you?" Grayson offered.

"As a matter of fact there is," Enman answered.

He told him what he needed and after a few bits of small talk said simply, "Good-bye."

19

Leslie Phillips, the Governor of California, drove his pickup truck through the side streets on the outskirts of San Francisco. Since he was a strikingly fit man with that type of appearance it took no convincing that he was probably a construction worker. He looked very natural behind the steering wheel of this vehicle. And with the demise of trivial news casting and newspapers, very few average citizens knew who he was; therefore, being discreet was easy.

His security staff was aware of his need to ditch them, so they were easy to elude. A not-so-secret part of his private life was his desire for dalliances with his stable of women. It was a rumor that he had carefully cultivated within his political power chain. Even his wife was aware of it, since she originated the idea in the first place.

Initially it was useful in securing votes in Southern California. The ultra-left saw it a "cool" badge of honor and gathered him not only a large group of donors and a significant increase in votes, but also a foot into doors that were not open to most Republicans. His endorsement of Madison and the appointment of a liberal as a running mate helped secure him a second term, and he needed all of the help he could get. Marion was a genius and he loved her more than anything, even his career.

He parked his truck on the road that ran parallel to the ocean highway and walked to the end of the block. The chance of his vehicle being noticed was fairly slim as it looked like every other one in the area and it had a fake license plate for specific use in these circumstances. It never left his possession when not in on the pickup.

Security knew this too and thought it was all part of the game. He and Marion trusted no one including them.

His mind was always in turmoil when he drove through the sections of California's cities that suffered the most from the broken economy. There were homeless everywhere, walking back and forth on the streets past boarded up houses. Their eyes spoke of lost souls from other times, and it ate him alive.

After forty years of mismanagement the piper had finally been paid. Many of the state's residents thought that the federal government would bail them out, but when the Obama administration tried, the backlash throughout the country almost cost him his second term.

California had passed so many laws and referendums providing low cost and no-cost education and public services for everyone including illegal aliens, that eventually it was proven unsustainable.

The state and local employees were allowed to be unionized, demanded and finally received salaries above and way beyond the private sector. This in turn generated outlandish retirement pensions which could never be funded, and never were.

As an example, all of the state parks were free for anyone to visit for most of that time, and when there was talk of charging a fair and sustaining entrance and use fee, it was voted down. Ultimately all of their treasured parks were turned over to the National Park Service, fees were charged, and when hard times hit everywhere they were neglected anyway. However, the buck had been passed and the feds got most of the blame.

Instead of taking the correct courses of action such as making cuts in spending, reducing taxes to encourage business, and sending the illegals home, they raised taxes on the "rich" which sooner or later always meant anyone making over minimum wage. They increased entitlement programs even more for the "undocumented" residents and for everyone else on the lower end of the pay scale to buy votes so they could continue their political existence.

California had the highest taxes in the country until the whole system collapsed. Businesses left the state along with the highest wage earners, leaving only the poorest and neediest behind. Even most of the film community abandoned ship. Many relocated permanently in Canada when Washington passed laws controlling broadcast media. It had only been a brief time until the pressure was on to regulate the motion picture industry. The irony of that fiasco almost made up for some of the pain.

All of this was constantly in the governor's thoughts. He had truly ran for office to make a difference, but the bullheaded left was still in charge, and was still wallowing in their own fantasies.

He turned at the corner and walked about half way down the block and then onto the back service road of the townhouses he had just passed. When he had reached the third on the right, he punched in a series of five numbers and the gate opened.

After entering he walked to the back entrance and it opened as he approached. A beautiful young woman, Nina Blair, met him at the door in her negligee, threw her arms around him, and gave him a passionate kiss, in case any passersby recognized him.

When the door had shut, she released him and gave him a warm smile.

"How's my girl Marion doing?" she beamed.

"Great. I know she misses the hell out of you," he responded as if she was a long lost friend.

They had been friends since high school. In fact, she had introduced Marion to him, and talked him into dating her in the first place. Every time he thought of it, he couldn't believe she had had to do that.

They walked into her hallway, opened a door that led to the basement, and descended the stairs to an amazing bedroom that they, Marion and Nina, had designed years before. She went into the bathroom and very quickly returned fully dressed, and they went to a side door and opened it.

The entrance led to the basement of the house next door. A similar situation was setup on the opposite house combining the three homes sitting next to each other.

What was truly unique and completely devious about all of it was that the couple that lived in the middle home had no idea there was a basement in use. They rented the building and were told the owner wanted it for storage and had it sealed off, which was the truth. It was also soundproofed, and had high-end security, close-circuit cameras, and alarms.

When they wanted to have meetings he entered through her house and the others entered through the front door two houses down the block. In the past this would have seemed like something out of a paranoid fantasy, but today it was looking as if someone had a lot of foresight.

That someone was Marion Conrad-Phillips. She even hyphenated her name to blend in. Unlike the former First Ladies of California who had liked and drew attention, the press seldom mentioned her and thought of her as rather bland and lack luster: were they ever wrong.

She was a distant relative of Senator Barry Goldwater, the first modern conservative, and she idolized him. Though she never met him, she had read everything available and not only studied, but also lived by the principles he espoused, probably better than he did.

A lot of people would have thought this all silly and a little weird, but she was deadly serious, and yes a little compulsive. After delving deeper into history and the twentieth century she was convinced that there was trouble ahead for the country.

Like Hilary Clinton before her with Bill, she was attracted to Leslie because she felt he was going to be a significant leader one day. But unlike Mrs. Clinton, she was not only willing to be in the background, she knew and relished the power she had accumulated behind the scenes.

Her husband was not only smart, educated, and had a ton of common sense, but she loved him for the great guy he was. She felt that they made an awesome team.

Each time he came to this room, he thought of all the planning and resources it had taken and the pride welled up in him for her.

The Patriots now used this place for upper echelon gatherings, and tonight was no exception. There were only four members that had access and knowledge to get this far; he (Cal #2), Nina (Cal #3), North Cal #1, and South Cal #1. Obviously Marion was Cal#1.

Though they evidently knew each other, they never used names at any times so that, if ever overheard, identifications could not be advanced, and slips of the tongues could be avoided.

The other two were waiting for them when they entered.

"We just got word," Phillips began, "that a large contribution has been made that will finance us for some time."

They were all totally pleased. Money had filtered out of some of the disaffected Hollywood elites that were still solvent, or too old to spend it themselves, but it had been dwindling. It was great news.

"Now let's get down to business," Nina said authoritatively.

20

Friday, April 22nd, 7:52 PM, CDT

Marsha Willard sat next to her father's indoor pool trying to read an article in one of the two remaining fashion magazines. This was something she hadn't done in years because they were such garbage anymore, similar to what must have been published in East Germany three decades before. She had been making the attempt to keep her mind on them for several hours with no success.

Still staring at the same page, her mind kept going over the details of her life until this day. A smile came to face more often than tears, just as life does in the continuum.

When she had called home and could not reach her father, she naturally got through to Tom Davis, his Chief-of-Staff. Noting the fearful tone in her voice, he contacted one of their people in Washington and two security men had accompanied her to Reagan Airport and flew back with her to Houston. Since there were only a couple non-military flights a week, it took an enormous amount of pull to get a seat even with the fact she was a member of the President's cabinet.

Davis and two more people met them. They swept her into his classic Hummer as the other two secured her luggage and followed in a second vehicle.

He was almost like her second father, since he had known her from the time she was a child. Her father had started with nothing and had built an enormous oil business almost like the mythical Ewings on the golden age of television.

The main difference was his utter contempt of most of the corporations that had acquired his colleagues. So in a fit of anger and dismay with these U.S. companies, he had sold everything for a huge profit to a Dutch conglomerate in the late Eighties.

He and her mother had lived a full life until she died suddenly. Even with the consumption of his time by the business, she was always his first and only love. After several months of mourning, he determined that if he were to stay sane and fit, he would have to get back into the fray.

When the bottom fell out of the market a decade later he had bought that deal back and several others for a fraction of the money he had received. By then he had diversified into many other areas of business, winning and losing, but mostly accumulating more money than any several thousand families could ever use.

Tom Davis had been a ranch hand on one of his first spreads, starting fifty years ago. He had worked his way up on it, and then to completely run the business, and then later all of them. Today he was in charge of security operations for the whole enterprise. However much work he had, there was always time for Marsha, even when her father hadn't had it.

That was not to say, her father was absent, he wasn't. They did many things together, especially traveling, going to concerts, and even shopping.

When she remembered all of the moments with those two, both emotions surfaced and tears of joy welled in her eyes. Obviously she had spent a great deal of the last few hours crying, and was feeling much better for it.

Tom hadn't told her when her father would return. Most likely he knew, but such business was as they say, on a need to know basis, and quite frankly, she didn't need to know. She understood.

Having basically worked for the enemy for the past few years, how could she blame them? Her short political life had opened her eyes and she really hadn't liked what she had seen.

In the midst of some exceptionally deep contemplation, she was brought back to the moment with a huge booming voice.

"Baby Girl! Thank God you're home!"

She turned and saw her father standing there in all of his grandeur, and like the little girl inside of her, she ran and hugged him, tears streaming down her cheeks.

He held her tightly in return.

If anyone had seen that picture, they would have been astounded. This petite gray-haired woman and this enormous six-foot five-inch man greeting as if they hadn't seen each other in fifty years would have warmed the dourest soul alive.

"Papa, I'm so sorry!" she let it all pour out.

"For what, honey?" he questioned.

"For not understanding you all of these years. For letting you down and embarrassing you." She was now sobbing dramatically.

"What the hell are you talking about?" he said as he grabbed her shoulders.

"I was an abject failure in the White House cabinet! I really wasn't very good in congress, I…" He stopped her before she could continue.

"Whoa, there darlin! You seemed to have slipped off here. You accomplished everything you set out to do. I especially like when you pissed off Madison the other day." He burst out laughing at that.

She wiped her teary eyes and started a little smile. "That was fun."

"Every report you sent back to Chicago was important; however, the main duty you had was to divert attention from some others who needed to be let's say more discreet."

She hesitated, and then said, "You used me as a decoy?"

"You bet. I knew you could handle it, and I would have bet my life you wouldn't have succumbed to the dark side. You are too damn decent." He gave her another hug.

"All these years and I was a… a pawn?" She started to get a tad peeved.

"But a beautiful one, yes siree Bob!" That rated another hug. His use of little colloquialisms around friends helped him to stay grounded, and he would die before he quit using them.

She pushed him away and lightly started to beat on him, again like a child.

"Do you understand how important you were? Honey we are about to enter a shit storm, and we needed all of the intel we could get. We could not have done it without you, and I promise, you will not only know everything from here out, but I expect you to be at my side constantly." He stopped for a moment then continued.

"I'm getting up there in age, you know."

"You're more fit than I am, you old coot!" She laughed, not wanting to face the truth in his words.

"Yeah, sure! The point is I have no one I trust more than you, and I have some extremely important plans for you." He became very earnest in his demeanor.

"What's that?" she asked.

"In due time," he answered. "Have you had supper yet?"

She hadn't heard dinner referred as supper in ages, and for some reason, even that made her feel safer.

"No, I really wasn't hungry, until now."

"I'm sure someone can rustle us up some grub," he smiled with every word.

"Yeah, me," she beamed feeling oh so much more human.

They turned and went to the kitchen.

21

John Enman sat in front of the computer screen for a long while. He had no idea whether he should call or not, and could easily foresee the repercussions of not contacting him, but his fears dwindled as the hours passed.

His wife, sons, and their families were as safe as possible, thanks to Mitchell. Even he didn't know where they were and wasn't about to even venture a guess since Saranoff seemed to be able to read his mind.

"God, I am paranoid," he thought.

Tired fingers finally beat out the necessary keys and the screen came to life; however, he sat there for over twenty minutes before there was a response. In this past decade this had seldom happened, especially on a return call. He had been summoned a few minutes before he had come into the house.

As he waited, he thought of the beating he would take over shutting the network. The picture changed and shortly focused on a slightly disheveled Saranoff.

He felt like speaking first, and he eventually did, "My friend, what is wrong?" That felt good.

The old man raised his finger for him to wait a moment, and then began, "Just an old man's ponderings, my dear friend."

When he hesitated again and dropped his head a little, Enman realized he was listening to someone, probably with an earpiece. That was indeed interesting, another first.

"John," he began, "I'm extremely perplexed."

Enman waited, noticing he had suddenly stopped breathing. Almost gasping, he fought to control his reaction.

He still thought Saranoff was trying to listen and talk. Eventually he became very animated.

"John," he started again, "I have no idea what is going on over there. I certainly hope you can enlighten me."

"All I know is that some very important people are either quitting the administration, being discharged, or just disappearing. My sources have lost track of some of them. There have even been rumors of arrests." Enman paused.

"I fear there may be a lot more to this."

"My thoughts exactly," Saranoff said stoically.

Did Enman sense a note of fear? "That was impossible, wasn't it," he thought.

"I became very leery when I saw that your network closed. Who would do that?"

"How the hell did he not know?" Enman pondered as usual, but by now he shouldn't have.

"Who do you think did it? I haven't been able to dig up even a hit of a clue and I own it." Before he would have never lied like that, but it seemed fine now.

"No idea, I must say apologetically."

"Pigs were now throwing snowballs at each other as they flew through hell," he imagined when he heard those words.

"Some of my best people in Washington are not responding to me," he simply said with a hint of emotion. "I don't like that at all."

"I can try to find out more, my friend," Enman offered.

"No John," Saranoff said emphatically. "I want you and your family to disappear."

"I can't do that, my friend," Enman said, thinking that maybe this old fart was his friend, but immediately discarded that notion. "But there is one thing I would ask, if I may." He was hoping to catch a break.

"What is that?" he quickly asked.

"I have some property in Canada and South Africa I would like to liquidate off the books for gold or something equivalent." Enman waited for the response he wanted, but didn't anticipate.

"Not a problem, my friend."

"You can take twice your usual percentage," Enman felt he should sweeten the deal anyway.

"Not necessary my friend, you have always done what I needed, and this time while I can, I will return the kindness."

To say that he was stunned was to minimize the very existence of that word.

"Thank you," was all he could muster at the moment for a response.

"Just send me the information and I will have it handled immediately." He paused and for maybe the second time since Enman had met him, Saranoff seemed to see him as a real person.

"And John… be careful. Please contact me at least once a day."

"Of course," he said.

Saranoff was gone and Enman sat there for several minutes absorbing what had just occurred, suddenly starting to comprehend the extent of the coming maelstrom.

22

Friday, April 22nd, 8:32 PM, EDT

Senator Childress walked as quickly as he tired body would let him from his office to a waiting town car. The day was etched into his mind as no other had ever been. If he lived long enough to have a moment to recall it, he doubted he would believe his memories.

For the past two days the House and the Senate had been in session almost without stopping. Fistfights had occurred regularly on both floors as if the British Parliament had suddenly moved into town.

Word had spread that the President was going to announce several new measures that would alter everything, absolutely everything. Without knowing a single fact, the factions formed and the battle had begun.

The left accused the right of all manner of ill-behavior and collusions with big business. The right responded in kind. The members who normally brought calm to most debates took sides and there was no buffering the emotions pouring out of all of them like molten lava.

Childress had been there for forty years and was totally perplexed. Never had he envisioned a future this disconnected with reality. Just as he thought he was about to go mad, a voice whispered in his ear. He turned to see who it was, when it occurred to him, it was his inner self. Suddenly he saw it all for what it was.

He rose as quickly as possible and worked his way back to his office. As swiftly as he could, he gathered as much paperwork as he was able. His assistant ordered him a car and two security people he could trust.

When he was as confident as he could be that he had as much as was necessary or convenient to carry with him, he had two of his assistants help him get it all to his car.

He quietly told all of them to go home and not return until they heard from him directly. "If they heard from him," the voice spoke again.

When he had everything loaded, he instructed the last two to do the same thing. They insisted on remaining with him, but the adamant tone of his voice won the day. Afterward, they literally raced to their own vehicles as his demeanor scared the shit out of them.

The town car left quickly, but not so fast as to draw too much attention. It continued in the same manner as they moved through the streets of DC.

When they drove out of Washington to Maryland he had them stay on side streets and avoid Rts. 95 and 295. Paranoia was not his normal pattern of behavior, but if what had flashed into his mind was correct, it was time to act.

He had moved his family to safety in Ecuador a few months earlier, and he was very tempted to join them. As he knew, that was not his way and he had explained that to them before they had gone. He had to call in a lot of favors to enable them to go. It wasn't mentioned, but they all knew the distinct possibility of never seeing each other again.

Now he knew that was how it would be.

23

Saturday, April 23rd, 10:00 AM, EDT

President Madison had called a Saturday morning broadcast, which was virtually unprecedented. To anyone familiar with politics and the media, it is normally a time in which you bury a story in the weekend cycle, when theoretically no one was watching. However, news had spread that Washington was in turmoil and most people were living in such fear that they listened constantly and were anticipating the worst. He was ready to give it to them.

As the camera moved in a little tighter, the director gave the go-ahead and he began.

"My fellow Americans, I come to you today with a great deal of sadness. It appears that not only are our enemies outside of the country continuing to terrorize us, but we also have enemies within our borders."

His appearance was both stoic and concerned.

"Many of you may know that our home-grown terrorists have finally struck in the halls of Congress. After the death of Senator Hampstead on the floor of the Senate, I have had the National Security Force arrest thirty-two Senators and one hundred and fifty-three Congressmen in the House of Representatives. All of these members are believed to be conspiring to one degree or another to overthrow the government.

Three of them are being held in a Federal Detention Center under the Second Patriot Act, and the remaining traitors are under house arrest. Three have managed to evade capture, and warrants have been issued for their apprehension."

He paused and lowered his head for affect.

"When I took office, I would never in my wildest imagination have thought I would see the day that we would be faced with this extent of treason. Both Branches of Congress will meet in a special session tonight to consider what can be done at this time.

I will send a press release to all media this afternoon, detailing the names and status of everyone involved."

He looked directly into the camera, and again paused.

"I can not express the amount of sadness weighing on my heart at this moment. I…we have been deceived by the very men and women that we elected to the highest offices in the country; people in whom we placed our trust. They ignored the very standards and honor that they swore to uphold. No punishment will be too great for them.

However, we have everything under control and this menace has been stopped. You may go to bed tonight knowing that our system will be preserved and will continue as it always has.

Good night, and May God Bless us all."

The red light on the camera blinked off, and the President motioned all of them to leave. Thinking he was totally caught up in the moment, they quickly exited.

Jim and Madison looked at each other and smiled.

24

Saturday, April 23rd, 2:32 PM, EDT

General Higgins and Gloria Martin had decided to meet at a small takeout stand just inside of Fairfax, Virginia a few days before. It was one of the very few left as hardly any people had enough disposable income to spend on prepared food. The owners made no money from the operation but simply ran it out of habit and the love of feeding their customers, many of whom were their friends. After today they would probably close and never reopen. He wanted to eat there for one last time, the nostalgia of age.

Now as they neared their destination, they both knew the plans they were reviewing were passé.

Madison's newscast form the Oval office had changed everything. Higgins knew the hammer had finally dropped, and she reviewed continuously the strategy for a rebellion.

They were having a rendezvous in the open as they now feared the roads into the countryside were being watched more than activity in town.

The traffic was very light for a Saturday, and somehow they figured the bars were open early and now packed, as were the churches. Both of those establishments would probably have their hours and events curtailed or ended, he reasoned; maybe not for a while, but it would eventually happen.

When Martin arrived from around the corner she found him chewing on a polish sausage and drinking a diet soda. She went to the window and ordered a giant hamburger and fries. After paying her twenty dollars for the meal, she walked over to the small table and joined Higgins.

"This may be one of our last meals together in public, or anywhere" she offered.

"You're most likely correct," he answered.

They had learned long before to speak extremely soft, but succinctly, so that anyone passing by would think they were whispering and trying to be intimate.

"Do you think we should talk to our friends?" she asked.

He nodded, and said, "The time to act is upon us. As much as I knew it would happen, I always hoped and prayed otherwise."

They ate a bit, and then he continued, "Mr. C. made it out of Washington, but I don't know how long he can remain free."

"We can't expose ourselves just yet to protect him," she said sullenly.

"He knows that and wouldn't ask. The last thing he would want to do is to endanger our operation. His family is safe and he is mentally prepared," he said with more regret in his voice than he ever would have expected. He and Childress went back a long way, a long, long way.

"What do you want to do next?" she asked.

"Plan 2B," he answered.

Martin knew this was the order for the alert of all involved. It meant that a state of readiness and preparation for the forth-coming signal to respond when given was now in affect. Hopefully the training and logistical planning would be enough, and that the enemy had no idea what was in store for them.

The announcement of the arrests with no regard whatsoever for the law had taken them back for a moment, but now it had cemented their resolve on the state of the nation and their need for action.

95

She nodded, finished her sandwich, and got up.

"Bye Dad, I'll see you when I get back next week," she said in a voice that anyone close could hear. Then she leaned over and kissed him on the cheek. It all meant something to them in signs and passes, but there also were deeper meanings for both of them.

She waved as she left, and he felt a sudden pain in his gut. He might not ever see her again. "Oh dear God no," he prayed silently.

25

"That son-of-a-bitch. I'm going to..." Gregor Saranoff caught himself as John Enman watch his benefactor in a state that he would have never believed possible.

"That can't be good for your blood pressure, my friend," Enman tried to calm the disheveled man on his computer screen. This was indeed a sight that almost stopped his heart. Could it be he actually felt sorry for him, well maybe just a little bit?

"It probably is, but I can't help myself. I have not felt so violated in all my life," he fumed.

"I'm sure others have by your actions," Enman thought.

"John, Madison is a lunatic. What is he going to do next?"

"I have no idea Gregor, but it won't be good, I can assure you. How much do you think you lost?"

"About three hundred and fifty billion," he bemoaned.

"Maybe you should just hold on for a while, maybe the market will correct at least somewhat," John offered.

President Madison had announced early this morning that the United States would immediately stop buying oil from the international markets. This included from their allies Canada and Mexico. The turmoil from this statement was instantaneous and violent. Suddenly, there was a worldwide glut in oil reserves and the price of crude dropped by half within an hour.

As he was talking everyone had the same thought, what in the world would happen to what remained of American commerce? The next words out of his mouth nailed the coffin lid shut. When he took office he had ordered the expanded North Slope and off shore drilling to proceed on the Q-T as rapidly as could be completed.

He also increased natural gas production and shale oil research without a bit of publicity, and these fields would begin production within weeks. All of the restrictions the previous administration had enacted were instantly dissolved.

The United States had enough known reserves to last at least a hundred years at the old rate of consumptions; however, with the massive decrease of the last few years and the expected problems in the future, it would probably go a lot farther than that.

These deals were easily accomplished since the government had taken over the energy sector of the economy after the elections in 2012. With the precedent set of government ownership of a huge portion of the financials, automobile production, and the health profession, the purchase of oil and gas companies was completed before anyone noticed.

Congress should have been involved and have oversight in all of these matters, but their rule was diminished to the point of irrelevance in a very short time. After the 2010 elections, executive orders were issued in such numbers, that the legislative and judicial branches were made thoroughly extraneous. The whole system of checks and balances was relinquished to a footnote in history.

"How did that happen? I thought you had bought physicals, not futures?" John asked him.

"Even so I leveraged a lot because I thought it was a fantastic opportunity, but for this piece-of-shit takeover, it would have been. I had to sell because I needed cash. The cascade of problems has disrupted most of the other markets, especially real estate. I had to cover a lot of cash calls in Canada, Central and South America, and the Middle East. So far the European and Asian markets were closed or restricted, but it is just a matter of time."

"I hate to ask right now, but what about the properties I ask you to liquidate?" John suddenly was personally concerned.

"They were taken care yesterday. Hopefully no one will back out, but who knows," Saranoff responded.

"Do whatever you have to get something out of it. It is really important," John asked almost begging.

"Don't worry I should have it finished by the end of the day. I have called in a few of my remaining favors. Believe me; I know it is important to you, and to the others."

John was a little baffled. Did Saranoff know for what the proceeds where intended?

"I will courier the results to you immediately thereafter," Saranoff offered.

"Thank you Gregor," Enman said sincerely. "You said there were repercussions in the in Mid-East, anything in particular?"

"You have no idea my friend. The impact on the economies there will be disastrous and extremely dangerous. Most of those governments are leveraged to the hilt and will have to forego most of their expansion and construction plans. The end result will most likely be riots and much discontent. They will either start attacking each other, or most likely Europe. Either way this tsunami will have a worldwide effect. And I believe Madison knows this and planned it all along."

"That should satisfy many Americans, at least at first," Enman inserted.

"Until they understand his ulterior motives," Saranoff finished, "total and absolute domination."

"It might not be that easy," he suggested.

"I hope you are right, dear friend. I sincerely hope you are right." Saranoff was clearly exhausted. "I'll contact you later tonight."

"Get some sleep Gregor."

"I will when this is over, or I am dead." With that he signed off.

Enman sat there and pondered all that had happened over the past ten years, and could not believe how much he had participated in bringing the country to this position.

All of their promises and expectations were simply fabrications. They had not only lied to the nation, but to themselves. By removing individual risk, responsibility, and accountability from society, they had unleashed this monster. By constructing a huge ever-devouring government, this was the result. It was only a matter of time. If Jake Madison hadn't come along, it would have been someone else.

Progressives had worked at it for over a hundred and twenty years, but he and his ilk finished the job overnight.

"I hope they are satisfied now," Enman said out loud. "No, I hope they all rot in hell. That's where we are all going."

He got up and went to his bedroom and looked out of his window into the night and cried.

26

Senator Leonard Childress sat in the office of a summer home located just outside of St. Michaels on the Eastern Shore of Maryland. It belonged to a friend of his, but was owned on paper by a shell corporation in the Bahamas.

He and Higgins had originally gotten it for the movement, but had only been using it as a safe house a few times. After everything that had happened over the past year they figured it would be confiscated along with any other foreign holdings in the U.S. in the near future. For the time being it was as secure as anywhere could be.

He was sipping his favorite brandy and reading Ayn Rand's Atlas Shrugged for the tenth or eleventh time.

It was a valiant attempt to rid his mind of thoughts of his family. The knowledge that he would never see them again ate into him more than he ever thought it would.

Curtis Schulman, the senator from Wyoming had been caught earlier in the day crossing from Virginia into Kentucky and was killed resisting arrest.

"Of course he was," Childress thought, picturing his eighty-six year old friend beating on the Security Forces. It a very implausible sight, but the idea brought a smile to his face.

The inevitability of the situation was surely flooding over him and somehow he felt a degree of comfort in that. He had sent his security people away as soon as he had arrived yesterday, since he did not want their deaths on his hands. They would definitely be needed much more elsewhere.

As if on cue, the door burst open and three men entered the room: others remained in the hall. Simultaneously the patio door was smashed and two more stood in the frame where the glass once was.

"Senator Childress... you are under arrest," one of the NSF said.

As he raised his glass he answered, "Ah, the Federal thugs have arrived, just in the nick of time."

"We have some questions," another spoke.

"I'm sure you do," he said as he smiled and took a sip of the brandy. It did taste so wonderful. "But gentlemen, and believe me I use that word reluctantly, I have no intention of relinquishing to any of your demands."

"We will see about that," the first man said as he approached the senator.

Childress sat his glass down as he moved his chair back a bit. It was placed strategically on a pressure pad. Instantly the deck on the patio burst into a fireball under the two soldiers that were standing on it. The hall exploded simultaneously killing the two positioned there and the third man next to that door.

The detonations were set to avoid his end of the room and in the seconds during the confusion, he casually raised the revolver he had on his lap and shot both of the other men, one bullet each, in the head.

As he made his way out of the house, he climbed over broken glass and splintered lumber. He crossed his yard and ran as quickly as his old legs would carry him to a small dock about one hundred yards away.

He quietly thanked Higgins for his refresher course in firearms. It had been over fifty years since his military days, but as they say about riding a bike, many of his instincts were still functioning.

Sounds of people shouting rang from the sides of the house as the others with them got up and started to gather themselves for a search. He just made it to the small boat that was docked there. As he untied it, a shot buzzed past him and hit the water. A shout from the shooter was sure to bring more of them.

He got in as fast as he could move, hitting the ignition switch as soon as he landed. It immediately started and he pushed the throttle forward.

Several more shots rang out and he couldn't believe his luck at not being hit. When he had the opportunity to turn his head, he saw that four of them were on the dock. As he reached for another detonator switch rigged on the boat, a bullet tore threw his right shoulder and knocked him against the dash. He slid onto the floor, exhausted and in enormous pain.

With every last bit of his energy he hit the switch and the dock exploded under the four men blowing them straight to hell; at least that was his hope.

He reached into his pocket and pulled out another remote, and his last thought was, "God I love a good show." His boat blew up with such force it knocked down a man standing of the shore, the only survivor of the raid.

27

Ramon Ramirez moved quickly and quietly through his neighborhood trying not draw attention to himself. In the old days this would have been impossible, but gang colors no longer mattered in the same way as then.

Some of the smaller groups had members leave and join the National Security Forces when the new President had ordered a total clamp down on gangs nationwide, sometimes simply shooting them and not even bothering to arrest anyone.

That procedure worked miracles, as activity ceased almost immediately. The country applauded, at least at first. The old ACLU type warriors began to take it all into their sights and tried to sue anyone and everyone they could; however, when the Feds started IRS audits and other forms of retaliations, including sudden disappearances, that too was history.

The larger gangs such as his guys, lost a few members to the raids and a couple to the NSF, but the rest went underground and waited for the right time to resurface.

When Ramon had discovered, quite by accident, about the Patriot Movement, his interest was totally piqued. He not only got involved, but convinced most of his boys, and several other former gangs to join.

In an amazingly short period, men that were shooting and killing each other were training to defend their people. Incredibly, the seed of pride and patriotism was planted and began to grow. Many of them were becoming men that could not have been imagined just months earlier that they would ever consider ideals and people other than themselves and their own interests.

The gangs formed loose alliances as instructed so that no one knew the other members and could not give up any information if questioned. This intrigued many of them and helped promote the whole cause. Initially it felt like a live video game.

It was just a guess on Ramon's part but he was quite sure their membership was in the thousands. "Let those bastards attack East and South L.A. again," he thought, "and they will get the shock of their miserable lives."

He finally reached his destination. In his original negotiations, he had gathered the five most powerful leaders in the area and worked with them. Even knowing each other as well as they did, they immediately began to refer to themselves as SLA#1 through #5. The system was continued right down the line as with the other cells in the country.

Since the farther away from the leadership the fewer members were known to each other, it would take an enormous effort to get information from them. They were all used to keeping their mouths shut, and looking out for each other. These were extremely useful traits now.

Ramon walked into a building that would have been guarded by some gang's members before, but now appeared to be totally unwatched. Appearances were becoming more and more deceptive as there were at least five sentries from non-related gangs watching the area, ready to kill or be killed.

The other four leaders were already present.

"Sorry, I'm late guys," he offered.

"No prob, man," one of them answered, "we were just giving with some shit."

"I just got some really wild info from South Cal#1," he was excited.

They looked at him with anticipation and said nothing.

"This old white dude from South Carolina, Senator Childress, and get this shit, he was seventy-two years old man. They came for him and he wasted nine of the ten bastards. Blew their asses to hell."

Murmurs of adulations and respect rose from all of them.

"We, mi amigos, are going to help write the history books. If some old white guy can do that, we can do a hell of a lot more." Ramon was smiling from ear to ear.

"No shit," rang out everywhere.

"Tell all your guys about him, and get his name right. He is the first martyr for the cause, and gets our respect, you hear?"

"Damn straight!"

"We want everyone in this damn town to know who he is and what it means. Get it? He will be avenged!" Ramon swore.

"They are sending some more trainers. We have to be ready as soon as possible." He continued.

"We'll teach them a few things!" one of them shouted.

"Maybe so, but we don't have time to be assholes. If you have ideas, don't be afraid to give them, but hear me, no lowlife shit. Maybe one day, your grand kids will sing songs about you.

And, if you need some dinero we have money coming in."

"What the hell do we need money for, we already have the guns. Tell them to send it to some poor white guys," shouted #3 proudly.

"Yeah, we can still take care of ourselves," another said.

"Ok. I'll pass it along," Ramon said smiling. He was proud of these guys, and of himself. "But we just might need our savings for other things, just a feeling I have."

They thought for a moment and agreed. The future was not something to laugh about and they were all getting that sinking feeling in their stomachs that suddenly cut deep into their machismo.

Yes things were changing and so were these men.

28

Governor Leslie Phillips was just wrapping up a meeting with four of his staff members when his secretary showed Marion into the room.

She went to her husband with a wifely dutiful show and gave him a kiss on the cheek. Everyone smiled as they left. All of them were thinking "that poor unfortunate woman".

Marion, on the hand, was thinking the same of them.

"We have to talk," she whispered in his ear.

After they had all gone, he reached into his desk and got a handheld device in a box, and moved to a side door. Upon opening it, he scanned the next room, and neither of them spoke until he was finished.

He had soundproofed it and made it virtually bug resistant when he first took office. Even with this knowledge, he checked it each morning, and before he used it, just in case.

His wife was the first to speak.

"Madison has gone over the edge. He just had three Supreme Court justices arrested. They are being held under the Second Patriot Act for treason with no legal representation allowed."

"Looks like we're close to the end," he said simply.

107

She nodded.

"I wanted so damn much to be wrong. You know as well as I do, if it wasn't him, it would have been someone else," she continued. "What makes him so damn disgusting; I think he believes he's right."

"His kind always does. That's what makes them so believable in the beginning." For a moment he paused.

"I wonder what shoe will drop next," he mused. "I sent word out earlier that everyone should be prepared and on stand-by. I'm still not sure how we are to handle all this. It will be difficult until our backs are in the corner."

She knew what he meant. Although, there were still many in California that wanted the cause Washington represented to succeed, thankfully, their numbers were steadily dwindling.

They had heard on the grapevine that several states were considering making an attempt to secede from the Union, but they had been muttering that for years. You could not put much credence in that, or hope. Maybe Texas might try, but it was probably the only one that could actually succeed in doing it.

Though legal scholars had debated the issue, many were convinced that it was possible for secession under the original documents that were written for them to join the United States. Prior to that they were the Republic of Texas and over a million Texans wanted it be known as that again.

"As bad as our economy and social situation is here, they might want us the leave," she offered.

There had been calls for years for California to divide into two states, Northern and Southern California, because of the diverse differences in the political structure, and the size of its population. At one time they had the eighth largest economy in the world, comparing them to nations.

As the song said, "but that was yesterday, and yesterday's gone."

The number of people in the state was higher than before, but the GNP had dropped precipitously. Debt had increased more than in other states, and a lot of people had to wait in food lines just to get one or two meals a day.

"Who knows, with all of the trouble Madison is taking on, he just might want to get rid of us. In the long run that could be a good thing," the Governor offered.

"Regardless," she said, "the crap is about to hit the fan, so we had better shut it off."

They kissed and went back to his office.

29

Tuesday, April 26th, 1:22 PM, EDT

John Enman feverously punched the keys on his computer and tried to get through to Saranoff. He had been trying for hours, but no luck.

The president's mouthpiece Ron Gibson had casually announced at a morning news conference that the United States was going to repudiate all foreign loans that had been made to us over the years.

In addition, any foreign government or legal entity that owned property or shares in American business would forfeit said equity to the Federal government to be held in escrow until the balances could be worked out.

Obviously that day would never come. Madison had succeeded in bankrupting the entire world and throwing the financial markets into a state of unmitigated turmoil in one small announcement, which he didn't even feel necessary to give himself.

Since the U.S. was for the most part energy independent, the country came out on top.

China, India, Japan, and several smaller countries were at this moment official pauper nations again. Within days there would be riots and death world-wide. There would be so much internal fighting that none of them would have the time or ability to strike out at America, at least not in the immediate future.

Madison had just secured a degree of national security so he could handle the forthcoming internal struggles that were damn well going to occur.

"Why can't I reach Saranoff?" he thought.

Much to his credit Gregor had kept his word and gotten Enman's property sold and gold had been delivered as promised. It had cost him maybe ten percent more to ensure its safety and to keep it on schedule. It had already been dispersed throughout the country. With what had just happened that gold was worth twice as much today in real value, so he was way ahead of the game. The properties he had liquidated were virtually worthless after the announcement this morning. Of course no country's currency had much validity either.

He was sure Saranoff had been awake for days and was thoroughly exhausted. Taking a break, he tried to get through to a website that a pirate-type group occasionally was able to get up in Bulgaria. He had been given the way to get to it, if it was available. It was constantly moving as one government after another tried to shut it down under pressure from Washington. Maybe now they would be left alone.

He found it and gasped as he read the title banner. "Gregor Saranoff, World Business Leader and Philanthropist Assassinated." Three hours before a group of terrorists had attacked his office building, killing him and most of his staff.

"Terrorists, my ass!" he thought.

Suddenly John feared for his safety, shut everything down, pressed a self-destruct mechanism on his equipment and left the room. The computers had immediately erased everything in the room, and a sprinkler system of sulfuric acid had backed up the destruction.

Enman had prepared for this day weeks before. He had thought at that time it was to flee from Saranoff, but now he knew who the real enemy was. Now he was even more terrified than he ever thought was imaginable.

He was long gone before the house began to burn. Hoping the destruction would be complete, he never looked back.

30

Marsha Willard knew she would never leave Texas again. As she sat staring out of the window at the Lone Star Heraldic Restaurant on the top floor of the Hamilton Building in downtown Houston, she was pondering her future. Would she just sit on the back porch rocking back and forth until they carried her off to the funeral home, or would she have a chance to do something meaningful?

As darkness continued to fall on her beloved state, her consciousness was awakened by a familiar voice.

"Baby girl!"

Her father had entered the dining room and for some reason was calling attention to her and him.

He strutted like a weather-beaten George Hamilton as he moved through the diners. The thought of the comparison brought a smile to her face.

The two men with him beamed quite genuinely as he glad-handed everyone he met walking across the floor. Even though she had noticed this as a major change in him since her return, she wasn't exactly sure what was prompting it.

Joe Boudreaux had moved with his family from Louisiana to Texas in the late forties and had grown up in the oil fields north of

Houston. His father was a well wrangler and worked hard to support his family. An accident had taken him when Joe was sixteen and he immediately succeeded his father as the family income source.

It didn't take him long to come to the conclusion that breaking his back hustling on an oil rig was not what he wanted for his life. Wildcatting came to him almost as an instinct and it wasn't long before he had his first gusher. Within no time he parlayed his money into a company.

Not wanting to put all of his eggs in one basket, he began buying acreage and became one of the largest ranchers in the state.

By the nineties with his acquisitions, he was one of the most influential men in Texas. He was always determined, hardworking, and persevering. Risk taking was second nature to him, but he tried to buffer that with prudence. Through it all he marched on with a quiet majesty. This was not the man that approached her at that moment.

She had wanted to ask him before what it was all about, but hadn't had the nerve. Now it couldn't wait any longer.

When he arrived at the table, he immediately began with the introductions.

"Marsha, this is Lloyd Ferguson of the State National Bank, and Mark Wilson, the State Senate Leader."

She had heard of both of them, but had never made their acquaintance.

"Pleased to meet you gentlemen," she said as she shook their hands.

They sat down and instantly a waitress was standing there to take the drink orders.

"I'll have a Diet Squirt," Marsha said. She had waited to order until they had arrived, and had simply sipped her water.

"I'll have tonic water," her father ordered. Both of their drinks were shipped in from bottlers in Mexico as soft drinks were impossible to get in the states.

He had never had an alcoholic drink to her knowledge since her mother had died. Although not knowing why, she never asked.

She had stopped drinking twenty years earlier when she had a revelation that it was getting out of hand. It was not part of her nature to lose control, and even the thought of it simply could not be tolerated.

The other two men ordered their drinks, and excused themselves to go to the restroom.

When they had gone, she leaned over to her father and said, "Papa, I have to ask you; why the sudden gregarious cowboy routine?"

"You will find out shortly Marsha. Please go with me on this, and be patient," was his answer in the manner she was accustomed.

Her mind was indeed perplexed to say the least.

"But you've been like this ever since I returned," she further prodded him.

"Practice, my dear, practice," was his answer.

The men returned and he continued in his business voice, "Gentlemen it is time to alter history!"

He raised his glass, and they all followed suit.

Marsha was now intensely interested in what was going to happen.

31

Higgins drove slowly through the back roads of Virginia working his way to Charlottesville. He had turned on his GPS re-router and hoped it worked. Traveling like this would become common place, he was certain.

A 9mm automatic lay at his side at the ready. He didn't think he would have any real problems as most of the National Security Forces and what few local police that were still employed no longer worked the highways, but he was prepared.

Riots had broken out in Richmond last night and most if not all of the immediate area "law enforcement" most probably NSF would be there administering "justice." His blood boiled at the thought of it all.

Madison, through his stooge Gibson, had announced late last evening that all of the media, including television, radio, and the few newspapers still in existence were now totally under Federal control.

In itself this didn't amount to a change per sie, but it simply was a statement of complete power consolidation.

To his surprise, a patrol car pulled up behind him, flashing it lights.

He pulled over to the side of the road and waited.

A young man in an oversized uniform came up to his window. He rolled it down part way.

"It's after curfew old man! Get out of the car!" he ordered.

Without giving it a second thought, he pulled the trigger and blew the kid half way across the road. Pushing his foot to the floor, his car shot down the road.

When no one followed he knew the "officer" was alone.

"Individually, they are sitting ducks, but en masse, who knows?" he thought quoting Gloria. He also wondered when his ears would quit ringing.

His mind raced. "God, is this what the future will be; killing kids?"

Tears began to well in his eyes.

32

Madison was ready to speak directly to the nation. Everyone and everything was prepared when he walked into the Oval Office.

The production crew scurried around quietly like neutered mice.

When the director gave him the cue, the President began to talk.

"My fellow Americans, the past few days have been exasperating beyond description. I know all of you will agree with me that nothing like this would ever have been imagined, that enemies of the state both inside and outside of the country would have become this brazen.

We have had to face many difficult revelations and make many hard decisions."

He paused for effect as usual.

"This is the toughest one thus far."

His words had not been very presidential, but he wasn't reading from the teleprompter, hoping that he would sound friendlier like one neighbor to another. Then he changed dramatically and began an authoritative and demanding oration.

"I am now declaring a National State of Emergency. Under the powers granted to the President in such cases, I will now proceed in trying to rectify the conditions that presently exist.

I have directed the Federal Emergency Management Agency to carry out its designated responsibilities. Complete details will be distributed to the media immediately after I finish."

The emergency powers that Madison was referring to in his declaration were accumulated over the years, quietly and deliberately. Many presidents signed off, most likely not even suspecting the dire consequences of their actions.

It all started innocently enough in 1962 with Executive Order EO 10990 under the pretense of re-establishing the National Safety Council. In actuality its true purpose was to take over all modes of transportation and control highways and seaports in case of an emergency.

In the fifties the Constitution was bypassed to establish the Interstate Commerce Commission. After court rulings made it law, it was then possible to refer to those decisions and use the ICC to make other deviations from it. When case law became the norm and constitutional law was passé, the die had been cast.

That was followed by these Executive Orders.

EO 10995: This allowed the government to seize and control the communications media. This was a mute point that day since the progressives had virtually done that years before, and Madison had already declared it law.

EO 10997: This allowed the government to take over production and distribution of all electrical power, gas, petroleum, fuels and minerals. Here again the President and his predecessors got ahead of themselves.

EO 10998: This allowed the government to take over all food resources and farms.

EO 11000: This allowed the government to mobilize civilians into work brigades under federal supervision.

EO 11001: This allowed the government to take over all health, education and welfare functions. Again this had already been accomplished in preceding years.

EO 11002: This designated the Postmaster General to operate a National Registry of all persons.

EO 11003: This allowed the government to take over all airports and aircraft, including commercial aircraft.

EO 11004: This allowed the Housing and Finance Authority to relocate communities, build new housing with public funds, designate areas to be abandoned, and establish new locations for populations.

EO 11005: This allowed the government to take over railroads, inland waterways and public storage facilities.

EO 11051: This specified the responsibility of the Department of Emergency Planning and gave authorization to put all Executive Orders into effect in times of increased international tensions and economic or financial crises.

EO 11310: This granted authority to the Department of Justice to enforce the plans set out in Executive Orders, to institute support, to establish judicial and legislative liaison, to control all aliens, to operate penal and correctional institutions, and to advise and assist the President.

This list was easily accessible decades ago from many independent and government sources. It was not hidden.

EO 11490: This assigned emergency preparedness functions to federal departments and agencies. All in all, it organized and codified 21 previous Executive Orders, including those above, and 2 Defense Mobilization Orders: VI-2 & I-12. All of these beginning in 1951 and became law under this order.

There were those that tried to convince people through the years that all of this evil executive order talk was promoted by crazies on the old internet. They stated that all of the previous orders from the Kennedy-Johnson era were nullified by this order, but they were dead wrong. Each and every one of those provisions and more were simply incorporated under different wordings and codified in this new EO.

EO 11921: Under a State of National Emergency (the preamble mentions Nuclear War, but does not state that exclusively), this allows the Federal Preparedness Agency to develop plans to establish control over mechanisms of production and distribution, of energy sources, wages, salaries, credit and flow of money in U.S. financial institutions. It also provides that when a state of emergency is declared by the President, Congress cannot review the action for six months.

This order solidified all previous orders and was the origin of what was later to be known as the FEMA. You might think that this was directly out of the Obama administration, but you would be wrong. Richard Nixon signed this order into law forty years before.

Many other orders supplemented EO 11921 and almost every president after Nixon signed addenda to it. Obama became the master of the Executive Order to bypass a Senate and Congress elected in 2010 that would not give him the legislation he wanted, forever destroying the Constitution and the law it represented.

Madison had some very good teachers, and truly appreciated their efforts.

The U.S. Supreme Court only ever overturned two Executive Orders: the Truman order integrating the Armed Forces and a 1996 Clinton order that attempted to prevent the Federal Government from contracting with organizations that had strike-breakers on the payroll.

The court also ruled in the mid-eighties that Congress may only overturn an executive order by passing legislation in conflict with it or by refusing to approve funding to enforce it. In the former, the president retains the power to veto such a decision; however, the Congress may override a veto with a two-thirds majority to end the order. In normal times this is impossible for all practical purposes, but after Madison arrested a large portion of both houses, it was a cinch.

Instead of arresting them as traitors under the Second Patriot Act, he could have simply issued an executive order arresting them. Richard Nixon could have theoretically done that and prevented his Impeachment proceedings; however, he was too much of an American to do so. That would lead one to believe he had no idea what EO 11921 was and simply bought it as public necessity by some liberal progressive at the time. He did that with other agenda they suggested, such as wage and price controls.

Madison wasn't finished yet.

"For this next week all USPS, Social Security Administration, and other designated offices will be open twenty-four hours a day to register each and every citizen so that we may be able to determine who is with us and who isn't. At that time you will each be issued a Federal Identification Card for that purpose.

Law enforcement at all levels will be instructed after one week to arrest anyone without the proper papers when they are asked to present them.

My fellow citizens, we will take our country back, and with God's help make it better than ever before.

Thank you and good night."

It was over, and Madison was pleased. All of his work, all of his training, everything had prepared him for this time, his time. He was now a real leader, the most powerful man in the world, and it felt good, damn good. As a true savior of the United States, he was pleased.

33

Wednesday, April 27th, 7:43 PM, CDT

At the end of the 700 block of Michigan Avenue in the Southeast Little Rock, Arkansas sat the Empire Hotel and Bar. It was built in the 1930's and for a time was a high class establishment. By the period of time the President had issued his proclamations it was the home of the most desperate, despondent, and down on the luck miserable clientele. Even most of the homeless would decline an invitation to stay there.

In room 342 a man sprawled across a filthy bed in a space that hadn't seen a cleaning in months. He was dressed only in a torn dirty t-shirt and underwear that were for the lack of a better word, foul.

He was in his late fifties, totally out of shape, and with the skin complexion of a confirmed alcoholic. His liver would most likely give out at any moment.

A thin layer of vomit ran down the side of one cheek and dropped to a puddle on the floor. His eyes were not closed, but the vacant stare into another world confirmed that no one was at home.

It started out a typical evening of wading through a drunken stupor and continued thus until there was a knocking on the door.

Anything similar to recognition could not be found in his eyes.

Again, the knocking occurred, louder and longer.

One eyelid moved a faint bit; a nano-flutter, it possibly could be called.

Again, the sound rang out, even stronger.

This time a nerve somewhere in the body covered with decaying fetid grime fired, a small burst to be sure, but it was something.

A moan of sorts frothed through the stench of his garbage caked lips.

Whoever was at the door was certainly persistent. Again and again the banging continued until the door almost burst from its hinges.

Voices could be heard in the hall complaining but were silenced almost as soon as they spoke, by a fierce look from the intruder.

More banging and rattling of the door knob was heard.

Now the man stirred a little, and tried to roll over and only succeeded in falling off the bed into his puke.

Crawling as best he could for what seemed like an eternity he finally reached the door. He tried to grab the knob and after several attempts was able to hold on to it.

With all of the effort he could muster, he pulled himself to his knees and turned the lock. Falling back a bit, he watched as the door opened.

There, with the dim hall light surrounding his tall muscular body, stood a handsome black man.

He looked at the pitiful heap of fleshy humanity lying before him, and with a stern but not unkind temper to his voice simply said, "We have to talk."

PART 2:

Civil War

1

August 3rd

General Higgins walked slowly through outskirts of the small town of Boonesville, west of Little Rock, Arkansas on Rt.10. He was taking in the sweet smell of freshness given off by the many grasses, shrubs and wild flowers covering the sides of the road.

If he hadn't known better, life from this viewpoint would have felt idyllic. It was the stuff about which poets wrote.

It didn't take long to dispel those feelings. His trek carried him past several cars simply pulled into the grass, left there to rot. Some were only a couple years old.

The owners had abandoned them for many reasons. They had no money to pay the finance companies or banks, if they still had been in business to come after them for repossessions. There was no money to buy gas; that is, if there were gas to buy. The thinking was why not simply park them there in hope of a better tomorrow. Nobody was going to steal them because they would have to have the where-with-all to operate them and few had that luxury.

Back East there were supposed to be areas that even now had those utilities and services a lot of the country had to do without. It had only been about fifteen weeks since President Madison had

126

declared a state of emergency, but in many places all of the normal life to varying degrees had come to a sudden and catastrophic halt.

Higgins had parked his own ride a couple miles back so as to not to raise eyebrows and have to answer the questions that would surely ensue. He was here for a single purpose and that was to get the necessary papers he needed to get to Colorado.

His people had made him quality passes and government identifications through Virginia, Kentucky, Missouri, and Arkansas. They did not have all of the proper items to copy other states as the Feds had made different grade papers and codes for each state.

The federal computers and workers still could churn out what they needed; however, very few private people had that ability. They had shut down most everything after the week everyone had finished getting their ID's and Interstate Passports. With the promises of a better tomorrow and the threat of prison, most people had complied with every regulation; however, a significant portion had not and had gone entirely underground.

A large number had tried to flee to the Western states. Many of those were caught and imprisoned, but more had gotten through. The National Security Forces were much stronger than anticipated and extremely brutal. After a few weeks when a lot of the people had gotten hungry, the number of enlistees increased dramatically. Desperate people always do what they deem necessary for their own continued existence. It's just too damn bad so many reverted to their basal instincts when they devolved.

Higgins knew many eyes watched his every move; however, he wasn't too concerned. First, most people were afraid to touch a stranger not knowing whether he was a Fed or not. And second, once you passed the Mississippi River, folks still were fairly civil, scared out of their minds, but civil.

There were times as he moved through some of the Mid-Atlantic States that he began to feel as if he were in a post-apocalyptic film. As the weeks went by the tensions and tempers rose until all hell broke loose.

Madison had known from the beginning that he had to secure most of the East Coast and the Mid-West. With the exception of the Upper Third of Maine, New England had capitulated like France did to the Nazis.

New York, Pennsylvania, Ohio, Indiana, and Illinois had pockets of rebellion which were quashed almost immediately. His military background had led him to deploy his NSF troops strategically before the announcements, so they were on the ready.

When the Pittsburgh "riots" as they were referred to, broke out in the South Hills area, there were five thousand of them there within three hours. Over seven thousand civilians and six hundred NSF were killed and about ten thousand more locals seriously injured.

Since the poorer sections of major metropolitan areas were affected first, the subsequent "rebellions" that took place there were easily controlled. They were the least equipped, armed, and financially able or prepared to resist, especially after the wholesale confiscation of any and all guns a few years before.

Upper New Jersey, Akron, Indianapolis, Richmond, and Virginia Beach were the hardest hit. Higgins had heard that unofficially there were over a hundred thousand dead on both sides, mostly the civilians.

Initially as the word got out, anger and resentment were the emotions of the moment; but, as more and more deaths accrued, that changed to demoralization and melancholy. It took only four weeks until the populace was shell-shocked and subservient. That had come to a real surprise for Higgins.

The loss of basic freedoms had occurred slowly but consistently for over fifty years and this was the result. Ironically all of the talk of bolstering esteem, character, and individuality as furthered in the public schools and broadcast over the airwaves, was just that, talk. The progressive approach in education through its fairness and noncompetitive methods destroyed the essence of the very traits they espoused.

Individuality, sense of personal freedom, responsibility and accountability became meaningless notions. With them the necessary

128

survival instincts of the population had been altered and in most people had ultimately died. Now they simply waited in food lines for government handouts or went to work for government agencies such as the National Food Agency which oversaw the production and distribution of groceries and related products.

Since it was going into summer, some of the diehards had tried to plant gardens and grow their own food in whatever space they could. Seeds and fertilizer had been rationed immediately and permits had to be obtained. You could only receive both if you promised half of your few crops to the government co-op.

Seeds and starter plants became a new species of currency on the black market. Because of the complicated and overbearing tax structure which had been in place for a hundred years, an under ground economy had always flourished, but now it was larger than ever and growing by the day. Even though it was tolerated to a certain extent, it was best not to be too open about your activities as there were laws in place and some pretty nasty penalties if you were caught and prosecuted.

Through all of this Higgins had wanted to be more active. He did as much as he could through the channels they had initially organized; however, not all of the recruits were as fervent and valorous as they had imaged in their hearts and minds they would be. It was extremely difficult to be thus when you saw your neighbors and family decimated, and resisters you knew imprisoned or executed on Main Street for all to see.

Madison had been deployed during his career in some God awful areas of the world and a lot of it rubbed off on him. He also had studied every play book on war and subjugation he could find over the years. His knowledge was applied with an iron fist. He and his four stooges were adept and without one whole conscience between them. Unbelievably, they still felt intensely they were doing the best for the country.

It had taken over six weeks for Higgins to reach Boonesville. He had to backtrack many times, especially in Kentucky, and layover hidden for days at a time. The NSF was fairly imbedded after the

Louisville "riots". He had almost gotten tripped up on his initial ID for that area.

The local Patriots eventually had engaged an exceptionally good forger for the work of replacing it. Not caring which side he worked for, he only wanted the gold he was paid. His honor was eventually tested by both the NSF and the Patriots and he passed with flying colors. He was indeed good at what he did, to play both sides and stay alive.

Higgins's current papers were good for Arkansas and Missouri, but he needed the Colorado IDs. This operative's work was supposed to be some of the best in the country, and he was one of the originals Patriots. Even though he didn't charge for his services, the group kept him supplied with money and materials and had smuggled his family to Northern Montana.

After turning the corner onto Crescent street, he stopped cold and edged to the right into some bushes. About a half block away were six very loud and angry men. They were bitching and moaning about the authorities and every other problem of the day.

He would have been more than sympathetic except that type behavior and decibel level of noise could draw the wrong people. Not knowing the area well enough to gauge the possibility of the NSF swooping into the situation, he gave them a wide berth.

Continuing onward for another block, he even avoided eye contact with the group, doubting they saw him, so intense was their fuming and ranting.

He circled the rest of the block and eventually came back onto the road about two hundred feet beyond them. They were loud, almost shouting. He hustled along as quickly as his old legs would carry him, expecting the worst.

After finding the house with the coded marking on the mailbox, and he went three doors beyond it. Turning left he followed a path running between two fences until he reached a grape arbor behind the fourth house.

A man was working in his garden. He looked up as Higgins approached and said, "Good day friend."

"Good Morning to you," he answered.

"Do you think you good spare a cup of water?" Higgins asked.

"Wouldn't you rather have a Pilsner?" the man responded.

"I would if I could, but I can't."

At that the man wiped his face with his checkered handkerchief and pointed to the basement door of the house behind Higgins.

"You'll find your refreshments in there," he said calmly to him.

He turned and went to the steps and descended. At the bottom he entered an open door.

The room he walked into was rather sparsely furnished and he immediately wondered if he was in the right place. He didn't have long to ponder that thought as almost at once an unnoticeable door opened in the paneled wall, flush with the other sheeting.

A man in his late thirties stood there and motioned him to enter.

He did so and it shut without a sound behind him.

The next room was a different story. It was filled with modern computers, printers, cameras, and all of the necessities of a first class forgery operation.

"Did you have any problems finding the place?" he asked.

"Not really," he answered, "but those guys down the street sort of worried me."

"Oh, the bitches of Barkley Street, all bark, no bite. You needn't waste a bead of sweat on them. They spend everyday shooting the shit over there."

"No one comes after them?" Higgins queried.

"Nah. The nearest NSF installation is about fifty miles south. They're supervising the regional NFA farm production."

That meant they were overseers of the workers, just as there were in the old South. Someone had to keep the help in line.

"They assume this dinky village offers them no real problems. Besides most of them are locals who try to keep confrontations to a minimum. It's not as bad as I hear things are back East."

Higgins was glad of that, but he knew that there were roaming bands of NSF nationals and the roving bands of private security forces that had been hired and placed all across the country months ago. That was one development that he had not anticipated.

The private troops were mostly mercenaries from Europe and Latin America and they were not to be encountered at any cost. Just like the Hessians in the Revolutionary War, as they were more publicly involved, they were instantly hated. At first their presence was just a rumor, and many thought a really weird kind of urban legend, but the stories were too consistent and frequent to be discounted. He had never seen them and really didn't want to have that dubious honor.

"Have you heard anything from the rest of the country?" he asked.

As if on cue another voice spoke behind him.

"I can help with that," it said.

Higgins whirled around and reached toward his hidden gun.

"Whoa," the woman standing behind him said, putting up her hands. She was in her late twenties and had a nerdish look. Her glasses dangled precariously from her nose, and she constantly pushed them back in place to little avail.

"Oh, this is a close friend of mine. I asked her to come over and fill you in with whatever you needed to know," the man said.

Higgins found out she had stolen a great deal of communications equipment from her employer before the government had come in and closed the doors. Everything in the company had eventually been confiscated. It wasn't really theft as the former owner got a heads-up and skipped town before the Feds arrived. All they found was a half empty abandoned warehouse. She offered no details as to where it was or what company it had been, and he didn't inquire further.

"I think Texas is planning something. I'm not sure what, but it's going to be big.

There are rumblings of major discontent in the North Western states.

But the big news is in Europe. I hacked into a satellite feed from one of the mini-mites over Mexico. While most of the U.S. forces are tied down trying to get all of the troops out of the Mid-East, the Arab nations have gone to war with Iran, Iraq and others. This hasn't stopped the conflicts between the European Muslims and the nations they now inhabit.

Israel has defended itself admirably and seems to not have dropped any nukes. It isn't a favor to Madison but to the armed forces that are retreating from that region. In turn the Americans are supporting them for the time being. At some point I think they will pull out and all hell could break loose.

They are surrounded since Lebanon, Italy, Greece, and the smaller countries north of them have fallen and are in total Moslem control.

It appears that France and the Netherlands are literally burning down with mass riots and civil war.

Spain and Germany are holding there own. They have put whatever armed forces they have on the borders, and have used local law enforcement to round up anyone of Arab descent and deport them. This in itself is brewing major trouble; there is no way to tell who is friend or foe.

I haven't heard anything from Asia, but I doubt if it is peaceful. Before the news barriers went up and the last of the internet died, I heard most of the economies had collapsed."

"What about Mexico and Canada?" Higgins asked.

"Mexico suspended diplomatic ties with Washington when Madison started gathering Latinos without papers and shipping them to Mexico whether they were from there originally or not. The word I get is that he might try sending back naturalized citizens too.

Canada has sealed its borders as tight as a drum, and only allowing their own people to return, even if they had become U.S. citizens. They are one of the few countries in fairly good shape and they want to keep it that way."

Higgins didn't hear anything he hadn't expected, but the knowledge that this had come to pass did hit him hard. He couldn't get out of his mind that he was too damn old for all of this.

She filled him in on much more as the man worked on his papers. This woman was a wealth of knowledge and he knew she enjoyed having someone new with whom she could share it.

Finally the forger handed him the Interstate Passports and Colorado papers, and he got up to leave.

"Thank you both so much," he said sincerely.

"Our pleasure," they both said almost together.

"Keep the faith and pray for tomorrow," she said.

"I do that almost every minute I am awake," he replied.

They shook hands and he exited into the afternoon sun.

He made his way uneventfully back to his car and got in. After referring to his map to find his next refueling stop, he turned and retreated about a mile to a back road he had passed. There he made a left turn and continued his journey.

2

August 3rd, Morning

Even though it was the middle of the summer, Houston was not hot. That was a blessing, considering the temperature of the average Texan. From the beginning, none of them took the matters developing in Washington well, and many were calling for secession.

Governor Richard Pearson did his diplomatic best to respond to every new dictate coming from DC on what felt like an hourly basis. He tended to his orders with a smile, while the entire time he was making the wheels of change of a different sort turn as quickly and quietly as possible.

Anticipating much of what had happened, he and a cadre of close allies worked night and day to prepare. Joe Boudreaux and his friends were among them.

He had called in favors from his long time buddies in the military and quietly had most of the Texas National Guard brought home, long before Madison had any idea what was occurring. When a call went out to the general citizenry to join, enlistments in the organization skyrocketed.

The National Bank of Texas and the other large financial institutions in the state were organized and geared up for their part in what was about to happen. All of this preparation had occurred over the past eight years. Texans had been motivated by anger since the 2008 presidential election, and the resulting idiocy of manic liberal legislation.

While twenty-eight other states had declared their sovereignty and tried to fight Washington directly, they had started their own internal movement. They had leaked just enough in the press to make everyone think any talk of what they were doing was just the ramblings of the lunatic fringe.

The day before, Governor Pearson had called for a statewide referendum on the motion of Texas leaving the United States and returning to its former status and name of The Republic of Texas. Even though the voters had only been given a twenty-four hour notice, the turn-out was almost ninety-eight percent.

There were few problems at the polls, because each was guarded by several dozen local men and women. This was necessary because all of the State's National Guard's units had been posted to the North and Eastern borders.

The lone major confrontation was from a group of NSF near Austin, and they were neutralized almost immediately.

Texas not only had a large part of their citizenry carrying weapons, over half of their people had been issued valid carry permits and were armed to the teeth.

To many the results were a foregone conclusion. The referendum passed by a ninety-six to four percent margin.

Saying there were celebrations in every street was to understate the whole matter. They were short lived though as a lot of work had to be done.

First, Governor Pearson agreed to be the President of the new republic until elections could be held. He asked Marsha Willard if she would be the Vice-President and she accepted without a second thought.

They were on the front steps of the State Capital building in Austin waiting to be sworn in.

"Well Joe, it looks like we did it," Pearson said to Boudreaux who was standing proudly beside his daughter.

Joe smiled and nodded. He stood there in his large white Stetson surveying the enormous crowd witnessing the ceremony. Later it was estimated to be over five hundred thousand very excited and noisy people.

The Chief Judge of the Texas Supreme Court walked to his place on the platform and faced the President-to-be. Pearson's wife handed him her parent's family Bible and he held it out in front of his body.

After he repeated the oath of the new office, the gathering went wild. Finally calming them down with several raises of his hands, he motioned Marsha Willard over to take his place. She repeated the process and the clamor arose again. It was deafening and continued for more than twenty minutes.

The new President and Vice-President stood before the masses and waved until they thought their arms would fall off.

Finally President Pearson moved to the podium a few feet away and asked for a moment of silence and offered a short prayer. In that few minutes you could hear no sound except his rhythmical words asking God to bless the new republic.

When he finished, the uproar commenced again even louder than before, if that were possible.

It again took a long while to restore a modicum of order to the event. When he had their attention Pearson began.

"My fellow Texans, it was with an enormous amount of regret that I asked for the referendum yesterday. After a lifetime of being an American citizen, I was truly saddened to even contemplate leaving the Union."

There were quite a few boos when he mentioned America, and a lot of "Don't be" and "their loss" shouted.

"However, it was necessary to protect our God-given rights that were in the original Constitution, those which we agreed to defend when we became a state. When that document was destroyed by the powers in Washington we had no choice. We had to act to preserve our freedom and liberty, and act we did."

Another round of shouts and applause rang out for over ten minutes, and then he continued.

"We will operate under the constitution of the State of Texas for the time being; however, I am calling for a Constitutional Convention to begin in two days so that we may incorporate the finest parts of the U.S. Constitution, our State Constitution, and the old Republic of Texas Constitution. I do not want to delay this process any longer than is necessary."

He was brought a folder with one paper in it.

"To that end I am as my first official act, signing the order for that convention."

He stopped talking and signed the paper.

"We are on our way to..."

He never had a chance to finish his words. Even his mouth continued to move no words were uttered because his head exploded as a large caliber bullet did its work.

There was immediate pandemonium on the staging area as the body guards threw themselves at him and pulled Marsha Willard onto the floor and covered her with their bodies.

Another shot rang out almost at the same time missing her and hitting her father in the shoulder. She screamed as he fell.

The short lived silence from the shots was replaced with a new form of clamor based in terror and anger.

Two hundred and forty years earlier a shot rang out in Lexington, Massachusetts that was said to have resounded around the world. This one was destined to be no less audible.

3

August 3rd, Afternoon

President Madison burst into his staff meeting.

"Who was the damned idiot that ordered the hit on Pearson?" he yelled, as if he were going to kill someone on the spot.

Sonfeld, Curtis, Murdock, and Wilkins were silent.

Madison paced the room muttering to himself. He used almost every expletive ever invented and some even these guys hadn't heard.

"Mr. President," Wilkins said. He was the only person in the room with the guts and leverage to speak. "I believe it was a holdover order from before."

Madison glared at him.

"Two months ago we told Blackpool to do something to silence him."

"We never said to assassinate the man," the President fumed.

"Over time I guess it took on new meaning. We had to move several units around and new personnel were sent to the area and the orders were passed on as a matter of course," Wilkins continued.

"Isn't that just grand? Do you shitheads know what this means? We now have another martyr to contend with, and he's a hell of a lot bigger name than Childress."

Blackpool Security had taken on larger and more difficult work as the weeks had gone by. New mercenaries were pouring into the country from all over the world. Control was becoming a significant problem.

"Mr. President, there is another repercussion from it already. Mexico has called their Ambassador and Consulate Staff home, and have recognized the new Republic in Texas," Wilkins announced.

"I could give a shit about the damn Mexicans. We just put up with them all those years for their damn oil," the President ranted, even though he knew there were other reasons. "But it sets an example we don't need."

Already, several countries had pulled their people from Washington. The first were Ireland, Luxembourg, Spain, and the Baltic States. Mostly this occurred because of the lack of finances to keep them here. With Mexico, the total consulates withdrawing had increased to twenty-two.

"China has made overtures wanting to know our intentions in Asia," Wilkins went on. "What should I tell them?"

Madison smiled and said nothing.

"I'll put them off until after the announcement tomorrow."

"How long after I throw out those money grubbing bastards are we giving them to clear out of the building?" the President asked.

The next day he would tell the world that the United Nations was no longer welcome on American soil and that all of the representatives would have to leave. In his heart he thought that it was long overdue and he really looked forward to kicking their collective asses. He had always detested their ability to take money and then use it to piss on the country he served and loved.

"I would give them a week," Wilkins said.

"Seems long enough for me," he responded. "If they have not packed and left by then, start doing it for them.

Back to this Blackpool situation, I want the person who gave the order in here, yesterday."

"That may be difficult as most of the team that carried out the order were caught and executed on the spot," Wilkins said. "They said they resisted arrest."

"I'm sure they did," Madison mused. "I learned a long time ago, don't piss off Texans."

He stood and continued.

"That's what I'm worried about. Rebellions are contagious. Obviously we don't need them economically, and we knew there would be secessions, but we have to keep it down to a minimum."

When they were planning the take-over, they all had agreed that some states would secede or try to and that would have to be tolerated until power could be consolidated especially in the Mid-Atlantic and NorthEast.

"Again, I want someone to take the blame for that order, and I don't care who it is. An example must be made."

"I have a call into Blackpool now." Wilkins as usual was already on top of it.

"I don't want some grunt. It has to be someone known to most of their people."

He knew they would comply, what choice did they have? Mercenaries and their commanders were a dime a dozen. Someone in middle-management would have to fall on their sword, literally. The business Blackpool was doing now was a once in several life-times opportunity, and there was no way they wanted to lose this contract.

Murdock and Sonfeld had said nothing and had been busy writing on their notepads.

Madison looked at each of them almost defying them to speak.

"I have the copy for your speech tomorrow ready for you to review," Murdock said, passing a folder to Wilkins.

The President looked at Sonfeld.

After several uncomfortable moments, he spoke. "May I ask a question?" He was sweating profusely.

The President nodded.

"When we began, I thought we were going to institute more progressive policies, like controlled health care, financial controls..." He faded out. "I knew we were going to be... I had a long list of things..." He soon realized he was rambling and mostly talking to himself. If he ever imagined he would be Madison's Himmler, he at that moment knew it was not be and finally realized he was finished.

Madison nodded his head to Curtis, Sonfeld, and Murdock; they got up and left the room.

After they had gone, he said to Wilkins, "It's time."

Sonfeld was never seen or heard from again.

4

August 5th

Ramon Ramirez walked through the streets of his beloved South L.A. Everywhere he went, he was greeted with "Hola", "Gracias", and many kisses. Over the weeks since the changeover in DC, he and his gang and not only changed in status but as human beings.

It wasn't long until food supplies had become a problem. They had used old connections in the drug trade to bring in provisions for his people, if not from other parts of the state or from out of state, then from Mexico. At first he was able to bring in some from Asia, but that dried up quickly as they had their own shortages. Many places were now in various degrees of famine.

The border had been closed almost immediately, not from the U.S. side, but from the south. Expecting the worst, many illegals were returning home as best they could. Mexico may have its own problems but at least it still had a government and food.

In fact, within two weeks all of the U.S. Border patrol had been called back to Washington. Most didn't comply and simply went home or disappeared to wherever. No one wanted to come into the country anyway, and of course the pay checks stopped.

Mexico was allowing anyone who had not become an American citizen, and had not been in the U.S. longer than two years to go back, if they could prove both conditions. This was not always easy.

Through Ramon and his men supplies at first trickled, then moved at a fairly fast pace. He was still able to buy border guards, local police, and the Federalis with very little gold or trade.

Over the weeks they had also developed a community conscience, and did what the War on Drugs was never able to do, Southern California was virtually drug free. Dealers became businessmen or they found themselves dead, or worse.

The California coast had been in and out of a drought condition for over a hundred years. The first decade of this century had been one of the worst, so much so that it was parched brown from San Diego to San Francisco.

Cattle ranching had diminished to a fraction of its former size. However, starting in 2010 that all changed with the weather, and for the ensuing years it had become a picture of verdant fields and ever increasing herds of cattle, emus, and bison.

The San Joaquin Valley had been handcuffed by the Department of Interior until it had become a wasteland, all for the benefit of some damn fish that no one cared if it became extinct or not.

Governor Phillips had tried to contact the Department of the Interior and other appropriate agencies concerning this after Madison had taken over. He not only didn't have his calls returned, but couldn't get one person to answer any phone on the list. Many of the numbers were no longer working.

Within a few hours of concluding that no one was going to contradict him on the Federal level, he issued orders for the water supply to be diverted to the valley. He also extended all the help he could in opening the area to farming once again.

In a short four weeks the first crops were planted and growing nicely. For the first time in twenty years, California was going to be in full bloom.

He had become aware of Ramon Ramirez and called him to Sacramento. By working together, the people of Southern California were working with their Northern brothers not as migrants but as co-workers with mutual respect.

This should have been a satisfactory outcome especially considering what was happening east of the Rockies, but there were still die-hard lunatics mainly in the Bay area that were mentally still in communes, and worse, thinking they were still in charge.

There were marches and sit-ins within hours of the orders to bring water to the valley; however, the few hundred that showed up were driven from the street by groups that out-numbered them ten to one. Some were beaten just for good measure, and the police looked the other way unless it was carried too far.

After being a bastion for the lunatic left, California was emerging as a light in a dark age that was progressing over the continent. It had a long path to travel, but it was taking the initial steps in splendid fashion.

None of this went on without notice in DC. In that first week of August, Blackpool and National Security Forces were on their way to dim that light.

There was probably never a more unlike pairing than Phillips and Ramirez, but they needed each other and much more for the battles on the horizon.

Just three years earlier all of this would have happened in a matter of days, but with fuel supplies rationed even for the governments, communications at a pre-World War II level, and the uncertain knowledge of who was friend and who foe, the tide of war was ever so slow. But there was no doubt it was coming.

5

August 6th

Gloria Martin had thought she had trekked through hell during her service in the Mid-East, but she found out there were even lower depths you could traverse, and it was in her own country.

She and her Richmond-Charlottesville cells had been caught off guard when the crap came down from DC. Their intel was massively faulty and she now understood exactly why. DC knew more than they had let on and there had been traitors embedded in several of the groups. When she had given the marching orders, the firestorm began.

The NSF had moved several thousand troops just outside of the area and when the reaction to the proclamation began, they poured in. The fighting was brutal and bloody. The actual losses were never reported on any news outlet, since they were all government operated.

Thousand of civilians who had no intention of submitting to dictatorial commands and most of her people were slaughtered under "take no prisoners" orders. She and Doug Houston, her second in command were the only ones she knew to survive. He died before they reached the Kentucky border.

146

After escaping that carnage, they had moved quietly at night and hid during the day. The progress of getting out of Virginia was nerve-wrackingly slow.

It seemed that roving bands of NSF were everywhere. Although they were small, usually four to six plus a squad leader, that person was an experienced mercenary. He or she was an English speaking foreigner and that pissed her off.

As much as they tried to avoid them, it was not always possible. They eliminated three groups. On the fourth encounter Doug was shot and killed early on and she went berserk. She let one of them live until she got some answers. He told her that the squad leaders worked for Blackpool. That explained it all.

She never had to take on any more of them, but it still took her four weeks to reach Louisville. Even though her niece and sister had been murdered there by the NSF, she wanted to see her other sister before she headed west.

Helen and she had not spoken since the massacre, mainly because she blamed Gloria for their deaths. Even though they had been in the "food riots" and were simply hungry, Helen thought they were foolish for trying to get help, and simply did it because that was what "Sis" would do.

Even though she and her family were just as destitute, they hid in their tiny home and waited for "better times". John, her husband, was later killed by some asshole he had confronted in the street.

Gloria had found out about it long after his funeral. She had not been able to be there for them then, but she was damn well going to try now. She had some gold left over from their work in Richmond and she was going to persuade them to go with her to Colorado.

Getting to their house took her another two days. Louisville was crawling with NSF, but she finally made it.

She took a position in an abandoned building almost a block away and watched during that day, and then moved in closer and waited until almost midnight.

No one was seen coming or going during all of that time, but there was activity inside. When it got dark, the lights were on, probably some form of candles because electricity was rationed or not available. There was no way to determine if her son Jeff was home alone and she was out working or if they were both there.

Cautiously she approached the house. As she peered through the windows she saw her sister washing dishes alone. Jeff was fourteen, but still probably in bed, because the upstairs lights had been off for over a half hour.

She went to the back door which entered into the kitchen and tapped lightly. She could see her sister approach the door smiling. However, when she turned on the light and opened it, the radiance disappeared and was replaced by a startled appearance like she had never seen before.

"What are you doing here?" she asked in a frantic whisper. Helen's physical build was much like Gloria's but definitely not as fit. The comparison stopped there as they looked nothing alike otherwise. She was a graying dirty blond with a round face and Gloria was a dark brunette with a thinner face and high cheek bones.

"I just wanted to see you." Gloria said trying to restrain the tears that were trying to form.

"Where were you when I needed you?" she was asked in that same voice, almost with trepidation.

"I'm sorry, I was really tied up, and I didn't know about John until weeks afterwards."

"You were part of that mess in Richmond, I assume." Anger was in her voice, but so was more fear.

"I lost a lot of good friends, yes," she responded quietly.

"Well, it's too late now. You had just better move on."

"I want to help out. I know it can't be easy for you," Gloria pleaded.

"We're doing alright," she said.

"How could you, with John gone and … everything?" As she spoke Gloria moved into the door and started to step into the kitchen.

"Please, don't." Helen gave her a little push. "You don't belong here and we are fine."

148

They both reacted as the front door opened and closed, and a voice called out. "Helen, I'm home."

She pushed again and quietly urged, "Please go, you'll just cause trouble."

A tall average looking man in an NSF uniform came into the room. "Who's this," he asked. His demeanor was one of a working man thrown into a supervisory position with no training or education to back the advancement.

"Just someone I knew a couple years ago," she tried to explain.

He then noticed her boots and caught a quick glimpse of her pistol in its holster inside her jacket, and said, "What the hell?"

He reached for his gun on his hip and yelled, "Get out of the way Helen!"

She moved in front of Gloria and begged, "Please don't Carl. She's my sister."

He stopped cold and looked at her. "You never mentioned you had another sister."

"She's been gone for years."

"The gun?" he asked.

"She's ex-military." Helen was shaking and speaking with a breaking voice.

"It's a dangerous world out there," Gloria interjected. "You should know."

"Which side are you on?" he asked bluntly.

"My own," she answered strongly.

"So you're a rebel, a traitor," he egged her on.

Gloria wanted to say more, but hesitated for her sister's sake.

There were a few moments when no one said anything, and the silence was deadly.

"What do you want me to do?" he asked Helen.

"I...," she started to speak but couldn't form the words.

He looked at Gloria with the same question in his eyes.

"I want to get them to safety and help them financially with what little I have," Gloria responded not knowing where the words were originating.

149

Carl looked down at the floor, holstered his gun, and walked toward the hall. He turned and said, "You two figure it out. I'm tired and I've seen enough crap today."

Helen turned to her sister, "He's really a good man."

"Will you and Jeff come with me?" Gloria asked.

Helen shook her head and said, "I can't." She went to a chair and sat down. "I'm tired and… I'm not well."

Gloria went to her and knelt in front of her. Now there were tears in her eyes.

"Tell me," was all she said.

"Cancer," she said as she held one of her breasts.

"What did the doctors say?"

"It took me six months to get an appointment and another six weeks to get tested, by then it was too late. I'm over forty, a woman without an education; therefore, I didn't qualify and couldn't get treatment anyway. They gave me a three months supply of pain pills and sent me home to die."

She took Gloria's head in her hands and then wiped the tears from her eyes, and said, "Don't. I've done enough crying for both of us."

Carl came to the door with a young man, her nephew Jeff.

"I don't know what you are up to or where you are going, and I don't want to know. I've only been with Helen a short time, but I do know her well enough that she wants the boy to go with you. All hell is about to break loose and he shouldn't be here. He deserves a chance at least."

Leaving Jeff in the doorway and walking to Helen and he put his hands on her shoulders.

"He's right," she said desperately try to stop her forming tears. They both knew that she would soon be dead and he would probably die on the job.

Gloria was going to beg them both to come with her, but they knew what she was about to say and both shook there heads. They were more than aware that their presence would cut the chances of an escape and would probably get all of them killed.

They all looked over at Jeff. He stood there with his hands in his pockets saying nothing.

Carl went to the hall closet and came back with a 30-30 Winchester rifle and several boxes of ammunition. "Give me your back pack," he said. "I know these were your dad's and you know how to use them. Treasure them and try to be safe."

Jeff reached around the door frame and retrieved it. Carl had come to his room and woke him, told him to dress and pack as little as possible. As with most teenagers he had his favorite clothes so it wasn't that difficult to do. His shyness was evident when he realized they were all staring at him, and he reddened totally.

Carl and Helen had been discussing Jeff's fate for weeks and though this was not the answer they had in any way anticipated, it was probably the best that would ever come along.

Helen got up and went to a drawer and got a small picture album and put it in on top of the bullets, and gave her son a hug.

He returned it with a force that should have hurt her, but with the drugs and the adrenalin coursing through her body she felt no pain. They stood there and cried in each others arms for a long while.

Carl moved in and said, "You had better go. It will take you the rest of the night to get out of town."

When the two of them had separated, Jeff picked up his back pack and the rifle. Gloria was still in such a state of shock, denial, and outright confusion that was so strange to her, she hardly moved when Helen came to her and put her arms around her trying to comfort her.

Gloria responded with such unexpected emotion that she collapsed in her sister's embrace.

Helen put her lips to her ears and whispered, "You take care of my son, and yourself. I love you both."

It took Gloria several long minutes to breathe normally and was still numb when she finally moved.

Carl had been writing something on a sheet of paper. He handed it to her and said, "Here is what I think is a safe route out of here. I assume you are on foot. It will help you avoid most of the patrols.

Try to get out to there," he pointed to an intersection he had drawn, "by daybreak."

He got up and went to Helen, "God help you." There was a break in his voice, "God help all of us."

The sisters kissed each other again. She went to her son and held him for a brief moment, turned, and left the room.

Carl shook his hand and gave him a man hug, and then he too left.

Jeff looked at Gloria, she returned his gaze, but neither knew what to say.

Her training kicked back in, and she went for the door.

"You ready?" she finally asked.

"I guess so," he said.

They went out and crossed the lawn and disappeared into the shadows.

Helen and Carl sat in the dark silently, not knowing how either would face the emotions that they both knew were going to attack them the next day. At least now they had hope for Jeff, and that gave them some much needed solace.

6

August 7th

John Enman had made it to Fargo, North Dakota sixteen hours after Madison had made his grand announcement. His broad inner circle pass held up almost to the end. Sometime as he was crossing Minnesota it had been revoked, thankfully not before.

As he crossed the mid-west states, he used the interstate highways as much as possible. Although the NSF had set up intentional detours to side roads to keep everyone on their toes and slow them down for inspections when they desired, he moved rather quickly. With his internal GPS set for unlimited travel, he was always waved through as they scanned his car. Nonetheless he held his breath each time.

His luck ran out in the early morning of April 28th. A Minnesota State Police Officer pulled him over and approached his car with his hand on his holster.

Enman rolled down his window and asked the officer, "Is there something wrong?"

"Are you John Enman?" he asked.

"Yes sir," he replied honestly.

"Do you have any ID?"

Enman reached for his wallet, opened it, and passed him is driver's license and one of his company pass cards with his picture on it.

The officer looked at them and shook his head.

"You must have pissed someone off," he said.

"Why do you say that?" Enman asked.

"Your travel papers and auto transponder have just been pulled."

Enman almost pissed his pants.

"Look, I know who you are, or were that is. If you made someone that angry, you're alright in my book. My suggestion is you keep heading west out of here." He pointed down the road in front of them.

Enman couldn't believe his luck.

"You're about fourteen miles from the border. I should be the last of your worries in this state, but you never know where those NSF assholes are. Don't stop for anything or anybody until you're over the line."

Enman just nodded that he understood.

"The Dakota boys don't care what orders are being barked, so you should be alright once you get there, at least for a while." Then he muttered to himself, "I might not be far behind you."

He did a u-turn and sped off into the fog that had started to form.

Enman wasted no time getting up to speed and moved as quickly as he could to the border, though not wanting to race and draw any more attention.

He crossed into North Dakota with no further encounters, and made it to Fargo by noon.

One of his company offices was located there as well as many of his contacts, and a lot of his gold. He immediately went to the company compound.

In the following weeks, it became not only his new headquarters, but also his command center. In his mind and heart as he watched his house begin to burn, he had started to change. By the time he reached Fargo, it was a new man that emerged from the car and entered the building.

One afternoon in May, he saw a tall imposing figure walking on one of the sidewalks and immediately recognized the State Trooper who had advised him to high tail it out Minnesota. He pulled over and asked him if he could buy him a drink.

Over a cup of coffee and lunch, he hired him, and he became the head of security for the operation in Fargo.

Since most news organizations were out of business or government propaganda machines, one of his first objectives was to make as many inroads into intelligence gathering and communications as he could. He knew that not only would his people need it but so would the others that would not give into the new regime.

Even though Canada immediately shut its border tighter than Mexico, his companies and contacts there enabled him to accomplish more than most others could, even state governments.

By working every angle he was able to keep up with what was happening around the world, or at least as much as was possible. The internet, though outlawed in the states, was sporadically functioning elsewhere and some news filtered through.

He learned over time of the total societal breakdown in Asia and the old hard line tactics that were being employed more each day. This time it wasn't as easy as when Mao took over. A taste of economic freedom is hard to give up, even if it was for the most part illusionary. The masses were fighting back and the bloodshed was horrific.

As Higgins had learned, much of Europe was on fire, literally and figuratively.

When he learned that Texas had declared independence, his heart raced and his mind began to work overtime. He called in everyone he knew in the Northwest for a conference.

Madison had to concentrate his forces east of the Mississippi until those states were firmly under his control. So far the NSF and Blackpool had left the states with small populations to wander on their own, but they all knew that it was just a matter of time before that strategy would end.

His efforts and operations were made available to the underground movement that he had helped to fund, and together they would make a stand when that time came. The resistance would not be taken down easily, if at all. He swore that to himself and God.

7

August 8th

President Madison was walking at his usual fast pace through the top floor corridor in the White House. I that moment his mind was totally engulfed by the agenda of the meeting in the War Room that was his intended destination.

Ron Erickson raced behind him and called out rather urgently.

"Mr. President!"

Deep in thought Madison kept up his speed, paying him no attention.

"Mr. President!" Erickson called out again.

This time the he stopped and turned to him.

"Yes," he said bluntly.

He handed Madison a file.

"You need to see this sir, before your meeting."

Madison opened it and swore, "Son of a Bitch."

He slapped it closed and simply said, "Thank you."

As he turned to leave, Erickson spoke again.

"Mr. President, I need to ask a favor sir."

"Yes."

"There is an NSF transport going to Lincoln, Nebraska in a couple hours. Would it be possible to take it? I have a family situation I need to attend to," he asked rather meekly.

"Is it that important?" Madison asked.

"Yes Sir or I would not have asked."

"Of course," Madison said as he turned to go.

"Thank you," he said. "I'll get back as soon as I can, Mr. President."

"Whatever," the president muttered, not too quietly.

Erickson's face reddened as one of the security detail with Madison cracked a little smile. He walked slowly to a nearby staircase and descended with his shoulders drooping.

Madison had immediately reverted to his previous mindset only angrier than before.

When he walked through the door into the situation room, he was wrapped in a knot almost unable to talk. This was a first for him. The room got silent immediately and stayed that way until he finally began.

"I knew those Texan assholes would pull something, but we can't be everywhere at once, and besides who gives a shit about a bunch of cow herders and old fart oilmen with dried up wells. But this," he slammed the file Erickson had given him on the table, "this will not be tolerated."

He stopped and became his normal self, the seething turmoil under control, at least for the moment.

"I will not let a bunch of backwoods idiots stop the national progress we are making. How did you morons miss this?"

"Miss what, Mr. President?" asked Jim Wilkins, as no one else including the military brass seated around him had the balls to open their mouths.

"The Separatist Party in Alaska has somehow gotten the Governor to hold a referendum on secession."

"It was always a possibility sir since some of them had considered it in the past, but I did think he was one of ours," Wilkins offered.

"There is even a report in here that they have been talking to Canada for support. Why have none of you known of this before now?" He was getting heated again.

"We have limited NSF operatives there," Wilkins answered. "They have been getting ready to start a cleanup operation in California."

"Admiral David," Madison asked an officer sitting two seat past Jim, "What do you have in that area?"

"There are two destroyers cruising just south of Fairbanks," he answered. Admiral Paul David wasn't afraid of Madison, but he still maintained a formal military barrier as much for personal safety as protocol.

"How soon can one of them be in Juneau?"

"About twelve hours, sir."

"Order one of them there, and the other one to Fairbanks. Make sure they are menacingly visible to everyone there. That shouldn't be hard in that little piss-water capital.

Colonel Martin, coordinate at least one bomber with a few occupying jets to do low level flyovers during the day tomorrow. I want those voters to think it over about any damn referendum. Those North Slope and ANWAR wells have to be protected at any cost." Madison was adamant.

"Sir, are we going to fire on our own people?" someone asked.

"I sincerely hope not, but we will do what ever is necessary," he stated flatly.

"Jim, gather whatever NSF and Blackpool units we have available up there.

Deploy them into those two towns, and also Ketchikan and Skagway. Tell them to just make a very strong presence, and try not to overreact if there is any trouble. I want to threaten them, but I don't want to rile them into action.

Now let's get down to regular business. Let's start with the Carolinas. Have we finally secured the coastal areas, especially Charleston?"

159

As they got on into their agenda, Madison calmed considerably and was back into his beloved element, strategy.

8

August 9th

President Marsha Willard was sitting at her desk reading when her office door opened and a young man entered after lightly knocking.

"Madam President. There is a call for you on line one," her assistant stated. "It is President Madison."

"Thank you," she said, smiling as she pressed the speaker button. "Mr. President, what can I do for you?"

"Marsha," he stated coldly, "I ..."

"That would be Madam President," she said equally sober.

"Not in my lifetime," he growled.

"Again, what can I do for you, Jake?" she was about to lose her temper, but controlled it admirably.

"How far are you people going to carry this nonsense?"

"Just what nonsense are you referring too?" she countered.

"I get it. You are so damned independent that you think you can go it alone. I have let you play around for the last while, but that is going to end." He obviously was determined.

"Jake, we are not playing around, and if you must know we have been preparing for this for over twenty years. You and your ilk have been trying to destroy the country for decades and now you have," she responded in kind.

"The Supreme Court will never allow it, and we will have to enforce the law. The United States must stay intact." He was beginning to bluster.

"First of all Jake, since you murdered half of the court, I'm sure the others will give you what you want; however, calling what is left of our former country, the United States, is laughable. The U.S. died on the day you made yourself dictator."

"I don't want to send the military in there, but I will if I have to," he said in an even colder voice, if that were possible.

"I don't think that would be a good idea Jake. Not only do we have a fairly nice Navy and Army thanks to you, but we also signed an alliance with Mexico about an hour ago, and have their full support. They don't particularly like your explicit ethnic slurs.

We also were recognized by forty-three other nations as sovereign, and are preparing alliances with several of them." The pride in her voice could not go unnoticed.

The garbled sounds emitting from her receiver made her feel as if Madison had almost swallowed his tongue.

"Jake, you have enough problems insuring your own existence. Don't fret about us."

"You have a great deal of U.S. property down there, as well as captured U.S. citizens," he continued.

"You can consider it a down payment on what you owe us. When the accounting is finished, we will see you in International Court. As far as any of your so-called citizens being kept here against their will, any of them can leave at any time, and everyone who wanted to, I believe already have gone.

Also Jake, if any of your Blackpool people come any where near us, I have ordered them to be shot on sight. We are formally declaring them war criminals and as such have absolutely no standing here or I daresay anywhere in the world."

The pride in her voice was palpable.

Madison hung up on her without saying another word.

162

He must be getting frantic she thought, something she had never seen. She would have smiled and maybe done a little dance, but it kept gnawing at her that desperate people do desperate things.

In actuality she had understated the Republic's position. During the time of preparation, the banks had quietly increased their holdings of gold and converted most out of state real estate and bond holdings to Texas properties and businesses.

They were issuing the Republic's new currency in a few days and since it was backed five percent in gold and other tangibles, it would be accepted at once in most markets.

"Yes, we are well prepared," she thought.

The new Texas Constitution would be ready to sign in the morning. It had only taken days to work out the details, thanks to Pearson and his friends. As he had announced, it had the best parts of the original U.S. Constitution, the former State Constitution, and the old Republic's. It was a fine piece of work, she had to say.

With all of that, and a lot more that even her heart and mind didn't understand, she had that deep nagging that there would eventually be serious trouble. She knew they could not stay out of the coming conflicts even if it didn't come to them. Everyone had family and friends involved outside Texas and they would not be held back. How far they would go and how much would be their participation, only time would tell.

Her musings were interrupted again, by her assistant.

"Madam President, the Prime Minister of Canada is returning your call," he told her.

"Thank you," she said as she reached for the phone.

9

August 11th

Over the last one hundred and fifty years, people journeyed to Alaska for many reasons, the Gold Rush, to work on the oil pipelines, to get away from troubles of one sort or another, or just for the adventure.

Those who stayed had one thing in common; they fell in love with the majestic beauty, the way of life, and the loyalty of the people.

That is not to say they were all good folks, but there was an uncommonly high ratio of hardy, hard working, hard playing, industrious types to scoundrels, and there still was on the day of the referendum.

That is not to say there was any agreement on what the outcome would be. This was not Texas with its history of sovereignty, but they were a tough minded lot. The odds makers gave it an even up chance and took one point on the side of remaining a state.

The day before the vote there were fights on the airwaves and in the streets. Radio stations still functioned here even without the blessing of DC. The Alaskans were not going to give up that right no matter what the result. Sometimes they and the shortwave

164

transmitters and receivers were a matter of existence in their day to day work and life, especially now with the satellite feeds shut off.

George Ferrell like many of his fellow citizens of that state moved there twenty years before because he needed a fresh start. He had gotten into some trouble at home in a small town in Pennsylvania, and felt it was wise not to stay and get into more difficulties.

After the dust had settlement he had returned several times to visit family and old friends, but he always returned to the North. It had buried its claws in his heart and there was no way he would leave permanently. He had never married, at least not yet; but it was home nonetheless.

He had no idea if any of his family had been hurt in the riots and other reactions to the takeover of the government by Madison. The last word he had gotten before communications were stopped was that one of his cousins was dead, but everyone else was safe.

At first he had thought of going back and trying to help, but then thought better of it. Needless to say it was on his mind every hour of every day. He still was undecided as to which way to vote, since he saw the advantages of remaining a state and trying to change things and seceding and building a safe haven for anyone who could make it there.

He had worked the oil fields, done some fishing, and learned many of the trails by hunting and snowmobiling. The bottom line was he knew his way around and could take care of himself, so he felt he could handle what ever came to pass.

His hands and body displayed all the evidence needed to ascertain his hard but satisfying life. He walked with the grace of a hunter, the confidence of wisdom, and the authority of a leader. If he decided to ever offer himself on a permanent basis to a woman, most of those who knew him would stand in line for the opportunity.

"Command Base, this is Major Carlton," a voice boomed over the speaker in a room where a large group of military brass was sitting.

"That's one of the accompanying jets that are going to fly over Juneau," one of them said.

"This is Command Base, go ahead," another voice replied. All of the men and women in the room were listening very attentively.

"Base, we are about to do our initial flyover at one thousand feet."

"Roger that," the voice said.

A matter of several minutes elapsed and no one spoke.

"We finished the first flyover sir, and will circle around and repeat," Carlton said.

A short time later his voice boomed through again. "I believe we are being fired on sir."

"Repeat that Major."

The room was now on alert.

"I see bursts of light sir, probably rifle fire, in about five locations. The chance of any damage sir is negligible, but should we respond?" he asked. "It looks like we not welcome sir."

"Shit," another voice rang over the speaker. "Springer here sir, sorry for that, but one of those assholes actually hit me. No real damage, but how in the hell did he do it."

"Just luck Springer," Carlton replied. "Command Base, what should we do? I for one do not want to respond and possibly hurt some of our own down there. Please advise."

There was no response for a short time.

"Agreed, Major. All flights return to base."

"What the hell are they doing?" asked one of the men in the room. "Get the base on the line."

"Already done sir," an aide near him said.

"Put him on the speaker," the man said. "Command Base, this is General Howard. What the hell do you think you are doing? Why did you order your people back?"

166

"Sir. I am not going to put my men into a position where they might be in danger, no matter how small the risk, when they can't defend themselves," the voice form the Command Base responded.

"What do you mean can't defend themselves? They can return fire if there is a problem," Howard asked.

"No sir. I will not give the order to fire on U.S. citizens. First it is illegal and I swore to protect and defend them, not kill them, and second... I ask that you do not make that order, sir, as I will not obey it."

"Mister, I will have your ass for that," Howard barked.

"Yes sir, you can do that, but I will not fire on Americans, sir."

Howard slammed the phone with is fist.

"Get me Arnold over at Blackpool," he yelled.

The aide did as he was ordered.

Later that day men of an Alaskan Blackpool unit scoured the hills around Juneau, and drew fire themselves.

There was no compunction on their part about returning fire, and they did so, to their own detriment. Every man of the squad was systematically shot dead over a period of five minutes. When the last one had been killed, George Ferrell and his four compatriots moved back into the forest to continued obscurity.

The day was a waste of manpower, bruised egos, ended careers, and loss of life, for the referendum was decided by one percent, 50.5 to 49.5, to remain a state.

If it had been held a day later, after the events that unfolded in Juneau, it would not have ended with that same decision.

Lines were crossed on both sides and as in any civil war, absolutes were being further blurred, and with them, the future as well.

10

What was formerly the Situation Room in the White House had been given a total make-over. It was now a full fledged war room complete with maps, computers and all of the most modern communications systems available.

Even though the average citizen or business was regulated, limited, or outright forbidden to have access to anything other than government controlled news and any type of communications, the NSF and Blackpool had no such hindrances.

There were more than a dozen NSF intelligence officers and administration staff manning their stations. Since the area was rather small, it was a bit crowded. All personnel present had been cleared at the highest levels and that dictated the small group, so it fit.

When President Madison and Jim Wilkins entered, an immediate hush fell over the room.

"At ease everyone," Madison said, "continue what you were doing."

They rapidly resumed their work, but at a definitely lower decibel level.

"Should we bring in Paul Curtis for these sessions?" Wilkins asked.

168

"Not necessary right now. You can bring him up to speed on a need to know basis."

Madison turned to Wilkins and looked him straight in the eye.

"When we are finished, you and I will go down in history as the saviors of this country, after all we have been working toward this end for a long time. I don't need to tell you of all people, that everyone else was expected to do their jobs and they did."

"Yes sir," Wilkins affirmed.

A woman in her thirties dressed in an NSF uniform approached them.

"We are ready for the briefing sir as soon as the military gets here," she said.

"There will be no military today or any other day," Madison stated, and then he raised his voice. "Attention everyone!"

Of course the place became instantly quiet.

"My fellow Americans, listen to me. We are about to embark on a grand venture. For so many years this country has been going to hell, and we are going to change that and save the Republic."

Cheers were shouted from every mouth. He waited a few seconds and absorbed the moment, and then raised his hands for quiet and continued.

"The forces that were at work in Washington deepening the level of rot that has infected this nation have for the most part been removed; however, there is much more work to be done. After what happened two days ago in Alaska, it is apparent that the military can not be trusted to help with the settling of issues on our home soil. That, my friends, is up to us.

Since we have successfully removed our people from the Middle East, I have deployed them at various locations around the world to protect our national interests, such as Hawaii, Alaska, and the Territories. I know those damn Chinese would like a shot at annexing Guam and the Marshall Islands.

We are currently removing all of our troops from Korea. Maybe the North and South will annihilate each other, and take some of the Japanese with them.

I want updates continually on the progress from all of those areas; however, our main concern is the homeland.

Our NSF forces now total over nine hundred thousand. Blackpool will be at a level of two hundred fifty thousand by the end of the month, and will be bringing in another fifty thousand in September.

Over the next two weeks we must station all available troops at strategic locations and prepare for the worst as we try to get this nation moving again. The enemies of freedom and democracy are still out there and we must find them. We will have to flush them out, arrest them, and bring their sorry asses to justice."

He pointed to a man in the corner and to the woman that had approached them.

"General Hollis and Major Forrester will be in command here. You will direct all inquires and file all reports with them. They will answer directly Jim Wilkins," he pointed to him, "and he will keep me totally informed."

He did not have to state all of this, as they knew their positions and responsibilities to the nth degree.

The President waved the two officers to him and Wilkins.

"Our goal for the next few days is to make sure that we have NSF distributed all through the Mid-West and throughout the entire Atlantic seaboard. Pay particular attention to the Southeast and Gulf Coast. Those southern boys can be a handful. I think we have most of them subdued, but I don't want any surprises."

They dutifully nodded as he spoke.

He walked over to one of the maps, and pointed to the middle of the country.

"As you know we have been moving people into Kansas and getting ready to move westward."

He turned to Wilkins.

"Have you heard from Erickson lately?

"No Sir. I was going to ask you where he was, but I haven't had the chance," Wilkins said.

"He took a transport to Lincoln on a family emergency. Find out what's keeping him."

Without missing a beat, he went back to giving instructions.

"Get me reports on the status of the Blackpool people that are encircling Texas. Use the NSF mainly to occupy the states just east and west of the Mississippi. I don't expect any trouble from most of the other states, but North and South Dakota might present some problems."

He then brushed his hand to the western part of the nation.

"Our main concerns will be the Southwest, California, and the Northwest. For now, I want those areas blanketed with equal numbers of Blackpool and NSF. Mix the squads so that our people can learn from the experienced soldiers.

I believe if we handle this assimilation with speed and accuracy, we can have the country up and functioning well within a month or two, and root out the trouble makers.

I know you have all worked hard and will continue to do so. Thank you all, and God Bless you and your work."

Madison waved and left the room with Wilkins. As they did the activity and the noise level increased.

He looked over at Wilkins and said, "You and I both know it's not going to be that easy, someone somewhere is going to try to put a break on this. Make damn sure these people know when and where that is before it happens."

Wilkins nodded in agreement, knowing he would not be getting much sleep for a long while.

11

October 12th

When someone takes over a business or a country, several criteria must be met. The most important are intelligence, knowledge, confidence, planning, timing and a whole lot of luck. Jake Madison was certainly endowed with the first three of these attributes and his application of the third and fourth was impeccable. As the fates would have it, in the beginning he was more than blessed with a massive amount of good fortune.

The initial resistance to his maneuvers was immediate and hard, but collapsed almost as quickly as it began. Good intelligence work and the inherent weakness of the rebels were on his side. Also, he had Mother Nature watching out for him.

With California having some of the best weather in a half century, their plight was alleviated for the time necessary for his preparations on that coast. He had to secure the Eastern part of the nation for it all to work.

Again he was given the present of the mildest summer in thirty years. This was important for several reasons. People tend to be more agitated when the temperature rises, and plants grow much more productively with rain and moderate temperatures. If it had been swelteringly hot and hunger was the order of the day, who knows what would have happened differently.

Madison had immediately placed wage and price controls on an already regulated economy. He conscripted the unemployed and made them work wherever needed, and since one of his first orders under the National Emergency declaration was the confiscation of all food production and distribution, there were places for thousands of people to be put to work. The NFA (National Food Agency) was in control of it all.

Months before the takeover, he had put production of buses and train cars into overdrive. When the initial fuel supply was rationed, mass transportation picked up a great deal of the slack. The national stockpile of oil had been increased, and the new production sites of crude on the Alaskan North Slope came on line in mid-July. The problem as always was refinery capacity.

Rebels had damaged one of the refineries in Louisiana and another in New Jersey, but they were repaired and up again within weeks. The loss of the production from the secession of Texas was another matter.

However, Madison had even foreseen this possibility and had made arrangements with producers in the Caribbean and several Latin American countries, including Venezuela, to ship already distilled fuel.

He had worked out arrangements with Mexico, but obviously those were negated when he shipped a half million people back to Mexico, even though many were from other areas of Central and South America. Still upset and trying to accept the refinery capacity loss, it pleased him to no end that he had pissed off the whole country that he obviously distained.

A large part of the bargain was the deployment of American troops in these areas as "peace keepers". This accomplished two things, the military was out of the country and had less opportunity to interfere, and he could also keep an eye on his new "allies."

The United Nations had basically disappeared within weeks. It had lived on the support of the U.S., and when that was gone the rats instantly abandoned ship.

To a certain degree life in U.S. remained the same as it was. By the time the Madison administration had taken the White House, the government had already absorbed a large part of the economy.

The financial sector was either still controlled by DC directly or regulated to the point of indirect ownership. Credit had been so limited by these regulations that the government had to step in and be the lender of last resort, and of course with every loan came strings that were almost impossible to cut loose. This began with the outright confiscation of the student loan part of the business in 2010 in the Health Care Bill.

No one would buy the miserable "green" cars and second rate trucks that the government owned car companies produced. Instead of letting these businesses go away as footnotes in history, the politicians did what they do best, make a totally screwed-up situation unbelievably worse. They took over the other U.S. auto manufacturers so their cars and trucks would be just as bad, and people would have to buy what was available.

While gas was limited, it didn't make much difference, but as more would become available, it was important. Since imports were banned, the only units available were from these producers. Of course this did mean more jobs in auto repair facilities, a small benefit.

Almost every fire department in the country worked on as usual. Those brave men and women continued to fight fires, perform EMT services, and run ambulance crews. They were kept busy working extra shifts on a regular basis because of the "riots" and other disturbances. Adequate fuel supplies were mandated for these services. Without them the "rebels" would have had a much stronger case for their anti-government cause.

Police departments were ordered to follow federal law as the primary operating code, but also had to maintain regular order, which meant also enforcing state and local laws as needed.

174

The sentiment among the local cops was not universally pro-feds. After the problems in Virginia, NSF overseers were assigned to every police department in the nation with more than fifty field officers. The size of the contingency could be from one NSF officer to one or two squads. For obvious reasons larger forces were assigned to Richmond, VA, Lexington and Louisville, KY, & Indianapolis, IN.

In the southern states and those states west of the Mississippi, they became known as "Regulators" after similar federal officers in the nineteen century. In the north and northeast the derogatory term was "Pussyfoots", especially in coal mining areas. This term harkened back to the Coal Mining Police of the early twentieth century, which were sanctioned by the state governments, most notoriously Pennsylvania. Those forces were manned by thugs and criminal types recruited off the streets of cities such as Chicago, Detroit, and New York much like the NSF who now donned their infamous moniker.

Health care, once the envy of the world, was second rate at best. By 2012 twenty-five percent of the medical personnel in the country had left the business to pursue other means of earning a living. This was made necessary since very few could break even, let alone earn a profit at it. Again, this had been a planned move so that the government could take over one-sixth of the economy in one fell swoop when insurance companies went bankrupt along with hospitals, pharmaceutical companies, and medical practices .

Another move Madison made when he issued the FEMA orders was the conscription of medical personnel into that federal health care system. Even individuals who had retired and were in advanced age were made to join the system, especially when the "riots" filled the hospitals with the critically injured.

Because of the increased coverage and direct necessity of rationing of medical care, the health panels created in 2010 were expanded in 2014 so that every citizen could assessed and only those with a foreseeable productive future would be able to obtain the best care.

By conscripting labor and cutting services the government had indeed cut costs as they had promised. Health care and research workers, once the elite of the labor forces were on par with auto mechanics. The political A-list in Washington had always wanted to emulate Europe and in this area they accomplished their goals exquisitely.

One of the major ironies of the Health Care Act, the Second Patriot Act, all of the other regulatory changes, and the huge number of Executive Orders passed was the very people that helped put these culpable people in office were some of the first victims of it.

Hollywood had backed liberal after liberal with their sanctimonious drivel and prodded them forward to change everything. They cheered them on when they shut down all of the alternative voices to their own. What they didn't expect was when you allow another person to be silenced; you can easily be the next in line to be gagged. By the time Madison had been elected, all of the laws and procedures were in place and within a few months he had eliminated any source of expression of any ideas in opposition to those federally approved.

All of the media were totally controlled, the Internet was a mere shadow of its former self, and everyone was afraid to voice an opinion openly about anything.

When Obama had become President, unions only controlled a small percentage of the work force, mostly government workers. Within three years their membership had reached thirty percent again. The dreams of the union leaders of universal authority dissipated like the mist of a shriveling piece of dry ice in a matter of months.

Companies, and most especially cities and states, had to renege on their pension and health benefits not only for retired workers, but for the current work force as well. Of course the feds took over the health care as was planned, but the retirement benefits shrank to a modicum of the former promises. Since this was the backbone of the Union movements, they disappeared as well.

The result of all this was that everyone in the country, particularly in urban and suburban areas had to do a lot more on a lot less. To a certain degree people still went to work, came home, and tried to go on living.

What had disappeared were the every day luxuries that most Americans had taken for granted, any type of travel, individual choice and availability of products, especially food, and most importantly freedom and liberty. They had gradually over the years given it away for spectral promises that also vanished in the new dawn.

They say luck is a fickle lady; what she might give freely, may very easily and quickly be taken away. The magnificently serene summer turned into a horrendously frightful fall. At the end of September, the fourth and fifth tropical storms of the season hit Eastern Florida, both within four days.

Hurricane Don with winds in excess of 90 mph winds swept across the state after plowing through Miami and Fort Lauderdale. It cut a swathe of devastation a hundred miles wide.

Four days later Hurricane Emily bounced off the same area and then moved up the coast intensifying as it progressed until it maintained 90 to 100 mph winds. Never fully coming ashore in any state, it tore into town after town, city after city including Daytona, Charleston, Myrtle Beach, and Wilmington and everything in between. Cape Hatteras and most of the surrounding area virtually disappeared. Ocean City, Maryland became two islands as the water tore a new seaway through the middle of town.

The winds calmed down to 90 mph hour along the Jersey coast, over Staten Island, and into New England. The upper end of Cape Cod also became an island, and with the accompanying rapid erosion a very small one at that.

Since President Madison had scatter deployed the NSF throughout the country, and given that it had before made up the major part of FEMA, there was no one to come to the rescue or aide of any of the victims.

177

Most of our former allies were not in the position to bring much help either, though many of them tried to do a little. Our reduced military could not assist as it was strewn all over hell and creation protecting Madison's interests worldwide.

Thousands were killed or injured in the first week. Hundreds of thousands were homeless, fatigued, and hungry. Disease would sooner than later become a problem, and cause more deaths. Property damaged was incalculable.

The East Coast was a powder keg ready to blow, and then there was the incident at the Miller Barber Shop and Fine Salon in Butte, Montana. A small storefront on a side street of this small city was about to become the Fort Sumter of this Civil War.

12

October 12th

Calvin Miller opened his barber shop in 1896 and ran it continuously until his retirement in 1938. His son, grandson, and great-grandson carried on the tradition for seventy more years. The establishment closed its doors in June of 2005 when the last barber in the family was gone.

In all that time there was no talk of being anything other than a place where men could go, get a hair-cut, and share the local news and views of weather, crops, hunting, and the occasional heated discussion of politics. However, that talk got so intense in the late seventies that Mike Miller had to bar it for a while, and limited the exchanges when it was permitted again.

The building had stood empty for a couple years, and would have probably been torn down, but the locals fought to keep it as it was. They even tried to get a heritage designation, but failed. An attempt to raise funds began so the town could make it an historic landmark but that went nowhere: then Sal Calvino returned from three tours in the Middle East.

He and the men in his family had been customers there for as long as anyone could remember. After mustering out of the service, he was at a loss as to what he wanted to do for the rest of his life. He had gotten a rather intense education in truck repair during the eight years he had been in the army, but he really didn't want to do that any more.

One day as he walked past the old Miller place, he was hit with the thought of why not go into the hair business. If anyone had seen him pondering this, they would have most likely been astounded. Sal was six foot four inches tall, weighed in at about two hundred and twenty pounds, and was as strong as a proverbial ox.

Once he made up his mind it was a done matter. He started going to a local hair school and at the same time worked at fixing up the old shop for when he finished. His wife got involved and between them they designed a really sophisticated façade even incorporating the old red and white barber pole he found in the basement.

They acquired the storefront next door and opened the two into one interior, complete with all modern equipment designed around antique wood borders and trim. It was expensive and a great deal of work; but with an enormous amount of sweat equity, they realized their dream.

Obviously there was no way it would pay for itself with Sal as a lone barber, or god forbid that name that was banned for one hundred years, stylist. As it turned out he was extremely good at his newly chosen profession, and eventually had a waiting list of clients for three to four weeks.

In no time other stylists were approaching him to work there. He had planned on establishing some sort of arrangement to use the space available, and settled on a rental plus small percentage on each station. By the time the war came to the U.S., he had ten stylists, three washers, four manicurists, and three others working there, either as employees or independent contractors.

Under this plan, during slower periods, they all took the hit, and when work was plentiful, the wealth was shared. Sal was very particular about who he allowed to work with him, and considered all of them family, and they him.

Samuel Macon Harris was born and raised in Baltimore, Maryland in an area known in the old days as Fells Point. It was basically a white section of town that had changed over the years with an influx of Salvadorians and others from Central America. There was some conflict between the two major groups of Latinos, but in general most everyone got along.

Sammy grew up with an alcoholic father. His mother died when he was ten, and he had no brothers or sisters. As he got older, he got more arrogant and unruly, most likely as a survival mechanism.

One day when he was fifteen, his dad came home drunk as a human could get, and started to beat the crap out of Sammy for some undisclosed and fleeting reason. This was a big mistake as the boy had grown already into a large strong bruiser. He turned the tables and put his father in the hospital. It was touch and go for over a week as to whether Jim Harris would make it.

He lived but Sammy was tried as a juvenile for attempted murder. Normally in Maryland very little would happen to a minor, but for some reason, he was convicted and sentenced to jail until he was eighteen.

By the time he was released, he was a confirmed and trained criminal. He was smart enough not to get caught, and stayed ahead of the law. With that degree of education he was on his way to a career in the art of crime.

When several of his friends decided to join the NSF, he thought it was probably a good idea, and a ticket out of town. Figuring it was a great move into a broader range of opportunities to practice his main profession, theft and battery, he quickly went into the service too.

Boot camp and the training planned for the recruits were cut short. He and most of his friends were deployed in the Richmond area where half of them were killed or seriously injured. Sammy and his closest friend Frank were later sent west and ended up in Butte, Montana, complete with massive chips balanced on their rather large shoulders.

Instead of the preparation most troops got when entering the military, they and their attitudes were forged in the heat of battle, and really didn't have grounding in logic, reasoning, common sense, and absolutely no civility. In their minds they were the victims of everything that was wrong in the country.

On the day they entered the Miller Barber Shop and Fine Salon, they were prepared for trouble, and they surely found it.

When Sammy, Frank, his new pal Clayton, and three other NSF men entered Sal's styling establishment, they were aching for an opportunity to show those backwoods rubes what asses they were. He and the others had been stationed in small towns for over three months and they were sick of it, bored to death.

Butte was the first large city that had presented any prospect of excitement and a chance of making some extra cash by looting and pillaging. Right now they just wanted to break loose.

They walked in laughing, talking loudly all sorts of crap, and pushing each other around. In additional to Sal, and the other employees, there were customers at each chair and five sitting waiting their turn on seats against the wall.

The gang looked around and only saw local yokels getting their hair done, looking for all-the-world like easy prey. Yes Sal was a big guy, but the rest were lambs ready for the slaughter. Sammy thought, "What a bunch of losers!"

Just to talk shit, he pointed to one of the female stylists and said, "You know, she ain't half bad."

One of the others barked back, "But the other half ain't that great!"

Then they all howled with laughter.

Breaking through the noise one of the others said, "Yeah, he is better looking than all the rest!" He was pointing his shaky finger at an obviously gay hairdresser off to one side.

They increased their decibel level even more.

Sal moved towards them at that moment and said calmly but forcefully, "You boys are making a huge mistake."

182

Sammy pulled his sidearm and shouted, "Give me a reason asshole!"

Sal just shook his head with an almost unnoticeable smile.

One of the men sitting waiting his turn rose quietly and with authority. "I'm Sheriff O'Conner and this is my town. You boys are guests here…"

Before he could finish his sentence, one of the others pulled his gun also and it fired nicking the sheriff and hitting one of the women standing behind him, knocking her down.

All hell broke lose. Montana was an open or concealed carry state and by that time almost everyone was packing heat. The six NSF did not have a chance, and were all dead before they even knew what happened.

Ten revolvers and automatics from both men and women cut them down like so much dry wheat in a hail storm. Three others were ready but never fired.

Sal kept a shotgun and two revolvers near him, but didn't feel the necessity to even try to get to them.

One of the other stylists helped the injured woman up and was applying pressure to her wound. He said, "Looks superficial."

"Same here," said the sheriff.

"I guess the shit just hit the fan Marty," Sal said to the lawman calmly.

Sheriff O'Conner nodded every bit as stoically.

"Should we take them and get rid of them? I know a few places they would never be found," said one of the men.

"No," said the sheriff. "What do you think Sal? Maybe a good offense is due?"

Sal nodded. He and the others had spent a lot of time discussing the state of the country and what was surely headed their way sooner or later, and to a man and woman, everyone in the shop was of one mind on which side they stood.

Several of them threw the bodies into the back of one of the pick-ups. Sal and the stylists finished their work and got ready to leave. Several calls had been made and the local phone chain had begun to do its job.

By the time they reached the NSF office, there were more than a hundred armed and angry Montanans ready for a fight. More were continuously arriving.

They threw the dead men onto the steps of the building and the sheriff called on his bullhorn.

"You people inside. Get this trash off our streets and clear out of town. You are not welcome here and of no foreseeable need to us."

An officer and three Blackpool men opened the door and came out.

"You people are making a grave mistake. I want whoever did this taken in and arrested immediately."

"Kiss my ass!" someone shouted.

"Kiss mine too," several others rang out in unison.

The men started to reach for their weapons and the sheriff called out to them, "Don't do it!"

A shot rang out from a second floor window, and dozens of other troops poured out the doors.

The battle began and took more than an hour to end.

Every last NSF and Blackpool man and woman was killed, four hundred and thirty in all. The locals lost sixty four people and had another two hundred wounded. By the time it was over, there were more than two thousand Montanans armed to the teeth, defending their life and liberty in the first true battle of the Civil War that had just been fought.

The other fights of the previous six months could be relegated to history as civil rebellions, riots, and any of a dozen other euphemisms that the government could generate. This was entirely different and would always be remembered as much for what it stood for rather than for outcome.

There was no way it would be tolerated in DC, and Blackpool would not let the loss of forty-five of their men go without a substantial response. The news spread quickly and loudly to every last part of the country.

Both sides prepared for the coming battles.

13

October 13th

John Enman had worked from the day of his arrival in Fargo to organize as much of the country as was possible given the limitations from DC that he had to circumvent. He was in constant contact with other like-minded citizens, civilians and law enforcement alike, especially in North and South Dakota, Wyoming, Montana, and Idaho.

All of these states were very much made up of patriots who had been fed up with the Feds since them began confiscating land in the nineteen-seventies.

For decades a lot of Hollywood types had bought up half of Montana, and areas in the surrounding states. But when their fortunes turned sour many had sold out to cover debts or, unbelievably, became absorbed into the local culture. Remember the old saying "a conservative is a liberal who has been mugged"? These changelings proved it to be very true. After the new elite in Washington turned on them, they truly thought mugging would have been preferred.

Enman set in motion relocation efforts that would have made Harriet Tubman proud. He moved over a quarter of a million people from the East and Mid-West in less than four months. They virtually disappeared into the night.

Homes all through the Northwest brought family, friends, and strangers into their lives. They cared for and fed all who asked, and helped them adapt.

There were many people with large holdings and money that needed to leave the country knowing that if they didn't, they would most likely disappear in mysterious and covert ways. They paid major amounts of money, mostly in gold, to be scurried across the border into Canada. With his powerful contacts in the North, he could accomplish pretty much anything necessary up to a limit.

As distasteful as it was to him having to work with a lot of these arrogant people, Enman made each and everyone of them cover the costs of relocating those who couldn't pay their own way. He determined what they could afford and they were forced to oblige him before a crossing was arranged. One well known Southern family paid for the transferring of over ten thousand others from their part of the country. It took over three months to move them; therefore, they stayed in a small home near Fargo until it was complete. Afterward they moved to Canada a week before the Battle of Butte.

The only groups that his organization would not allow into any of their activities were the few crazy militias from Montana, Idaho, and other nearby states that he did not trust or could not abide their beliefs. Problems occurred on a regular basis, and several of them had to be eliminated for the good of the others near by. They were not assassinated but where simply stomped on when they got out of line, which is what they quickly did. The war eventually took care of most of them, because the Feds were well aware of their existence and loved pinning any and all the mischief and illegal crap on them that they could.

When the call went out for those who were interested in joining the insurrection, over two hundred thousand answered immediately and began to prepare. These were not the talk now and give in later Easterners who buckled after a few losses, but the hardy "my word is my bond" people that make up an enormous part of the populations west of the Mississippi.

The day after the fight in Butte Enman got word that over four thousand NSF were ordered into the area, as well as five hundred of Blackpool's best. They felt that the line had to be drawn there or controlling the rest of the country would be a lot more difficult than it should be.

Unlike what happened in Richmond, their intel was poor and they had no idea what was waiting for their arrival. It was going to be a bloody and brutal conflict.

Those preparing for the assault on their homes had the edge of local knowledge, personal defense, and the power of having right on their side.

The NSF and Blackpool leaders felt that any one of their troops was worth fifty to a hundred of the other side because of the experience of the previous six months. They had no idea of the strength or will of the opposition, or the whole scenario would have been changed.

The coming events would forever change the outward appearance of the nation, and the hearts and souls of many of its citizens.

14

October 14th

Jake Madison spent an inordinate amount of time in the War Room. It had the simultaneous result of energizing the staff and creating an extremely tense environment.

None of them had had much down time since the hurricanes had struck. With most of what was left of FEMA absorbed into the NSF, there was little that agency could do for the victims.

Major Forrester approached the president.

"Fulton Construction has moved all of their crews into Charleston. They report that it will take a week or so to clear the area and restore enough power and open roads just for the rescue needs," she said.

Martin Fulton had been arrested when he told Madison's people to go to hell after the President had issued orders for all companies that had any equipment or personnel to aid the effort to help. It wasn't that he and others didn't to support the cause. The directives were simply confiscation of property and staff without any compensation. This did not sit well with a lot of people, especially Fulton.

They were already working on their own because many of their employees were affected, but being ordered around just didn't set well with those boys.

"Most of the coastal areas have started burials in mass graves," she continued. "The number of able bodied workers is far fewer than the number of dead and injured. It will still take a number of days to move crews from the interior to the coast. They are basically working their way in, clearing and repairing as they go. It looks like the death tolls will probably climb dramatically as time goes on."

The NSF could get some troops into the area, but Madison was reluctant to pull many of them out of the current locations, fearing that the public would try something if not watched continuously.

The president had made an appeal to several other countries and some help was on the way; however, most of them had their own problems, and couldn't spare the troops or workers either. On top of that, he had to offer them compensation in gold for any and all of their expenses.

Jake had committed all of the military to the locations that were supplying necessities such as oil, gas, and food and could not pull any of them back. His main concern was that they would immediately join forces with his enemies. The desertion rate was already more than anyone had anticipated.

He and Wilkins walked over to the computer display that showed the movement of troops into the Northwest.

"How soon before we have sufficient manpower there to knock some sense into those morons," he asked. His contempt for the West was obvious.

"We're concentrating a large force in southwestern Wyoming and Eastern Idaho. We'll stage a wide sweep from there and plow over any opposition," General Hollis said confidently.

"Any spots of insurrection elsewhere," Madison asked.

"Not at the moment; however, some of our people say there are smatterings of discontent forming in Oregon and Washington."

"Oregon?" Wilkins interjected. "That's one of the most liberal states west of the Mississippi."

General Hollis just shrugged his shoulders.

"What about California?" the president asked.

Major Forrester responded.

"It's been quiet. They have been concentrating on rebuilding their agriculture and some construction projects corresponding to that, and may possibly be able to ship produce east again soon. It's the same in Arizona, New Mexico, Nevada, and Colorado. The moderate summer certainly helped."

Madison thought about it and wasn't convinced there wouldn't be any trouble there. Yes it might have been quiet, maybe too quiet.

One of the staff approached them.

"We have just gotten word from a Coast Guard vessel that approached Myrtle Beach," he hesitated to continue on, choking up. "Most of that area is totally devastated, whole sections are... gone."

They had not been able to get word out of nearly all of the North and South Carolina coastal areas, and this confirmed their worst fears.

Madison turned and left the room without saying a word. He had known it wouldn't be simple, but he had no idea that the tide would turn against him in this manner. He had to get some sleep if possible and think of what to do next. Deep in his gut he began to feel that some stronger measures would have to be put into place. He just was not sure what they should be.

Later after a couple stiff drinks, he finally passed out.

15

October 14th

Gloria and her nephew Jeff left Louisville on August 6th, starting their journey in the middle of the night. Not in her wildest dreams did she ever think that it would take her nine weeks to reach Colorado.

The first few days were mostly uneventful. The information Carl had given them proved to be correct and extremely helpful. Jeff had considered "borrowing" a friend of his' motorcycle, but she talked him out of it. It was not right to start a new life stealing from a friend. In that frame of reference, he totally understood. It was then she knew for certain he was a good kid.

On the fifth day it began to rain and didn't stop for three more days. They found an abandoned barn and holed up there for the duration of the storm. At first he was quiet, obviously thinking of his mother, which was exactly what Gloria was doing.

The tension built up in her to the point she burst into tears. She tried to control it for his sake, but that was impossible. The thought of Helen dying that young and for no reason other than the ideology of a bunch of mad men and women was more than her tortured mind could handle.

Suddenly Jeff put his arm around her shoulder and held her as she let all of the pent up emotion release. She knew as calm as he felt, tears were pouring out of his eyes too.

They fell asleep from exhaustion lying next to each other.

Several hours later she awoke with a start in a panic mode. She reached for her gun and heard Jeff quietly laugh.

"That must have been some dream, or was it a nightmare?" he asked.

She shook her head to try and clear it.

"I guess so," she said, "but I don't remember a thing."

She knew from that point on she had to go back to her training and pull herself together, especially now that she had the additional responsibility. Her promise to her sister was not an idle comment to calm her at the time. She meant to deliver him to safety, and by god, she would do just that.

Through the next days of rain they talked and talked until they passed out, and when they woke, they began again. In that short time, they learned more about each other than either one of them would ever have thought was possible, and a bond began to form that would soon develop into something that would never be broken.

During the storm they never heard or saw anyone. On the morning of the fourth day it stopped raining, and as they prepared to leave there were a series of distant rumbles. At first they considered it might be thunder but the sky was blue and cloudless.

They retreated to a ravine behind the barn and waited, watching the road in front of them. In about twenty minutes a convoy of military trucks, jeeps, and semis moved down the road past them in the direction from which they had traveled three days before.

Thinking of course that they were going to Louisville, they both had the same thought. Carl said that trouble was coming, maybe this was it.

After the troops had passed, they went in the opposite direction and kept to the brush along the way for a mile or so. Everything seemed so quiet. She knew they were off the main drag, but not seeing anyone was eerie.

They remained on the back roads and cut through fields and forests when possible. Later that day they came upon a house with a mailbox with a yellow cord hanging from it. There was no way the resistance was out here she thought, but they investigated carefully.

As they approached the house, a woman came around the corner. She eyed them as they came closer.

"It looks like it's going to rain," Gloria said.

"It very well might," the woman stated, "and then again it very well might not."

"Beats me," Gloria responded.

They stood there and looked at each other for a few minutes, causing Jeff a little unease. Gloria had mentioned the code language but he didn't think of it at that moment.

"I guess I'll take a chance on you two," the woman said. "Come on in."

They walked into her house.

"Have you eaten a decent meal lately?" she asked.

"Not really," Gloria said.

"Didn't think so," she said matter-of-factly. "Sit down and I'll heat you up something."

She motioned them to the kitchen and they sat at the table.

"Your code was from last month. How long have you been out in the woods?"

"Over a week, but I haven't had any contact for almost five weeks," Gloria said.

"Thought so," the woman said. "I'll catch you up on everything I can then you should move on. It's getting a bit unsafe around here."

As they ate what seemed to their stomachs to be some of the best food ever, she filled them in on everything she knew or had heard. One of the resistance members had a shortwave and some other gear and listened constantly. He never sent out any calls because he was afraid they might trace the signal back to him. Whether they could or would was irrelevant, he wasn't going to take the chance.

The woman gave her the codes for August and September. After they had eaten, drank several glasses of coffee and milk, and gone to the bathroom, Gloria and Jeff thanked her profusely and left.

She thought the woman was on the up and up, but they took no chances and veered from their regular path for about two miles.

When they saw another mailbox and cord, she tried the new code and immediately was ushered into the house by a tall thin man. He offered to take them about ten miles to another relay and by evening they had gotten almost to the Mississippi River.

It took them two more days and they finally made it. Their next problem was getting across. They made contact with another patriot and found out that every bridge and crossing he was aware of were either closed, guarded or being watched twenty-four-seven.

It took three days, but he found someone who would get them across, about fifty miles south. When they arrived there, it was a dead end: the man who was to take them was arrested the day before their arrival.

Finally after two weeks they made the trip in the middle of the night in a small boat with an electric motor.

The lady they had worried about had been a godsend, because without her nerve in helping them, they would never have made it to Missouri.

From there to Crystola, Colorado, took the remaining weeks. There were stops, starts, layovers, and almost-encounters continually. With her experience and his youth, they kept at it, and were successful.

As they approached a couple buildings in a valley just outside of town, they both were musing over the same thoughts and feelings they had had every day since they left Louisville, "how was her sister and his mother?"

An older, heavy man ran to them as they approached and yelled, "Oh my god you made it, oh my god."

General Higgins hugged her and held her as if she were his long lost daughter. In his mind, she was.

In the coming months they would find out that Helen had died about the time they were half way across the Mississippi. She was much sicker than even she had known or had let on, but her inner being must have sensed they were on their way to safety, and she was at peace.

16

October 15th

Ron Erickson had left DC on August 8th and had not returned. After a few days Madison had simply assumed he had jumped ship and went into hiding or joined the other side. He had always thought he was a miserable cowardly ass.

Since he had never really known him, he wondered if he even had family in Lincoln. Wilkins ran an investigation for his own edification feeling rightfully so that the president didn't give a shit one way or the other.

He indeed had a relative there, his mother. She had been in a retirement home but when the National Health Board determined she could no longer have that kind of money spent on her, she was sent to a relative's house to live.

Erickson had tried to pull some strings to help her but had gotten no where. Rules were rules he was told over and over again, until no one would take his call.

When he approached Madison to go back to Nebraska, he had gotten word she had had a severe heart attack, and he wanted to see her even if it were for one last time.

Before his plane landed she had died and he was too late. Witnesses who had been to the funeral said they had seen him there.

He had kept to himself and only answered when spoken to, and only briefly then.

She had been cremated. This had become the only option for most people as an old time burial casket was out of the range of most family's affordability. Since this had been her wishes he went along with it even though he could have afforded to do otherwise.

Erickson had been seen carrying her box of ashes to a military jeep that was to take him back to the Air Force base. From there he was to fly back to Washington.

It never arrived and he and the driver were never seen again.

Madison's doubts remained until the day Wilkins entered the Oval Office and said, "They found Erickson's jeep."

"What?" the president said, as he looked up from some papers he was reading.

"Ron's ride had not been found until today."

"Where was it?" he asked.

"Just outside of Lincoln on the way to the base in a ravine under some brush. It was discovered when the leaves turned and fell off." Wilkins waited for a response and got it.

"That son-of-a-bitch and his driver deserted. I knew it." Madison pounded the desk as he spoke.

"That may not be the case. Actually the evidence implies just the opposite," Wilkins interjected.

Madison became silent and glared at him.

"There was blood on the seats and his briefcase and ID card were in the dirt outside the vehicle."

The president said nothing for a long while. When he finally spoke, it was simply, "Maybe."

"We ran DNA on the blood and it was Erickson's and the driver's."

"Maybe," he repeated, over and over again.

At that point Wilkins began to worry a little. He wondered if his Commander-In-Chief was maybe a bit obsessive.

He turned and left the room.

Madison stared into space for a moment and then returned to his papers.

17

October 25th

One week after the Battle of Butte, NSF and Blackpool forces gathered in Tower Junction in the northwest corner of Wyoming. It is located in the northern section of the former Yellowstone National Park with easy access to most of the few major highways in the area.

The original number of NSF troops to be deployed was four thousand. That was later increased to over five thousand. Blackpool at the last minute had added to their number, bringing its staffing to over seven hundred.

Colonel Melvin Howard was in charge of the entire Northwest Division of the NSF, and at least on paper was leading the entire Montana campaign. General Ramon Alberto Hernandez was the Blackpool chief officer, assigned to assist him.

Men, equipment, and supplies had been flown in all week and a major headquarters established in a large area of open lands near the tiny town. Most of the terrain in that region was rather rough with hills and valleys which is why the local resistance preferred it.

Even though not much confrontation was expected, medical facilities and personnel had been brought in, and requisitioned from some of the towns surrounding Billings and Bozeman. This was more action than this area had seen since the Indian Wars over a hundred years before.

Recon flights had been sent since the first supplies rolled in and had nothing to report until two days before the campaign was launched. A group of people were spotted camping and training in a military fashion southeast of Bozeman near Bald Knob.

Colonel Howard called Washington and requested that they simply drop a few bombs and finish it. Madison had specifically forbidden that. He was concerned that it would be seen as a massacre and they would have more martyrs to rile up the opposition. He was entirely right in his thinking.

The plan of action was to send two series of groups, one to the East on Rt. 89 and Rt. 90 and one to West along Rt. 191 in a flanking action to go around the compound, and the remaining troops would fan out in a frontal assault.

There were very few towns of any size other than along the main roads that each division would be encountering. The troops were then divided into smaller groups, some as small as squads, so that they could requisition food and drink as they traveled and would not be burdened by having to transport supplies as well as arms and ammunition.

Theoretically this plan accomplished two goals, faster movement of troops and the ability to determine friend from enemy. They did not want to have any more collateral damage than necessary. Of course most of the troops involved couldn't care less, but DC and the regional leaders knew the repercussions of such losses.

The end result was that about one hundred groups of fifty to sixty soldiers fanned out across the countryside to surround what was thought to be a bunch of local yokels pretending to be minutemen.

The far ends of the flanking maneuver started and then every two hours another two squads left camp. From the air it indeed looked like a rope of troops proceeding to lasso the group.

Orders were that they were to encircle the area and wait for instructions on when and how to move.

No heavy armaments were brought in because of the weight and time necessary to do so, and no one felt there was any need. Most of them were supplied with light fully automatic assault rifles and semi-automatic pistols.

The whole operation encompassed an area of over four hundred and fifty square miles. A lot can happen in that much terrain and it did.

As the hours and days went by military and government procurement representatives forged ahead for food and water in every town, and group of houses that were in the path of the operation. Most of the time they were just feeding one squad and at the most two which didn't present a problem for many of the locals.

The townspeople and rural families that were confronted with the situation were for the most part friendly and helpful. They even laughed and joked with the military as they fed them.

At the end of three days the encampment was totally surrounded and all the squads waited for instructions. When the orders were given they were told that anyone offering any resistance was to be arrested and sent back to headquarters for trial as enemy combatants. There was to be strictly no engagement of firing unless fired upon. At all times it was to be remembered that the publicity of killing fellow Americans would certainly play against them.

On the morning of October 25th, fifty-seven hundred troops began to close in on the suspected five hundred militia types training in the center of the circle. No sooner did the maneuver begin than each of the squads was fired upon from behind. As they had flanked the encampment, twenty thousand Montanans and others from neighboring states had out-flanked them.

The local yokels had high powered rifles, were good shots, and the home town advantage. As each group had eaten and laughed with the people on which they had imposed themselves, information had been sent to those assigned to trail and attack each squad.

With the exception of three or four squads, during the first hour of the action clearly half of each group was eliminated. Several of the NSF had tried to surrender, but they were either picked off by the local snipers or shot by the Blackpool men in their own squad. Running was not tolerated by either side.

The reasoning for this by the resistance was entirely understandable. Any American that was willing to fight against another American didn't deserve to be taken prisoner. That may sound horrible by modern standards, but these people felt violated by there own brothers. They were fighting for a cherished way of life, and had not started the whole thing.

The Blackpool people were considered as low as the Hessians were in the Revolutionary War, that is, mercenaries and beneath contempt. Since almost to a man, they were foreign soldiers, that idea was not a stretch.

For the most part the invaders were sitting ducks, and with the exception of two squads were annihilated to the last person, stripped of their weapons and equipment and left to rot.

Four members of two of the remaining squads were allowed to escape to report back to their people what had happened. The resistance disappeared into the hills.

When questioned later, all of the townspeople were aghast at what had happened and to a person denied any involvement.

Madison and his people had made some classical mistakes. They had also underestimated the will of a people used to freedom and liberty and their ability to defend those rights.

The Montanans had lost a few hundred of their numbers, and sustained a considerable amount of injuries; however, to a man they were pleased, and felt damn good about the whole thing.

The local constabulary, a group of fifty plus lawmen, and almost a hundred deputized citizens surrounded the headquarters and arrested the NSF and Blackpool regulars. The medical and non-affiliated personnel were released and sent on their way.

The prisoners were taken by bus to the nearest correction facility that would hold them in Bozeman. The handcuffs and chains were kept on them for the duration of their stay because all of them were considered dangerous, especially the private security forces.

Blackpool executives were furious and immediately dispatched a squad of specials ops personnel. They attacked the prison without warning and slaughtered every last person there. Almost all of the victims were law enforcement.

When they freed the prisoners, only the Blackpool men and two of the NSF ran. The remaining men were more afraid of leaving than staying.

Two days after the massacre, the area was blanketed in an early blizzard with over a foot and a half of snow.

The resistance rallied every snowmobile and gathered all of the fuel they could find. Using those and the NSF's own trucks they hauled every last body from the original battle sites and stacked them in a mound along Rt. 90, fifty seven hundred dead troops.

They placed banners across the area so that they could be seen from every viewpoint including the air. Each of them read, "May All You Rot In Hell", and "You're All Dead Men, You Just Don't Know It Yet".

Pictures of the horrendous scene were sent to every possible transmission source and with a couple weeks everyone in the world knew what had happened.

18

November 14th

Thanksgiving was almost upon the country, in most areas there was little to eat and not much to be thankful. Most people were just grateful to be alive.

The Northwest and Midwest was blanketed with a more than normal amount of snow as winter came early, hard, and continued unmercifully. It helped keep the DC troops at bay, but the shortage of supplies and food took its toll.

The West Coast and Southwest states had sporadic fighting almost daily. In the little sea port town of Eureka, California, a four day fight between twenty-five Blackpool agents ended with all of them dead and over a hundred townspeople killed or injured.

NSF and Blackpool surrounded the area and threatened to kill every last one of them if the survivors of the battle were not arrested and given over to them. Governor Phillips sent in the National Guard and forced them to leave. When some of the Security Force resisted they were shot on the spot. For California, the line had been drawn in the sand.

Philips had quietly built the Guard from new volunteers and returning troops that had deserted and come home to fight those they felt were the real enemies. Several crews of Navy ships had mutinied and brought their vessels with them. Many of the officers simply joined with the regulars and sailed home. California had the start of a small fleet.

They were immediately assigned to guarding and patrolling the coast which with its size was quite a job.

Spotters were organized the entire length of the expanse and with several thousand pairs of eyes watching very little got by them.

Several forces of NSF and Blackpool people attempted to land but were dispatched with speed and regularity.

Troops tried to enter California from Nevada, Utah, and Arizona. The problem was that they had to get through those states first. Most of them did not make to their destination.

When a joint effort of the surrounding states was functioning, it began to solidify their relationships and bring them together as cohesive area.

Madison would like to have multiplied his reach in the west but after all the storm damage had been assessed, he had to pull back personnel for the rebuilding of the cities and keep order on the East Coast.

New England was affected the most as the damage was compounded by the winter weather which was as early and harsh as in the northwest. Thousands were destined to die, and that generated an enormous amount of ill temper and consternation.

It took until the following spring to bring order from chaos from Virginia to Florida. The smell of death destroyed the morale of many, but built the resolve of others who were preparing and waiting for the right moment.

Much of what Blackpool had done had not been authorized by Madison or anyone in his command. They were now so big and so essential that he had to tolerate their existence. To compound matters, it became necessary to import even more forces from out of the country.

With the spring would come many decisions, more tribulations, and as an entirety it had become increasingly very complicated.

19

November 27th

Gloria and Jeff had become very much acclimated to their new home. General Higgins had welcomed them with open arms, literally and figuratively. He had no family and now neither did they. Though his best years were behind him, he was determined to see that they had a future. He spent every waking hour trying to figure out a way to bring it about.

Higgins had acquired and prepared the safe house years before under an assumed name. He had given her instructions on how to get there before he left the East Coast in case they had no other choices. That became the scenario when everything went further to hell than even he could have imagined.

By the time she finally arrived, he had almost given up hope. All of the news from back East had been so depressing that he began to have thoughts of ending it all. Her arrival had given him a fresh start and a purpose that he richly needed for survival. The addition of her nephew Jeff enlivened him even further as they hit it off immediately. Higgins made a wonderful grandfather figure.

Gloria and Jeff were thoroughly exhausted when they had walked into his life and slept for days afterwards. He watched over them like a mother hen.

Higgins had been trying for weeks to contact some of his major collaborators from before but had very little success. This caused him a great deal of apprehension, but he tried not to show it.

The three of them were sitting in the kitchen planning a real Thanksgiving meal when a knock was heard at the door, just loud enough to be audible. Even with that it was a jolt and both he and Gloria automatically reached for their weapons. He had no idea who it might be.

The next knock was a recognizable pattern from the past. They both looked at each other then walked cautiously to the door.

Higgins opened it as Gloria covered him with her 9mm. The sight he saw made his jaw hit the floor. There was Mitchell Grayson standing as tall as ever, and appearing just as confident as the last time he had seen him.

"May I come in?" he asked extending his hand.

Higgins grabbed it and pulled him into the house.

"I thought maybe you were dead. I sent out feelers and never heard anything," he stated with a sigh.

"I know. I heard but I couldn't respond. I was in the middle of something extremely big and important."

"What the hell was that?" Higgins asked, but then remembered Gloria. "God, I'm getting feebleminded."

He pulled her over and introduced her and then called to Jeff so he could do the same for him.

After relating something of each of their backgrounds, he suddenly became quiet, thinking maybe had had gone too far.

Mitchell sensed that and said, "That's fine General. We've reached a new road in this battle, and to a certain extent we'll be operating more in the open. That's why I'm here."

They had been standing at the door, and the realization hit him: Higgins motioned them into the living room and they all sat down.

"What's going to happen?" he asked.

"Do you remember John Enman?" Grayson asked.

"Yes, the corporate bastard!" Higgins snapped.

Mitchell smiled.

208

"The one and the same," he said. "He was the benefactor of our money at the end."

"No shit," he said in amazement.

"Oh there's much more," he added smiling.

He related to them everything that had occurred and what Enman was doing in Fargo, careful not to give out any more than necessary. Information was still a deadly commodity to own.

"I heard his buddy Saranoff had been assassinated," Higgins said hearing the word "commodity".

Mitchell nodded, and then said, "Saranoff had liquidated a lot of John's holdings and transferred them to gold and several other tangibles. What he didn't know was he has been converting his own holdings also, and just a few weeks ago discovered he had been given control over all of it. Much of it is in gold and other parts in real estate and companies. Some of it is no longer available because of political changes in the countries involved.

I have had an idea for some time and with his help, we have been able to bring it to fruition."

"What's that," Higgins asked leaning into him in anticipation.

"We have set up some radio broadcasting facilities."

This got his attention immediately.

"Three of them are located in Canada where he has a lot of connections. Two are 200,000 watts aimed at the West and East of the country, and a 100,000 watts aimed at Alaska."

"My god the air must fry around them when they are operating!"

"It actually turns blue," Grayson smiling.

"We have three in Mexico also. Two big ones pointing at the Southwest and Southeast, and one of the smaller towers covering Florida and the pan handle."

"How in the hell did you get them to cooperate?" he asked.

"That was due mostly to the negotiating of President Willard in Texas, and partly to the fact they hate Madison," Grayson explained.

"They will try and put them out of commission immediately," Higgins stated.

"The Canadian Air Force has fighters ready to answer any attacks to their air space, and the same in true in Mexico, plus the Texas Air National Guard is on the ready also."

When Higgins looked puzzled at that, Grayson added, "Most Texans have family scattered all over, and they have no problem being involved."

"What are you going to broadcast? It will have to be attention getting," Higgins asked.

"That's why I'm here." When the General started to open his mouth he continued, "No you're not going have to do it, though I'm sure you could if you set your mind to it. Excuse me."

He stood and walked to the front door, opened it and motioned for someone to come inside.

When the man entered both Gloria and Higgins stared in amazement.

"Guys, I want you to meet George Barnes. He's going to be Barnstorming America again."

This was the man that Grayson had taken from the flea-bag hotel in Little Rock all cleaned up and dapper.

"I thought you were dead," said Gloria totally taken back.

George smiled and offered, "I was, at least morally and spiritually, if not physically."

Grayson started to say something and he interrupted, "I have not seen my family in a few years. When the FCC ended our broadcasts and we received all those death threats, I got them out of the country. I have no idea where they are, though I have been told recently they are safe."

"Everyone knows I was an alcoholic before I was a successful radio host. Well I still am, and always will be. When Mitchell found me I had crawled back into the bottom of a bottle again and had almost finished committing suicide by drink."

Higgins stated bluntly, "I'm not going to say anything behind your back, I won't say to your face. How in the hell do we know we can trust you?"

210

Mitchell started again to say something and George took over as was his old way.

"That's fine, I don't blame you. Thankfully you didn't see me a few weeks ago. It has taken a lot of hard work by a lot of good people to get me into this condition, but let me tell you from the bottom of my heart, I will do whatever is necessary to stay sober and everything I can to bring these people down."

Mitchell finally spoke, "As he said, it has been difficult and a few times even I came close to giving up on him, but he has come a long way, and I believe he is the one we need."

"What about some of the others that were in the forefront of talk radio back then?" Higgins asked.

"Either they are too old, too tired, not trust worthy any more, too damn radical, or too damn dead," he answered. "George is a teacher as well as a communicator. I think he is perfect."

"It all sounds good to me," he said without hesitation. "How do we do it?"

"He's going to operate out of this area; hence, I need your involvement. We have made arrangements so that the signal will not emanate from here, but it will be transferred through several protocols and relays. Enman has been working on it and finished testing yesterday. He says it is flawless, but just in case, we will be rotating actual broadcast points for the first few weeks."

Higgins stood and went to George, "Well, when do we begin?"

"Thanksgiving afternoon about three," Mitchell answered.

"Then will you join us for an early lunch or a late dinner then?" Gloria asked.

"Late dinner," George responded. "I don't want to fall asleep on the air, or worse throw up. I am actually very nervous."

"I don't think there is much chance of that," Higgins said smiling, "none whatsoever. But you will be a target."

"I have been dead before," he said smiling.

20

November 30th

President Madison very seldom celebrated Thanksgiving, but given the general atmosphere and condition of the country, he felt it would be good PR for him to do so.

He had invited key figures that were still involved in or remained alive in his administration, some friends, and a few distant relatives that were still speaking to him. Of course some guests were there because they were afraid not to be.

Dinner went very smoothly all things considered. Afterwards, Madison shook everyone's hands and thanked them for coming. His aide was telling him how well he had done, and what they could do with all of the photos when Jim Wilkins motioned him over to another room.

After they had entered and closed the door, the President asked, "You look as if the world were ending?"

"That might be better," he said with a dark tone in his voice. "You should sit down."

When they had both taken chairs opposite each other with a coffee table between, Wilkins placed a digital player on it.

"This began about two hours ago. It was live then, but has been broadcasting on a loop ever since."

He pressed a button and it began.

"Happy Thanksgiving America," a voice boomed enthusiastically. "I know the holiday is late this year, but we are more in need of it than ever. This is George Barnes, and we're going to Barnstorm America today and from here on, so be prepared, be alert, and most of all have faith; faith in yourself, your friends and family, all Americans, and most especially in God," he began with a bit of hesitation.

Madison turned a deep shade of red. Wilkins stopped the recording.

"Where the hell did that come from?" he almost yelled.

"Broadcasting began at three this afternoon. We've located at least three high wattage stations in Canada and in Mexico. The whole country is blanketed with it," Wilkins informed him. "I doubt if many people heard it live, but they are continuously repeating it. He claims that he will add more to it and be live every day at three Eastern Time."

Madison said nothing more and Wilkins pressed the button again.

"My friends, it has been a long time since you have heard my voice and I have had the opportunity to come into your homes. I will bring you up to date."

He told his story as he always had with honestly and integrity. Leaving nothing out he related his relapse in drinking, the necessity for not seeing his family, the difficulty of his return from the bottle, and his abiding faith and trust in the American people and God.

The fury that was building in Madison seemed to be unfathomable. Even Wilkins was starting to worry where the rage would go first.

George continued.

"I don't know where this will lead, but we are going to have to take this journey together. As I told you over the years, none of what is happening to us now is new. It is the culmination of a hundred years of effort by the radical left and right. They set the ground work for what has happened to out dear country.

I always said that my most sincere wish was that I was totally wrong and dear God I wish I had been. I never thought we would reach this point, but we have. Now we have to do something about it.

I know you have been limited in ability to get information. It has been a real adjustment to go from unlimited sources on the internet and cable television, and then overnight be relegated to a situation almost as bad as before the telegraph. That is just one aspect of this administration. No, this is a dictatorship, not a duly elected government.

It is going to have to be stopped, and I will be here trying to do just that..."

The sound ended as Madison hurled the player against a nearby wall destroying it.

He paced and hyperventilated until it seemed he would pass out.

"I want this son-of-a-bitch. I literally want his head on that table, and I don't mean next week."

"I've had the best people we have working on it since I found out it was happening. So far we have nothing," Wilkins gave him the bad news.

"It appears they have relays and feed-back protocols that our people have never seen. The whole setup is state of the art and far beyond what we have."

"You have to be shitting me. Where is god's name did they get the brains, the money, anything!" Madison was even more furious if that were possible.

"The only thing we have is the location of the Eastern broadcasting sight. It is about fifty miles northeast of Windsor."

Madison looked at him.

"We have to take it out, and the rest of them. They shouldn't be too hard to locate. With the wattage they're using, a child could find them."

"But Mr. President, even if we could afford to start a war with either country, I don't think that would be wise." Wilkins was starting to fear what Madison might do in this state.

The president walked out of the room and went to the Oval office. Wilkins followed.

He went to his desk and picked up the phone and said, "Get me Bert Williams over at Blackpool."

A Blackpool Special ops squad was inserted into Canada to take out the Windsor area tower. They planted enough C-4 to annihilate half of the area. When it blew up the signal disappeared for about a minute then returned. Not only was there double and triple redundancy, but what they blasted was for the most part a decoy, and a relayed version of the real signal.

Almost immediately they were surrounded by private security from Enman's own forces. Blackpool wasn't the only game in town.

Canada was taking a quiet hand's off approach trying to keep some deniability; however, Madison received a dispatch from the Canadian Embassy as they were packing to leave Washington and return home.

The document was on formal paper; however, it was not the most diplomatic verse. It simply said, "Next time, we're at war." There was no signature, but he totally understood.

21

December 4th

Joe Boudreaux was John Enman's counterpart in Texas and other areas of the South and Southwest. For years he had established contacts everywhere north and south of the border.

For over a decade the drug cartels that had moved out of Columbia had taken root in Mexico and virtually ran the country. The amount of money involved in the enterprise was sufficient to buy off most of the government, judiciary, law enforcement, much of the military, and border agents.

Not everyone was involved, but there were enough people at the top that change was going to be slow if not thoroughly impossible. The old president was not the man for that job so interference was necessary. Boudreaux was asked by several of his friends in the country if it were possible to help. He was able to hire the right people to influence the election in a legal manner and an unknown by the name of Vicente Hernandez was elected by a slim margin to the office.

As soon as he was sworn in, a Mexican security company hired by the new government, "La Nueva Mañana", attacked the major strongholds of the cartels and totally eliminated them. In a six hour period most of those in the top echelon of the business including judges, officers and the like were arrested and jailed. Trials were held immediately and all concerned who were guilty were convicted, executed, or shipped into the wilderness for life imprisonment on work farms.

Over the next few months there were further arrests and trials. This was a demonstration of how an entire country could be resurrected in short order. Although it was thorough and efficient, particular care was taken to insure that no liberties were violated and no abuse was practiced. Joe had made this a condition of his involvement. That was how and why Mexico had come to the aid of and became an ally of the Republic of Texas in such a short time.

When Blackpool tried to attack the lower wattage facility in the Yucatan, La Nueva Mañana took care of them. To further demonstrate to the enemy who they were dealing with, they sent their own Black ops unit into Mississippi and took out a whole company of Blackpool soldiers. They were never detected and nor lost a man.

Blackpool was so embarrassed they didn't even inform Madison of the occurrence. They did however realize that Mexico and Canada were out of the picture for the time being. Efforts had to be concentrated on developing their role in the United States.

Washington and the security company had to accept that for the time being nothing could halt the broadcasts. It was a completely intolerable situation made even more so by Barnes upping the ante each and every time he spoke.

Within days word had spread and everyone that had access to a radio listened constantly as if there were finally a ray of light in a dark storm. They added short wave transmitters and translators so that other countries could hear the signal. Several other broadcasters were added over the weeks reporting on events in most parts of the globe which succeeded in pissing off a lot of other governments as well.

However, the biggest draw in and out of North America was George Barnes. His earthiness and neighbor next door approach not only made him acceptable to the average person, but added star power without a hint of phoniness. He spoke from the heart and all could feel it. This was exactly what the nation needed.

22

December 7th

"Seventy-six years ago President Roosevelt said this date would forever live in infamy. Well my friends, he had no concept of what would happen to his beloved country." Barnes began his daily broadcast.

"Even though he was one of the people who helped in an extremely large part to make what is now occurring a reality, I doubt he would have wanted this for us, or could have imagined it.

Here are the updates we have for you. Let me say as always, much of this is not suitable for the youngsters who might be listening.

There are reports that many in South Carolina and Florida are running out of food and some of the distressed, rightly now called homeless, are forced to forage in the rubble left by the two storms.

Since the edicts were made that looters of any kind should be shot on sight, dozens have died trying to feed their families. There have been many tales of retaliation against the NSF and Blackpool enforcers, causing even more shootings and death.

Outside of the urban areas the food situation is a lesser concern, as many of the country folk have kept much of their survivor mentality and skills. Their biggest problems are the city dwellers that out of desperation have started to form gangs and send marauders into the rural areas.

New England, my friends, is turning into a wasteland of death and destruction. The lack of supplies, food, heating fuel, and power is killing thousands every day. I am told that the president and his staff tried to help, but have had to, at least in their minds, write the whole area off. Whoever can survive the winter, might consider where their allegiances should be when the spring finally comes.

I urge anyone in my audience that can help any of these unfortunate souls, please do so. I know that most everyone in the world has their own problems right now, but we need your help. America has helped every nation on earth in the past, and when we get back on our feet, we will be there for you again. Presently, we are the ones in need."

He hesitated and had a long moment of silence, fighting back the audible tears.

"I'll be back on the air in a short while. For now, God Bless everyone one of you, and God Bless America."

Later when he had composed himself, Barnes came back and brought more news of the day. During his absence, millions of eyes had tears wiped away, and with the international broadcasts of his show untold numbers of people outside of the U.S. heard his words.

Within hours, dozens of nations did what they could in small and large ways to help. Cargos of all sizes began to arrive in Massachusetts, Rhode Island, Connecticut, New York, and even New Jersey. These were mostly from Europe and the Middle-East.

Canada had been clandestinely smuggling aide through Maine, New Hampshire, and Vermont, and was openly doing their part.

A lot of help for the South came out of Latin America and the Republic of Texas.

Madison knew he had no choice but to let it all happen. If it were perceived that he wanted his people to die, he would be finished in no time. He therefore, devoted his whole being into developing a consolidation plan for the spring campaign.

Regardless, it was going to be hard winter for everyone. The goal for most was just to stay alive.

23

Winter

One would have speculated that in its weakened condition that there would be those countries that would want to do America harm, take potshots at it, or even try a takeover. For many reasons this was not to happen.

Venezuela and Cuba were contemplating a series of forays into the southern states; however, the recently formed Organization of Latin American and Caribbean States sent dispatches forbidding any such actions.

Their reasoning was two fold. Many of them had Madison's military guarding their refineries and production facilities and were directly affected by any repercussions from that type of aggression.

However, the largest consideration was that America had become an enormous market for their natural resources and crops. Yes, everyone was having a tough time of it, but it would eventually be resolved and that source of revenue would return.

Many believed that even though there were problems between North and South American nations that the U.S was known to remember its friends and enemies alike. This too was a reason for the aid that was sent north when Barnes had asked for it.

Winter had calmed much of the turmoil in Europe or at least the resolve of both sides as the cold slowed everything down.

This was not the case in the Middle-East. Civil war had erupted most everywhere even more so than in America. Worldwide terrorism had taken a holiday as Moslem sects fought fiercely among their selves.

After Israel decimated Iran, all of the attention to conflict was internalized. Sunnis, Shiites, and others warred to have their version of Islam rule the area and hopefully the rest of the world.

Asia was out of the picture, at least temporarily. The Japanese economy hit the skids even more so than most other affected countries since a large part of the repudiated debt belonged to them, second only to China. They would have loved nothing better than to finally attack the weakened Americans, and desperately worked to convert their factories to war time production. It was a good idea since their existence would eventually necessitate it.

When the American military was removed from the demilitarized zone separating North and South Korea, any semblance of peace between them disintegrated. The North Koreans made the huge mistake of dropping a limited range nuke on Seoul and the South proceeded to wipe out half of the North.

They tried to concentrate on military and government facilities but there was a lot of collateral damage. Even though many in the south had relatives in the north, they knew it had to be done and stoically accepted the actions and consequences. For the first time in almost a century there was a type of peace in the region.

Even though the U.S. had repudiated the trillion dollars of debt that it owed China, they were not as affected by all of the affairs as might have been thought. During the good times the government and almost every citizen bought as much gold as could be afforded. Thus, they were not totally impoverished from the currency collapse as could have been the case.

In a few months China was well on its way to recovery. It would only be a matter of a few years, maybe sooner, before they would be able to set their sights elsewhere.

One of the reasons they said nothing when South Korea annexed North Korea was that they assumed that as soon as possible they would take their revenge on the Japanese for their treatment in World War II.

The Chinese also had not forgotten Nan-King and other atrocities from that war. Each and every family had their stories that were passed on; and, every school child was shown the pictures and films from that time ad nauseam. There was no way that it would be forgotten, no matter how much the Japanese tried to rewrite history as the defenders of Asia from the foreign invaders.

Though India had fared even better than China in the worldwide collapse because of their history of poverty and work to climb out of it, that part of Asia was a powder keg with a fuse in place ready to light.

Pakistan and India have been nuclear powers for almost sixty years and mortal enemies forever. The civil strife in the Mid-east had spilled over into Pakistan, a Moslem country, weakening the economy and government. When the U.S. pulled its troops out of the area, the destabilization was further increased.

Due to these conditions, India would have probably taken on Pakistan; however, the increasing presence of China in Tibet on its northern border gave them pause. The decision was made to rebuild the country and wait for another day.

That was the state of the world when spring finally arrived.

24

March 21st

President Madison and Jim Wilkins were standing in the War Room watching the staff scurry from one screen to another taking notes and asking each other questions.

You would have thought they were doing this for appearances because of the presence of the Commander-In-Chief, but that was not the case. There was much maneuvering of troops, construction crews, food distribution, and every other imaginable core business of the nation.

Madison was hands on enough that he wanted detailed up to the hour reports. There were sixteen people in the adjacent room simplifying and condensing these updates to a readable form on a continual basis.

Jim Wilkins received them and gave verbal comments until the president hit something that intrigued him. He would then retire to another room and pour over the details. The system worked quite well, but was tiring to all involved.

Most of the staff were vetted followers of the president's agenda and were the few people left that he trusted. Most of them had worked eight hours on and eight hours off for the past year. They had had very little contact with their families other than to know they were all well and had been receiving the best of everything. This and the promise of future high end positions kept them going.

During the winter, the state of the country had been treacherous at best and in some areas disastrous at worst. With the government takeover of most goods and services, and with total regulation of all aspects of the economy and business, the expected problems immediately arose and multiplied.

There were areas of dire shortages, especially of power, fuel, and food. Distribution was sporadic at best. Even though the summer had been very productive, the lack of motivation and incentives had left problems such as food rotting in the fields or in warehouses. Ignoring the past problems in the Soviet Union was idiotic, since they had been through it all before.

With the take over of the financial markets and the banks, a new system of credits and allowances had been initiated, purporting to equalize everyone's availability of resources, but as is always the case, none of it worked. Besides, what good would credit have been without businesses or consumers to use it?

For one thing, not all of the people were treated equally. High NSF members, government officials (at least those still in the country and remaining alive), Special Operation staff such as the War Room crews, and several others with close ties to, friends and relatives of, these people had privileges. These were based on level of authority and who you knew as always has happened in the past. This did not go unnoticed by the rest of the citizens, but private griping was about all that was done, since public speeches and the gathering of groups too were strictly forbidden.

Because most of the attention had been concentrated in the eastern part of the country, the western states had been allowed more leeway. Plans were in place to change all of that as soon as possible.

Efforts were moving slowly to rebuild a working infrastructure on the eastern seaboard. By eventually using much of the NSF in conjunction with business had generated its share of tribulations. Attitudinal problems between the NSF and private citizens were frequent and often did not end well for either side.

The other situation that would present itself in the future was that Blackpool hired even more staff and troops increasing its presence enormously.

On an occasion as Madison and Wilkins were discussing a problem that needed immediate attention, one of the officers came to them and handed Wilkins a report.

"This is the meteorological updates you requested sir," she stated flatly.

He looked them over and motioned Madison into their conference room.

When they were seated, the president asked, "Well?"

"It appears the sunspot activity we were alerted to last November is a lot greater than anticipated. The mild weather last summer evidently was a fluke, the lull before the storm, I figure.

Those hurricanes may or may not have been connected, but they feel that there is a definite possibility of some really severe climate change over the next few years, maybe beginning in a few months."

"Shit," Madison said forcefully. "What next?"

Wilkins continued.

"It may bring us some higher temperatures this year, but most certainly next year. "

"We have to really work on crop production this year, and storage. I don't want to go through the crap over food again," Madison mulled through his pursed lips.

"Especially since the southern hemisphere will be hit hard this fall," Wilkins added. "I don't know if they are aware of it yet, so we might want to see what we can import in the way of canned and preserved goods."

"I'll call in whatever favors I can and if that doesn't work, threaten to pull out our troops. Chavez would love that," Madison said with a little menacing laugh.

Then he added, "With those storms, that brutal winter and now this… If I believed in God, I would have to think, he's really pissed about something."

"There is one upside to all of this Mr. President."

"And what is that, pray tell," he said using the last word as if it were a pun.

"Barnes' radio broadcast should have a lot of interference soon," Wilkins said positively.

"Yes, but communications will be difficult for all of us. Get those guys working on that problem, now!"

"Already on it, Mr. President," he responded quickly.

"Ah, sir," he started hesitantly, "in their last report Blackpool stated they had increased their forces by another sixty thousand last month, and they are going to try to do that again each month for the foreseeable future."

"Why?" he asked forcefully.

"They claim it was needed because you pulled so many NSF from their ranks for the salvage and reconstruction projects. However, they so much as said the NSF holds them back and most of them are not qualified or dependable. They do not like to work for them or with them."

"Tough shit," Madison said. "They will and they will like it or else."

"Or else what, sir? Without them we wouldn't last a minute and they know it."

"They think they have us over a barrel," he responded.

"In fact they do. I have wondered why they have not pressured us for more per capita money. The only increased cost is a prorated addition for more troops."

"And you worry about that?" Madison said when the thought sunk in.

"I do sir. I have had a suspected an alternative motive for awhile now."

"Get Bert Williams and Casper Walker here to DC as soon as possible," the president asked.

"I will ask them."

"Ask them shit, tell them," Madison blurted out.

"I don't think that would work sir," Wilkins said simply.

Madison mused over that thought and a look of concern began to cover his face.

25

April 23rd

George Barnes opened his show with his normal patter, and then became extremely serious.

"My friends, I am sure most of you know that today is April 23rd. This is the one year anniversary of Jake Madison's overthrow of the United States government. He can call it what he will, but we now have a dictator that has been increasingly converting our poor country into a third world banana republic.

That may seem harsh to some of you, but deep in your hearts you know it is a fact.

Those of us who survived this last year, and the deadly winter, must take it upon ourselves to choose one side or the other.

If you have any lingering doubts as to whether what I have been saying is true, I have a special guest today. He has been relocated to a safe place in an undisclosed country and we have been able to set up a communication chain with him. I will not disclose his whereabouts or our technology to have him with us.

I will tell you that he is the real deal. Some of you might not recognize his name or voice, but many of you will. We have had onsite verification so trust me, and listen to what he has to say.

My friends, and my enemies, as I know you are listening too, I have with me today…" He hesitated for effect. "… Ron Erickson, the former Chief-of-Staff for Jake Madison."

All over the world his listening audience gasped in unison. Those who knew Erickson thought he was dead. The others could not believe he was going to speak out.

"Ron, thank you for being here today," Barnes began.

"It is a pleasure George, and I have to say my duty. I wish I had taken this step a long time ago. Maybe things would have been different," Erickson responded.

"We spoke earlier and quite truthfully I don't know exactly where to begin," Barnes said. "Can you tell us how you came to be Madison's Chief-of Staff?"

He answered that question and proceeded to detail as much as was possible his relationship with the president, his continuing demeaning attitude, and how he was left out of a lot of major decisions and meetings.

"What was the final turning point Ron? What made you turn your back on him?"

Erickson spelled out point by point what had happened to his mother and how the way she died affected him.

He did not go into detail his escape from Nebraska, but that had been an adventure.

His driver was a friend from high school, Paul Freeman, whom he had met accidentally in DC a few months earlier. They had gone out for drinks a few times and discovered that they still shared a lot in common. Paul absolutely did not like Madison and as Erickson became disillusioned, they started to form a strong bond.

When Paul was transferred to Lincoln, the pieces of the puzzle fell together. The final blow for Erickson was his mother's death. He arranged for his friend to be his driver.

They had prepared vials of their own blood to seed the wrecked jeep, and set the whole scene up before they took off. The jeep was left were they knew it would be found in the fall, adding to the hopefully convincing nature of it all.

With Paul's training they were able to reach the Texas border. Erickson convinced one of the Texas National Guards to have his superior quietly contact President Willard. She knew him well and immediately brought him to Austin.

Her father's contacts were able to get him to a friendly nation in Latin America and that was where he remained. He had not related what he was going to say to anyone other than her until today.

Barnes knew what was coming was going to be a bombshell, but even he did not know the details.

"Ron, we now come to why you are here? All I was told was you had information that would stun us all and possibly change everything that is going on out there. Are you ready to tell us?" Barnes asked.

"Yes," he answered.

"Then I will just let you do that," Barnes stated and held his breath.

"As I said George, everything that I saw and heard was beginning to disturb me. I had my suspicions all along but when I found evidence that confirmed them, that information was the final straw." He hesitated briefly.

"Jake Madison planned the attack in Houston on the Keiferland wedding party using a group of black ops men he knew and could trust. They killed all of those people.

Some of the same men blew up the two trains in the Chicago subway, and set off the blast in Seattle.

The whole affair of the bombs in Los Angeles was set up to place blame on Iran and the Middle East. Everything that followed was made possible by these staged events."

When Erickson had dropped this bombshell, even Barnes was at a loss for words, and he said so.

"I honestly don't know what to say Ron. I was not aware of anything at that time as my audience well knows. But I have tried to study and discern what happened through all of it. There were a lot of questions, but now that we know the President had Americans killed just to further his ambitions. Good God."

"Now you know why I had to get out of there. I have no family left, but I do have or had friends, some are already dead. I wanted to live long enough to tell my story. Also, I have turned over all of the evidence I have to someone who will introduce it into court either in the U.S. or the World Court. Madison needs to pay for his crimes."

Erickson seemed to be tired.

"Amen to that Ron," Barnes responded. "Amen."

PART 3:

Deconstruction

1

Jim Wilkins almost ran into the Oval Office. Before he could open his mouth he knew Madison had already heard about George Barnes' broadcast. He had never before seen the look that now resided on his face. If this was how a major defeat appeared in his world, it was the picture of utter misery and failure. It was indeed a rara avis.

Wilkins knew that Madison in his own deluded mind thought he had been doing what was the best for the country. At least that was what initiated everything years ago. The manic nature of success and power had pushed him onward as if it had a life of its own.

The day to day maneuvering and manipulating that was government service had taken its toll on this broken man and his country.

"You don't need to say anything Jim," he said finally breaking the silence. "We can try to salvage something of all this, but for the life of me, I don't see how."

"You knew the risks," Wilkins responded. "And we both felt it was worth it. Hard decisions had to be made, if the course of this ship of state was to be corrected. Those were your words and you were right."

"Maybe so," the president said. "But I doubt if history will see it that way."

"You never know," Wilkins added.

The silence returned. Finally Wilkins broke it this time.

"Bert Williams will be here in about an hour," he said.

"Is that fart Casper Walker with him?"

"No, Williams said he wasn't available."

"Have security in place. I don't trust any of them, especially after this. Hell, I don't know who we can trust anymore."

Wilkins left Madison to his musing.

All through the country people were talking, mulling over what had just been revealed to them. Many had suspected something, but few had given the possibility that it had all be ordered by their own president.

Most were as depressed as Madison at that moment, not knowing exactly what to feel or do. There was an undertone of anger surely emerging. It was only a matter of time before the pot would boil and blew itself apart. Only God knew what would happen then. For certain there would be a lot of death.

NSF troops would begin to leave their units. It would only be a trickle at first but everyone knew a lot more would follow. Many had enlisted out of desperation and possibly a sense that they were doing the patriotic thing too.

The only ones that remained after the first days were those opportunists that saw it as a ticket to act out by hurting people and looting.

Bert Williams arrived at the White House with his squad of body guards. He was shown into the Oval Office as quickly as possible. The Secret Service was stationed outside with a three to one presence with more waiting just a few rooms away.

Wilkins opened the door for Williams and they both entered.

Madison didn't get up.

"It's not bad enough I have the weather, Barnes, and god knows what other problems heading my way, but you ingrates are trying to pull something," he began.

Williams just stared at him and waited.

"I have reports that you have been increasing your armed contingents at a rate twice to three times what I recommended and you agreed to."

Williams still said nothing.

"Well, what have you got to say?"

Finally he spoke.

"You finished ranting Jake?" he said.

"Mr. President to you asshole!" he bellowed.

"Hell no," Williams responded.

"I could have you shot for that," Jake roared.

"Yes you could but you won't," he answered.

"You are cock sure of yourself," Madison fairly spit through his teeth. "You don't have your guards with you now."

"I'm certain you have already detained them," Williams answered.

That is precisely what had happened as soon as they had been separated.

"Look Jake, you served your purpose so why don't you retire and go live on some island."

Wilkins jaw dropped.

"Who the hell do you think you are?" Madison roared again.

"No Jake, who do you think you are, the president? You gave up that right long ago."

"You sound like George Barnes," he snared back.

"He's so far off base, just like you, that he has no idea which way the sun rises."

It was Madison's turn to sit and stare.

"Let me give you a little history lesson Jake. The progressive morons that basically set up everything for you to make your move were ideologues of the first order. Hell, some of them actually believed the shit they spewed forth, or mostly their followers did.

Wilson, Roosevelt, and the rest were simply evil. They were interested in only one thing, power."

"Forty five years ago our founders believed that the day would come that someone like you would emerge and take advantage of all the government control they had inserted into the country. Most of the regular citizens, the people who made this country great and kept it working under freedom and liberty, would be beaten down and ready to be ruled. It was all just a matter of time." Williams paused to let it all sink in.

"You're telling me you have been planning a take over all along?" Wilkins asked. "That's impossible."

"We didn't plan as much as knew what was likely to happen, and made preparations to take advantage when the opportunities presented themselves."

"What you two don't fully grasp is... it's over. The quest for ultimate power resides in planning, opportunity, and the will to do whatever is necessary. You were fairly good at it but just not good enough."

"I did all three and even got elected," Madison stated flatly.

"You really think you had much to do with that. When you came on the scene we knew your ego was just what we were anticipating all these years. Without us and our maneuvering you wouldn't have made it out of the gate. You have been our guy in town for all this time and never knew it. It is quite ironic: don't you think?" Williams leaned back and held his hands in front of him almost in a position of prayer.

Madison leaned forward and began, "What's to stop me from shooting you right here where you sit?"

"Nothing," Williams calmly answered.

"You have no fear of dying?"

"No. When I joined Blackpool, I was just in it for the money, but when I was made a member of the Inner Circle, I swore my life and substance to accomplish an end. In return, all of my family will be taken care of and I never have to worry about them.

We believe that our form of mastery is what is needed now, not only here but in most of the developed countries. Total domination of emergent nations is a given.

The era of personal freedom has come and gone. It is just not practical with the huge populations of today. There simply is no room for free will. You of all people should know that.

Therefore Jake, I have no fear of dying because my death is a foregone conclusion. I knew I would never be leaving here, but that's fine."

"If you're gone and we get the rest of you, how can that be a certainty?" Madison asked curiously.

"Jake. Jake. Jake. Do you really think you know who runs Blackpool? The upper echelon isn't even known to most of us. Furthermore, we already have operatives at every level of government and have for over twenty years. Now that's what I call planning.

As far as your concern for troop size and management, the numbers are far more than you know. By the end of the month we will have over one million units in the country and another half million ready to be brought in.

We have our own navy and air force stationed within striking distance so there is no need to threaten us with your puny military. What's left of it after all these years of down-sizing, is so disparaged and scattered there is little with which to be concerned.

You have done a fine job of preparing our way, just as we expected."

Jake reached for a button and several security men entered.

"Place him under arrest,' Madison ordered.

"You're nothing if not predictable Jake," Williams said as he was escorted from the room.

Madison stood, turned and looked out of the Oval Office window wondering how much longer he had.

2

April 23rd

Abel and Matthew Harrington were born on May 15, 1925. Their father and grandfather were in the industrial construction business for over forty years. They grew up around the work and the ups and downs of it all, including the crash of 1929 and the depression that followed. The company lasted through that period and came out stronger than ever.

Both boys enlisted in the army as soon as their seventeenth birthday came around. By the fall of 1942 they were landing in Europe where they saw the horrors of war first hand as infantrymen fighting their way through Italy. Somehow they survived it all fairly unscathed. Both had taken bullets but were still alive.

When it was over they stayed on the continent during the reconstruction period after they had mustered out of the service. It took them no time at all to figure out that for many years construction would be needed on a large scale, and the Harrington Construction Company became international. Their grandfather died in 1951; however, he lived long enough to see the fruition of all of the effort. By that time they were all multimillionaires.

The postwar rebuilding of Europe was especially full of opportunities if you learned the fine art of graft and corruption. From

Washington to Brussels it was vital to find who was for sale and make sure all of the contracts were forth coming when deals were made. Abel and Matt became experts.

President Eisenhower warned the nation of the dangers of the military-industrial complex. He could not have been referring to any group more viral than the Harringtons. Since they knew they couldn't compete with the armament and aircraft people, they specialized in the supplies, equipment, and construction that the military and governments world-wide needed for every day use as well as in emergencies.

By the mid-sixties, during the age of conglomerates, they had originated or acquired over fifty seven divisions under the Harrington Industries umbrella. When it became front page news that the government was paying five dollars for a washer and nut, or three hundred dollars for a toilet seat, they simply paid someone else off and it all went away. It was simply business. By the seventies they were worth billions.

After the Korean War, the constant turmoil in the world especially in Southeast Asia and Africa brought about a need for other commodities: men and women, troops, soldiers for hire.

Because of the Hessians that were brought to the Colonies by the British to help fight during the Revolutionary War, Americans had always been anti-mercenary. This, however, did not stop the Harringtons. Initially it was Matt's idea so he ran with it.

Most of the soldiers returning from Korea were fed up with war, but there are always some who once feeling the adrenalin rush of combat never wanted it to stop. Others liked the pay which was more than they could make anywhere else. To some this was the only thing they were trained for. There were probably as many reasons as there were people available. Other countries became areas for recruitment also, but the favored were the ex-military of the U.S. and Great Britain.

The division that handled what was to later become the Private Security business in the nineties was located off shore, as was its banking, planning, and training facilities. It had to be kept quiet as the legality of the whole company was in question for years. That did not stop them from growing and expanding exponentially. When it became a public corporation in 1988, it was known as Blackpool Security.

When Viet Nam ended, their recruitments sky rocketed as did the need for those men. As has often been said, there will always be wars and rumors of wars. That is one of the few constants in life and Harrington Industries was determined to use it.

When their father died in 1971, Matt had already developed this division of the company into a massive though clandestine unit. Abel became the director of the rest of the business. They had developed contacts throughout most major governments and had built a cohesive and loyal internal organization.

Quietly they had originated an internal sub rosa think tank in 1958 and it was discovered through its work that the machinations and corruption of governments at all levels, especially in DC, would eventually lead to the collapse of the constitutional system creating a void that would necessarily need to be filled.

They developed a logic line and determined the scope of this reasoning to include the extent of their business and the possible correlation with government. Through this process they worked out a fifty year plan for taking control of the United States and most of the world.

They felt so certain of it, and determined that it must occur or the peoples of the world were doomed to extinction, that the entire structure of their organization was rebuilt around the concept.

You could call them delusional, but they were set on saving the world through domination. Maybe they were right, but subjugation is so contrary to the human spirit that is seldom endures without massive force.

Harrington's Inner Circle that was created to propagate this ideology was prepared for a conflict and prolonged duration of fighting if necessary. They were hoping for an immediate capitulation but certainly didn't count on it.

243

During the fifty years of preparation they extended their reach into almost every corner of the governments of the G-20 and most of the others. Many of the smaller countries that were necessary for their natural resources were already on the payroll and the relationships would become public when the orders to do so were sent.

Madison had no chance against these forces; however, he was blinded by rage and would certainly face his ultimate failure. How he went down was the question of the moment.

The response of the rest of humanity would be a different manner. For the first time since the Romans conquered the known world, an empire dominated by a Corporate Oligarchy was about to make that attempt. All hell was unquestionably going to break loose.

3

April 23rd

Madison had moved Williams' men to a detention area about three blocks from the White House. Williams was kept in a holding cell several blocks in the opposite direction.

He had been sitting on a chair in the middle of the room. It was the only object in there. His hands were not bound and were folded in his lap, and his eyes were closed.

The door opened and Madison entered with three Secret Service agents.

Williams made no move and didn't even open his eyes.

"Taking a nap?" Jake asked.

Of course there was no response.

Jake knocked the chair over and Williams rolled to his feet at the ready.

"I thought so," Madison sneered.

"If you ever thought anything through Jake, you would never be where you are today," Williams said. His eyes were total blanks as Madison tried to read them to no avail.

"I won't go down without a fight you bastard. I'll finish you and your whole outfit. No one is that powerful, no one." Madison was fuming.

"You are a very simple man, Jake, with an extremely limited intellect. That's too bad really. If we had trained you, it might have been different, of course then you wouldn't have been as valuable as you were. Without you or someone like you, we would never have had this opportunity. We thank you, as will history."

Jake reached to one of the Secret Service men with him, "Give me your gun."

"I'm sorry sir, but I can't do that," he responded.

"Then shot this bastard!" he roared.

"I can't do that either sir," he replied.

The other two men looked at each other in surprise.

Jake went to the man, and grabbed for his gun. His training taught him to protect it, but with a moment's hesitation he realized this was the president. That was time enough for Madison to get it from his holster.

Jake raised it to shoot Williams when he heard, "Don't!"

He turned to face the other two agents who had their guns out and pointing them at him and the disarmed colleague.

His instinct was to instantly assess these two as enemies and he tried to fire at them. They shot Madison and the other agent without the slightest bit of indecision.

That was how it ended. Jake Madison, the 45th President of the United States died in utter shock and confusion.

Then it was their turn as Jim Wilkins shot them both in the back of their heads before they could react. He was seldom far from Jake and always tried to cover his back. That was his duty and reason de etre. It was that simple, but this time he was a moment too late.

He had begun carrying a weapon a few weeks earlier without informing the Secret Service. They would never have given their approval in the past, but under the present circumstances he and Jake neither one cared what they thought. His first thoughts were that the president should have been armed too, and that he had failed him.

He turned to Bert Williams who had been standing there taking it all in. His military instinct made him deal with him as a enemy combatant. Reaching for one of the dead agent's weapon, he got and it and handed toward him.

Planning to shoot him as soon as he touched it, he stopped in his tracks when he heard someone behind him.

"Hold it right there," a voice commanded before he could act further.

Wilkins turned to see Paul Curtis, the National Security Czar, holding a gun on him. There were two NSF officers behind him.

"Paul, it's good to see you. We have a very a real problem on our hands," he started.

"Yes we do. Somehow we have to tell the nation that the president's security advisor just killed him."

"You've got to be kidding. These two killed him and the other officer," Wilkins proclaimed.

"That's not how we see it, and unfortunately that's all that matters."

Wilkins immediately knew that Williams had been correct. He just wondered how far the tentacles of Harrington Industries reached into this government; unfortunately, he knew he would soon find out.

Ending it all right then and there was certainly an option, but the knowledge that they would simply declare it a murder suicide kept him from doing so. He was not going to make it any easier for them, and dropped his gun on the floor.

4

The word of President Madison's death spread like wildfire because Harrington Industries made certain of it.

Vice-president Lloyd Carlson, whose name had never been mentioned since the election, was formally sworn in as the 46th President. He immediately appointed Paul Curtis as the new Vice-President.

What was left of Madison's cabinet was sent packing, and most positions were not filled, and never would be. Harrington's think tank had designed the future around a Corporate Oligarchy which left little room for differing opinions.

The simple fact was Carlson and Curtis were their messenger boys, nothing more than figure heads. They had no problem with this as the pay and benefits were fantastic.

On his first telecast from the Oval Office, Carlson outlined the immediate changes in government.

"My first order of business is to declare martial law for the foreseeable future. It is necessary for the good order of society and the safety of the citizenry.

Also, the following changes will immediately be instituted. All local, state, and federal law enforcement agencies as of this moment are disbanded and no longer have any authority. This includes local and state police, special police units, the FBI, ATF, DEA, units of the Department of the Interior, and similar agencies. The Harrington Security Force is now the sole law enforcement of the land.

All local, state, and federal judiciaries no longer have any authority, and Harrington Justice Offices have been established in most locations central to the districts previously in existence until new district lines can be designated.

All local and state governments have been dissolved and governors will be appointed by tomorrow morning.

All financial institutions are now controlled by Harrington Financial Services and will be aggregated into the necessary units and locations.

All interstate and foreign travel will be curtailed until new passports and interstate visas have been issued."

He continued on for another thirty minutes, and then concluded.

"A complete directory of changes will be available shortly at the Harrington Postal Services.

My fellow citizens, all of these new directives have been put into place not on a whim, but as a plan of government that has been in development for almost a hundred years, and more recent work for the past fifty years. These are for your safety, benefit, and the good order of society.

I regret the following order, but it is absolutely necessary. Anyone not acceding to the new program will have to be removed from the community until they can be made to understand the necessity of it.

I thank you for your attention and wish you all a good evening."

It took most of the nation by surprise; however, it wasn't very long before the rumors and speculation began to take wing and fly, though they were never as harsh and diabolical as reality.

George Barnes had spoken a little not wanting to join in on the conjecturing but before long he had the ammunition he had been waiting for, and began his show with a bang.

249

"My friends, never in my wildest dreams did I expect our beloved country to dive so deeply into the abyss. If hell were ever expected on earth, we just may be seeing its appearance now."

He hesitated, obviously a little choked up.

"I am so glad that our mother's and father's generation are not here to see what has happened to their efforts and sacrifice. I have known for years that the big government movement had the potential to run amok and take us into economic destruction and slavery; however, that may have been extremely mild speculation on my part.

I seldom say anything on here without naming sources, but for security concerns, I must not do so at this time. I have it on absolutely authority that there is no longer the slightest bit of government left in Washington, DC.

What remains of the Congress, Senate, and the Supreme Court has been exiled from the town. In doing so there were no repercussions as none of those who would have objected in the past remain or in many cases are still alive.

Harrington Industries has for all intents taken over the country and are enforcing martial law with their troops. I am told that there is a standing army of over one million of their soldiers spread throughout the nation… or what's left of it.

No other country is objecting because none of them are certain how far the tentacles of this organization reach. I am further informed that several of the smaller nations of Africa, Southeast Asia, and South America have already recognized the new regime in DC as a government and some have sworn allegiance to it. Do you understand, not as allies but as part of it?

It would appear to me that there is no other ideology here than master to slave, and we are to be the slaves. I detest having to do this, but we have no choice. We must fight back and I am sure for some of us it will be with our dying breath."

Suddenly the air was silent. All over the world, people checked their radios to see if they were malfunctioning, but the signal was gone.

Gloria and Jeff had been watching Barnes doing his show as they did with every broadcast. In the beginning they had moved each few days to one of four locations. Then it was decided that was riskier than finding one isolated location. With Enman's equipment and means of transmitting through a Canadian satellite, it was possible to do it anywhere.

Higgins had found a small chalet about thirty miles north of his safe house nestled in a valley with extremely steep walls on all sides and that was where they had been broadcasting the show sometimes live several times a day. On some occasions they simply stayed there.

With what had been occurring for the past week they had not returned to Higgins' place at all.

He, Gloria, and occasionally Jeff took turns monitoring the few trails that approached the building from the front and one side. Today the colonel had been at the vantage point that overlooked the whole area. It was there that any movement could be seen for several miles.

Any attack would have to come from those two directions on the ground as there was no place for even a helicopter to land, and the constant updrafts made rope landings extremely dangerous.

Just before the show's transmission had been cut, Gloria got a call from Higgins on her small walkie-talkie.

"Get out, now!" was all he said and she reacted immediately.

Jeff ran in and grabbed Barnes by the shoulder and got him out of the room.

She had instantly grabbed her weapons and was on the ready.

Because of Jeff and Barnes' lack of training they had been drilled for an evacuation many times, and they each knew what to do. They ran down a flight of stairs to the small basement and pulled a set of shelves aside and entered a tunnel which led to a fruit cellar several yards from the chalet. After replacing the shelves, they crouched and moved quickly to the cellar.

The tunnel had been there when they found the place. The original owners had put it there so they could get to the storage area and exit to a spring in case they were unable to get out because of a blizzard, deep snow, or some other reason.

After passing through the fruit cellar they went through another opening which led to the spring area. From there they were able to escape over a very small path through the rocks to a cave-like structure that was totally hidden from sight from every direction.

The important aspect was they had a view of everything in the valley, and no one could see them.

At the end of the tunnel, the cellar roof was set to collapse when they left and it did so efficiently and silently.

When they approached Higgins he had his finger on his lips for them to be silent. Of course it wasn't necessary as that had been part of their training also.

He pointed through an opening in the blind he had constructed in the beginning and they looked out over the vista.

There were at least twenty men in Harrington military uniforms approaching from each of the trails that entered the area. None of them used the small dirt road on which they had walked yesterday to get into the chalet.

After the equipment had been installed, they never brought a car into the valley as it was impossible to drive out with any degree of safety.

They soldiers surrounded the cabin and cautiously moved towards it. Half of them stayed on the alert facing away from it, and the other half burst through the doors and firing as they did.

Within seconds the place blew into a million pieces taking everyone inside and most of those outside with them. The blast was so intense it blew dirt through the blind and into the enclave.

"Maybe I used a little too much C-4," Higgins whispered not knowing if they could even hear him.

They all shook their heads to clear the dust and the ringing in their ears.

"Not really," Gloria responded. "That should do it."

When the dust settled sufficiently, they could see that little of anything remained of the building or even the vegetation around it.

Two of the men on the outside were crawling back to the trail at the side of the blast site. It was the easiest to traverse and they were having great difficulty doing it. One passed out or died and the other left him behind.

It was very tempting to shoot him, but they did not want any evidence of them surviving.

They finally turned and slid to the ground.

Barnes was the first to speak.

"Holy Shit!" was all he could say. It was his initial foray into anything that approached action in his life, if you didn't count the few muggings he had endured when he was drinking. Somehow he figured it wouldn't be his last.

"They knew where we were," Gloria stated matter-of-factly.

"Yes and the timing coincided with Madison's departure and the new government," Higgins replied. "There are only two people other than us four that knew its location."

"I was just thinking that," she replied.

"Couldn't they have traced the signal somehow?" Jeff asked.

"It's possible," Barnes said, "but I doubt it. I have been studying the engineering plans. From what little I could figure out from this end it is not likely. Maybe Harrington has the ability, but I doubt it was from DC."

"We have to go on the assumption that one of ours is part of the plan, and we can't take any chances on contacting anyone for the time being," Gloria said.

"There are a couple people I know that I have trusted with my life before, and I still do," Higgins pondered. "It will be difficult getting there, but we will have to try."

It began to rain, so they rested for a while longer. When it stopped they left through a long roundabout path Higgins had discovered a few weeks before they had started to use the place. He had tried to think of everything and plan ahead, for which they were all now thankful.

At the end of that journey were provisions and transportation, hopefully still secure. Returning to the "safe" house was no longer a viable option.

5

April 29th

John Enman's headquarters in Fargo had been moved several times. Most of his communication equipment and computing facilities were in trailers and could be transported in minutes and resettled almost as quickly.

He tended to stay between the city and the Canadian border in case he needed to make a dash with everything into the North.

Many of his arms depots, factories, and assembly plants were located throughout the Dakotas, Montana, and Wyoming. His security force had been initiated almost from day one, and had grown exponentially with every incursion from the NSF and the Harrington Security Forces (now referred to in venomous breaths as the HSF).

The governors and other leaders from that section of the country were in constant contact, and the flow of information moved even more freely as they began to trust and depend on each other.

After the Battle of Montana, the HSF & NSF had stayed away for the most part. Any attempt to move into Northwest was met with an immediate and violent backlash. There were never any survivors on the intruding side.

Luke Masters, the Minnesota State Trooper who had helped Enman make it to Fargo, was now not only his Chief of Security, but also his confidant and chief advisor. His insight into what was happening had been extremely useful and through it all he had become vitally important.

Enman was not a micromanager, but insisted on delegating work and authority as much as was feasible. Many of the employees had been with him for decades, some from the very beginning. As he had helped people move out of the East and South into the Northwest and Canada, he had been able to assemble a good portion of them into the area so that he could work directly with them.

Eliot Norris and Jean Kilgore were two of his best. They were now intimately involved with the planning and staging of mock battles to be sent to the Northwest Defense Groups for training purposes. Both were ex-military and extremely knowledgeable and talented.

Up until now those three were the only ones in the company that had access to all of the records and the entire company data banks with the names and addresses of the NWDG and its leaders.

Since Harrington had usurped the former government, Enman felt he needed to allow a few more people into the inner workings of the group and deemed Masters would be the first and most qualified. After he was instructed in all of it, and his work panned out, they would consider a few more out of a very narrow list of nine candidates.

After Kilgore had gone over the background material and the logistics of the operation, Norris began to give him the necessary clearance work, complete with passwords and entry systems.

When they had finished, Norris gave him a data field and watched that Wilson could get in and work through the system.

"They are pretty much the same," he informed Masters. "You should be able to take care of anything on this level. Now we have something we need you to do with Alvin Neely and the Missoula Contingent."

256

He turned to pick up the instructions and Master pulled his service weapon.

"I won't need that," he said with a strange type of smirk. "I have everything I need now."

When Norris turned back to face him, he shot him directly in the heart. The fall backwards was complete with a resounding grisly thud.

Masters gathered the pile of papers and notebooks to leave the room. He knew he had to get all of this back to Harrington as soon as possible. With these passwords and entry parameters they could dispatch any resistance in the Northwest with little difficulty.

As he finished and moved to the door, a voice called to him from the rear of the room.

"I have to say, I am very disappointed Luke."

It was John Enman standing at the far end. Kilgore was with him pointing a large military rifle at Master's head.

"Those papers are worthless and the information we gave you is entirely wrong, so you really have nothing to take to Harrington."

"How did you know?" he asked.

"We didn't," Enman answered. "It was a test that was devised for all of you, and as I said, you failed."

A moan emanated from what had appeared to be Norris' corpse. He slowly pulled himself up to a sitting position, and turned to Kilgore.

"Next time you take this part. Even with the new body armor this shit hurt." He reached into his lab coat and pulled out the spent bullet.

Kilgore smiled and motioned Masters to go out of the door.

Waiting in the hall were four more security men. They escorted their former boss to a holding cell in the basement. He remained there for several days as they interrogated him unceasingly. What little information he had was extracted in a relatively short time.

He was turned over to the state law enforcement, which was still operating as before, and would be left in a cell for the duration of the conflict as a prisoner of war. Since he was a traitor in most of their eyes, he had no rights, and was kept on subsistence rations. He committed suicide after six months.

Enman continued testing the people on the list, finding that one more was a Harrington agent. He joined Masters and was killed by another inmate before the year was out.

When all of the information on the trials had been compiled, he alerted all of the NWDG contingencies with the results and an order to "trust no one". Further investigation found more than a hundred agents spread throughout the Northwest. They were handled in the same manner and had very similar life spans.

Trusted allies and members of the underground were also notified. The hunt for Harrington moles began in earnest. Many were discovered, and some escaped. Even though the numbers ferreted out were large, the sense of it all was there were many more to be found.

Every group was now on alert, and the initial edge this gave them was enormous, and as it would turn out, absolutely necessary for their survival.

6

May 1st

Ramon Ramirez and Governor Philips had grown quite close. In the beginning they had needed each other for the economic and political survival of California. The more they worked together the greater their friendship strengthened.

Ramon had gone from being a gang boss in South L.A. to a charismatic, hard working, and competent leader of not only the Hispanic community, but the population at large.

Through his efforts the majority of former gang members were now serving in the California National Guard. Most of them proved to be the same caliber of character as he was. They had just needed something larger than themselves to believe in.

Hundreds of Hispanic women from the old gangs and otherwise underemployed enlisted also. Most of them believed justifiably that their futures and those of their families and unborn children were at stake.

When the Guard members and other service people who were stationed in various parts of the world began coming home with ships, planes, and equipment, they were welcomed with open arms by the Governor.

Many military people from the Eastern part of the country came with them, knowing that they could do nothing at home but get arrested or court-martialed. The majority of them felt that the only way to save their hometown families was to be involved in an organized effort to free them. After the takeover by Harrington they knew this had been the correct move.

Most of the military personnel from the Western states returned to their towns and guard units as soon as possible.

Philips had been able to dig out a lot of moles in Sacramento and the former Silicon Valley; however, with one out of every nine Americans living in the state he knew their efforts were very superficial.

He and Ramon formed a Covert Task Force of people thoroughly known and trusted by them to work on this problem. They were very good at their job and immediately got results. When discovered, the Harrington agents were arrested as terrorists, and placed in maximum security.

The old-line liberal factions in the Bay area and Sacramento had people who were still core believers. They, as well as legislators that agreed with them, were given a choice, shut up or leave. Some were simply sent to the Iowa border and told to join their comrades. To accomplish this, Philips had to issue state executive orders and declare a form of martial law. After the Harrington takeover, few questioned his judgment.

Obviously the efforts of the Western States, Alaska, and Texas were affecting Harrington operations, and it was just a matter of time before they moved against the West.

Tying up the loose ends in the East was almost as easily accomplished as had been anticipated, since many of the former Americans were demoralized and desperate. There were thousands who objected strenuously and many were executed openly. This quieted a lot of resistance as the majority simply caved in and gave up, but thousands fled to the West. Many were killed in their attempts, but most made it by sticking together and protecting each other. The lessons in survival they learned would help them enormously in the near future.

After the NSF was disbanded, the greater part of them had gone home or otherwise tried to disappear into the night. There was no way they could run west. If their pasts had been discovered they would be arrested or shot on sight. For the most part, their lives were over.

About ten percent of them were such ruthless psychopaths, that they were allowed to join the HSF. It was not the wisest decisions on their parts. They were later assigned to the most dangerous suicidal missions and were eliminated over time. Their purpose was as cannon fodder, and to that end they served well.

Texas' Guard and Navy grew overnight. Since many of the service men and women had been assigned Latin American countries, getting to Texas was even easier than California, especially if they were coming from the Eastern coast of South America.

Harrington operatives had easily taken over Suriname, Venezuela, Cuba, and several of the Caribbean islands that had oil refineries. An attempt to include Nicaragua and Columbia had been thwarted by members of the Mexican security force who had infiltrated Central America and ended the coups before they began.

The rest of the world was not as clear-cut and it took months to learn who was with whom.

7

May 2nd

Higgins, Gloria, Jeff, and Barnes made it to their escape stash on the third day of walking. Their traveled path was torturous and dangerous, but they arrived without a major incident.

To their satisfaction and relief, everything was untouched as they had left it. It had been stored in an out building of a fellow underground member. After adequate surveillance and waiting, Higgins approached his friend's house.

Without hesitation, he asked him in and Higgins waved them on.

"Were you involved in that explosion a few days ago?" he asked.

Higgins nodded, and inquired, "Any word about it?"

"Nothing. Of course there was speculation, but more people were asking about Barnes's radio show. But now I see they were one in the same," he noted, seeing that he was standing in his living room.

He asked nothing further, and they offered him nothing more.

After a little more discussion they felt it was safe to head for the Utah border. They were fairly certain that if they made it there, they would be safe at least for a while. Colorado was obviously the one western state that had been penetrated by the HSF to a degree that had to be considered.

The friend gave them a suggested route that would take the party to just outside of Park City and a trusted contact in that area. He also supplied them with the locations of safe fueling stations.

The NSF was no longer involved but their experience back at the chalet dictated they keep to the back roads. The common feeling was that they should have little difficulty, but caution always had to be their first consideration.

Everything was already packed in a five year old SUV that should not attract much attention. They piled into it and drove off as the old man closed his door and went inside to pray.

They made it to their destination by late that evening. After again watching for any evidence of trouble, Higgins went up to the house he had been sent to and knocked. As before he was beckoned inside and the others followed.

He had been told that important individuals had come to see him and arrangements for their travel had already been put into place. They were to go to an air strip just northwest of Park City. A plane would arrive in two hours to take them west as soon as the sun set.

The new contact had them park the SUV in his garage and he drove them to the rendezvous point in his car. Shortly after their arrival, a twin engine Cessna landed and they boarded.

Though it all seemed authentic, in the back of each of their minds was the thought that this was too good to be true. Their concern was of course grounded in the knowledge that they had been betrayed by someone in their own movement once, and it could very easily happen again.

They were flown to a small airfield outside of Merced, California and were met by a large van. It took them a short distance to a restaurant which had been boarded up for years. They parked out back next to a nondescript grey sedan and entered the back door.

Inside were two men that had been waiting for them. Higgins had never met him, but he knew immediately that one of the men was John Enman.

He came to them and shook each of their hands.

"I am so glad to see you are safe, and so very proud to meet all of you," Enman began. This is Carl Murphy, special ops assistant to Governor Philips."

They all shook his hand, and Higgins asked, "What the hell happened back in Colorado? Someone had to have ratted us out."

Enman proceeded to bring them up to date on everything that had happened at his place in North Dakota and more. When he had finished he began a new train of thought.

"I know you have been through a lot but we need you to do something else."

He then told them of a secret broadcast facility that had been set up near Yosemite National Park in an area that was desolate and easily protected. A special unit from the California Guard had been assigned to keep it secure and running.

As with all of the National and State Parks, Yosemite had been abandoned for over two years. In the beginning it was a matter of funding, but later when all of government agencies were dismissed, the Park Services were the first to go. When things got tough, some people had turned to the empty parks to live in the deserted buildings, and try to eke out an existence in the forests.

The CG group would stay there and supplies would be shuttled in a manner that would not draw attention from any unexpected wondering eyes. Enman had installed a new system that at least for the foreseeable future would not be traceable even with Harrington's advanced systems. Also, a special type of booster had been added to all of the broadcast stations that for now negated any problems from the sun spots that were steadily intensifying.

He further told them how immensely important it was to get Barnes back on the air, and that he would have the ability to interview people as they became available to further magnify his points.

The nation was splitting apart and a whole new future was on the horizon. Every attempt was going to be made to defeat the Harrington government, but in the event that was not possible, they were going to do everything possible to protect the western regions and get family and others out of the new totalitarian regime on the East Coast.

That night they continued on to the new broadcast facility and were moved in before dawn. It was located in such a way that from the road and the air you could not even see that anything was there. A type of subsurface shield had been installed so that no satellite imagery could detect its existence and a slew of other detectors and equipment provided even further safe guards.

For the first time in quite a while they began to feel a degree of security, but Higgins and Gloria remained constantly on alert and immediately began to develop contingency plans as always.

The very next morning Barnes was on the air, and by evening a good portion of the world knew he was back and were listening to his every word.

8

"Good morning my friends," Barnes began. "Today we have some very good news. We have been able to set up an advanced system that enables us to not only add new broadcasters, but it also allows us to interview individuals world-wide. As far as we can determine, it is the only one of its kind functioning anywhere on earth.

Do you remember just a few years ago, all of this was common place? Free speech, round the clock news," he said wistfully, "Forgive me."

He paused then continued. "We are adding five new shows, and right now you will meet the wonderful people who are going to be bringing you the latest updates on world affairs.

First we have Guntars Wiesel who will keep us informed on the happenings in Europe. Are you there?"

"Yes George. Everything appears to be functioning perfectly," he responded.

"What is the news from Europe?"

"George, most of the Mediterranean countries, Italy, Greece, Southern France, Spain, Croatia, Turkey, and Lebanon are now under Moslem control.

France is again bracing for a hot summer, and anticipates more riots. A few of their cities have not even tried to recover from last year.

The United Kingdom has been under martial law for over fourteen months, as are most of the West European nations. Since the demise of the European Economic Community six years ago, little by little Russia has increased its influence in the Eastern countries. Last year's conflict with the Ukraine and its subsequent fall has demoralized most of them.

We will be developing more specifics and keep everyone updated as information becomes available. It is increasingly becoming more difficult to get reliable news, but we will do our best."

"What about the Harrington influence there?" Barnes asked.

"It is becoming more evident by the day that it is considerable; however, the Moslem incursions will be a thorn in their sides too. Thankfully they are still fighting among their own factions. If and when that is settled, it will change everything."

"Thanks Guntars," Barnes said. "Next we have Abdullah Ali Alazerha, who will be reporting on the Middle East."

"Yes George, I am working very hard to present the news from here with a relevance that the rest of the world can understand."

"How is that going?" he asked.

"It is going to be extremely difficult. As with any culture or religion, over time sects and factions evolve.

Consider that Israel bombed Iran in 2011, and then the old United States did it again last year and subsequently pulled out of the region. Iraq immediately fell into a civil war that spread throughout the region and then to most of the Moslem world. When their mortal enemy retreated to its homeland, they no longer could use you for the focus of their anger, and at least for now they have internalized it, as individuals often do.

I am preparing an in depth report for next week that might shed some light on it for all of our listeners world-wide."

267

"Thank you Abdullah, we will all be waiting for that, and thank you for your help in all of this. I know it must be tough standing alone out there."

"We have to do this George, if the world is going to survive all of this madness. You too have a massive struggle facing you. My heart goes out to all of mankind, my friend."

"As we pray we must pray together for understanding," Barnes added.

"Yes indeed," he answered.

"Next we have Soshi Moto who will work on Asia and the South Pacific. Soshi, how are you today?"

"I am well thank you," she said.

"I had the pleasure of meeting Soshi a few years ago when I was broadcasting out of New York. She was one of the most informed people I had ever met, and I know she will be able to help us all understand her area of expertise."

"You are too kind, George.

The tensions here are palpable to anyone who is able to get into the area. China has pulled itself back from an economic abyss more quickly than any other nation I know.

Korea and Japan have been crippled and it is only a matter of time before something happens between them or one of their other neighbors.

As always, Vietnam, Cambodia, Laos, and the others are just surviving. The results of the outbreaks of famine from the decreased rice production have been unbelievably gruesome.

India has had it problems as usual, and its unease from the threat from Pakistan on the West and China on the East, is certainly taking a toll on the nation's morale.

I too will have many reports to present over time."

"I'll be listening Soshi," he said. "You can count on that."

"Niels Hammond is working on the news from the African continent. Niels?"

"Yes I am here," he answered. "The reports out of this area of the world are bleak indeed. The Northern Countries are in constant turmoil as is the rest of the Arab world, and at last count most of the others are either under control of Harrington or will be soon.

There is really no one to come to their aid. In the past, when there was a threat of U.S. involvement that intimidation helped keep a lid on Africa conflicts, more than was understood. Since that is no longer the case, it has been open season for the thug dictators. Harrington now is either employing them or disposing of them. Either way the continent's vast natural resources are under its control.

All of the billions of dollars China invested here in factories, mining, and other businesses were nationalized into their empire, and that can not bode well for this continent."

"It's the same here in Latin America," another voice chimed in, "in the sense that we are a target of Harrington."

"That's Jose Verde," Barnes offered.

"I know Jose," Niels said. "The countries of Latin America must keep up the good fight. I hope they understand how important they are."

"I believe they do. Economically we have not been as hard hit as the rest of the world, and our leaders have been quick to act. After Madison's military left or stopped defending his pals here, the locals were for the most part able to fend off the Harrington attempts to take over.

The emphasis on the new Organization of American and Caribbean States has been able to cooperate in the fight of a common enemy. We were able to just this week remove them from Aruba and Bonaire. I will have a guest next week from the O.A.C.S. that will tell you all of the details from that battle.

They all feel that as much as possible, this alliance must be sustained in case Harrington solidifies its power in North America.

George, you and your people must stop them there, if the rest of the world has any chance to evade their tyranny."

"We will or die trying," Barnes said somberly, but inside his heart knew which result it would probably be.

The six of them discussed schedules and then Barnes continued with his regular show.

9

May 3rd to 6th

On May 3rd, the curtain fell on the states east of the Mississippi. The New Republic of North America as it was now designated issued a broad series of laws and regulations.

The basic tenets and scope of all this served to maintain control of the population. All new papers and identifications were issued. Travel was banned out of the country unless ordered by the government or approved by them, which was seldom the case.

Even though the old political divisions of states remained in name and for reference only, the concept of state government ceased to exist. In reality there were districts which were overseen by governors and government offices.

Iowa, Nebraska, Kansas, and Arkansas continued under their power and were well guarded by the HSF. The agricultural nature of the areas was fundamental to their success. Food production for this year especially had to be increased as much as possible as the imports would not be sufficient for another several months. This was in spite of the fact that Harrington had taken over other countries, adding the economics of their productions and resources into their family of nations.

In the short period of time leading up to this announcement, order had been secured and appeared to be complete in the northern and Midwest states. The fifteen or so insurrections ceased as quickly as they were initiated when the leaders and hundreds of others were executed in town centers on the final TV broadcasts.

Thousands of people were herded into reeducation camps. The end result was a very compliant society in short order.

The fact that the public had been inured into to complacency and abeyance by years of mind numbing television and film productions by the far left, an incompetent education system, and a lazy and liberal media made the transformation and subjugation of an entire society rather unproblematic.

The soul of the nation had been destroyed over the years leaving its citizens little self esteem and character, the very elements of humanity the far left elite had always espoused.

Having accomplished most of their goals in the East, they immediately set their sights on the western states. They felt that Colorado was the weakest link so it all began there. Its close proximity with the plains states was an extraordinary plus.

With the new setup no information was getting out to the western states; therefore, the movement of troops was easily hidden. Within hours of the closure of the Republic, ten thousand soldiers entered the northeast corner of the state and another ten thousand from the southeast corner.

The trucks and tanks moved quickly. The hope was to take Denver before anyone could resist. The desire was to capture the state and set up a front to annex all of the Four Corners (Arizona, New Mexico, Utah, and Colorado) rapidly and efficiently, without the loss of manpower as they had experienced in the North West.

This maneuver proved to be quit efficient and effective initially. Even though a valiant effort was made by the Colorado Guard and Homeland Militia, the invading hordes could not be stopped.

An immediate call went out to all of the surrounding states and the Republic of Texas for aid. The response was immediate and

272

strong. Everyone knew this was the first and most important battle of the new phase of the war.

New Mexico and Arizona sent half of their militias and State Guards directly into the southeast of Colorado. Wyoming and Utah deployed into the northwest corner. California and Nevada went straight to Denver to head off the attack.

After a short discussion with her advisors, President Willard sent the Texas Air National Guard to attack the HSF from the air. The Mexican Air Force was on alert in case they were invited to join in the battle.

The Harrington government had prepared for that contingency and an air battle ensued. Jets on both sides were shot down, but in the end the HSF Air Guard won the day over Colorado and chased them back to their border.

Several of the Mexican Air Force jets were waiting for them and half of the remaining HSF craft were destroyed. The rest flew back to Colorado.

Since the MAF had only been asked into Texas, the HSF planes were not pursued. This time interval gave the California troops an opportunity to get men and supplies flown into Denver and when the jets attacked the city most were destroyed with SAMs (surface to air missiles).

After two days of intense fighting, the invading forces pulled back but retained a large part of the state. An undeclared cease-fire ensued.

What was not known then was the whole attack had been a diversion so that over one hundred thousand troops which had been deployed in the North West to enter the Dakotas, Montana, and Wyoming could accomplish their mission.

Since Wyoming had sent much of its Guard, which was very large, to the Colorado border, the state was wide open and lost most of its land in the first two days.

The Dakotas did not fair any better. By the 5th of May both North and South Dakota were in enemy hands. Enman had just enough warning to get everything across the Canadian border before the downfall of the state. The Canadian Air Force was dispatched to cover their interests and shot up a small group of HSF that happened to cross into their space accidentally.

The Dakota Guards were forced back into Montana joining with their rather pissed off neighbors. With every able bodied man, woman, and child standing with them the border held, and the HSF was stopped short of getting into their state.

The ploy had worked and by May 6, the NRNA (New Republic of North America) had planted its flag in Colorado, Wyoming and the Dakotas. The future was becoming bleaker by the day. The war had now begun in fact, and had escalated in a few days into outright bloody conflict.

The West was now in the position of fighting not only for a way of life they cherished, but for their very existence.

10

May 13th

The fight continued unabated for ten days on both fronts, in Colorado and the North. It paralleled France in World War I, in that the battle lines moved back and forth almost daily.

No nerves gas was used; however, the losses on both sides were incredibly high and atrocious. The HSF lost well over two thousand troops in Colorado and thirty thousand plus in the Dakotas, Wyoming, and the border of Montana. The numbers killed or injured rose each day on the Free States side. Reinforcements continually arrived and joined the fracas.

During this period of time the nature of the society and governments of the attacked states began a metamorphosis that would continue into the future.

George Barnes began his broadcast with a very special guest.

"Hello my friends," he began gravely as was the usual character of his demeanor during this time. "We indeed have a lot of news today, a special guest, someone with a lot of extremely important information to present.

It is the former Lt. Governor of North Dakota, and now the Governor in exile, Alicia Fairchild. Governor Fairchild, how are you doing?"

"The best that can be expected George, everything considered," she responded.

"In case there is someone out there that does not know what happened over the past ten days, would you please tell everything from your point of view?" he asked.

"It's difficult George, but I'll do my best," she began. "When the Harrington forces attacked the Dakotas we had little time to react. I was at a meeting near the Canadian border and was able to be taken there to safety.

My dear friend Governor Bruce Leamer was not as fortunate. He was trapped in the capital and was assassinated on the spot with his staff and most of the state elected house and senate members that were in town."

She stopped for a moment obviously holding back tears. George said nothing.

"They did the same in South Dakota and Wyoming. Only Governor Hartman in Wyoming survived because he was in Idaho at the time. Both states lost fine wonderful members of their respective governments."

"You are now in Seattle?" he asked.

"All available governors and or their representatives of Alaska, Washington, Oregon, Idaho, Montana, and … we few from the Dakotas and Wyoming are here, along with special delegations from Utah, Colorado and California. We are forming an Alliance to coordinate the defense of our region."

"I believe the exact same thing is going on in San Diego for the Southwest," George said.

"Yes," she added, "representatives from Arizona, New Mexico, California, Nevada, Utah, and Colorado are attending with several people from our alliance."

"Why not a united group from the whole of the Western Free States," he asked.

"We had considered it, but at this time there are too many logistical problems to consider. Mainly it is a matter our ability to coordinate it all," she answered.

"It is my understanding you are actually developing an organization to be known as the Northwest Alliance of Free States, and you are the acting President?" he asked.

"Yes and the other states will be formally known as the Southwest Alliance of Free States. George, the feeling is that our people need some structured form of government to refer to and identify with. There are many sound reasons for this," she responded.

"I think you are absolutely right," he offered.

"I want to let the people listening know some additional facts that may give them some much needed encouragement.

I stayed in Canada for two days before I made my way here. The Canadian government has found over fifteen hundred Harrington agents in their country, even in the Yukon Territory. They are all in maximum security prisons held as terrorists. The Prime minister declared them enemy agents and gave them a status that did not allow them any legal representation even if they are citizens of Canada, just as it used to be in the States.

They are not taking this lightly at all. It was discovered that more than fifteen hundred ex-military work as mercenaries for Harrington, and over six thousand others are employed outside of the country. Orders have been given for any and all of them to return to Canada before June 1, or they will forfeit their citizenships and be declared war criminals and subject to arrest if they try to enter at a later date."

"That is all astounding," George said.

"The sad part is they are facing a similar situation as we did, many of them upon hearing this, immediately tried to go home. Hundreds were either executed or imprisoned before they could. I doubt if a lot will make it.

Canada has tried to stay neutral; however, in my opinion that will not last."

"What is next on the agenda Governor?" he asked.

"We are already working with the Southwest Alliance and have sent emissaries to the Republic of Texas, and Mexico, who as you know have been outstanding at helping with our defense."

"That is for certain," he added.

"At this time, I can't go into any more details George, but I want anyone who is listening from our people to hear this. Please do not be discouraged, we will overcome this enormous adversity, we will. And to any Harrington traitors out there, you will rue the day you began this. I guarantee it."

"Thank you Governor, and please come back anytime to update us."

"I will," she said, "and George, keep up the good work. You are one of the most valuable assets we have and I thank you as I know many others do."

"I don't know how true that is, but I certainly thank you for saying so, I sincerely appreciate it. My heart bleeds daily for those who are sacrificing more than I ever could. They are the real assets, and each and every one of them is a hero that will always be remembered."

"You are so right," she added as she said goodbye.

As the fighting continued, the world changed, minute by minute, more and more dramatically.

11

May 16th

As the battles waged on, events took place in all sections of the country that would mold the future into a shape never anticipated in any fiction that came before that era.

Harrington solidified its hold on the Eastern regions in a way that would have made old Joe Stalin proud. Resistance was simply met with force and death, and Liberty and Freedom became a memory.

Yes, there were still those hardy souls that would make attempts at fighting it, but they were more and more exposed by neighbors and friends that had greater interest in their next meal than honor.

Even George Orwell would have been shocked at the rapidity, thoroughness, extent of it all. Every human in that zone was afraid of his and her own shadows.

As each lost their home and was transplanted into a new house or commune as dictated by the government, the realization of their slavery put out the last spark of their humanity and spirit. They were subservient to the new society that would "save mankind", and more fully enrich their masters.

George Barnes began his afternoon broadcast.

"Hello, my friends. I have two guests today that you must listen to intently. My first guest contacted us to announce some truly important news. Please welcome President Marsha Willard of the Republic of Texas. Good afternoon Madam President."

"Good day to you also, George," she responded.

"Madam President, I have to say that even though I speak of all the change, it still hasn't quite sunk in how far we've declined from our glorious past," he proffered.

"I know what you mean George. I for one truly miss the good old days, especially when we were young. We may have thought it was difficult then, but this is… was, totally unimaginable."

There was a somber silence.

"I want to bring all of your listeners around the world some extremely relevant and imperative news and announcements," she began.

"Please do," he said.

"First, the Organization of Latin American and Caribbean States are happy to announce that all of the countries in the southern Americas have been freed except Cuba and Venezuela. Harrington agents have been ferreted out of most areas and have been imprisoned or executed as traitors. Obviously a lot more of their people will be found and handled appropriately.

Food production, oil distillation, and other vital industries are under the native nations controls.

OLACS has unanimously passed an intra-organizational edict that any citizen of any member country that is employed by Harrington in any capacity has until June 15 to return to their homeland or they will lose their citizenship and be declared foreign agents, and possibly terrorists. After that time they will face the consequences of such change in status.

It is my feeling that few will return as the promise and fact of wealth is probably too strong of an overriding factor."

"Speaking of oil refining," George asked, "you and California are the only Free States to have any appreciable capacity. How does the future look for that?"

"That is the next announcement.

The Northwest Alliance of Free States, the Southwest Alliance of Free States, the Republic of Texas, OLACS, and Canada have signed a formal Mutual Defense Pact and will be cooperating in whatever manner necessary to retain our freedoms. It will be known as the ATO, the Americas Treaty Organization after the old NATO.

Those countries with fuel production will be providing its resources as needed, and quite truthfully we will have enough for any foreseeable future.

Food, natural resources, and industrial production will be coordinated between our nations. We expect that we will be able take care of the needs of all of our people quite nicely."

"Wow, that is great news," he gasped.

"It was necessary for many reasons, one of which I must delineate now.

The Gulf of Mexico has still not recovered completely from the oil rig explosion, the subsequent spillage in 2010, and the idiotic use of dispersants, and it probably will not for another decade or more. As you know the turbulence of the last hurricane season stirred all of the pollutants that were thought to have disbursed, or whose existence was hidden for the past six years. It is indeed a sorry mess.

When the discovery was made last year that the combination of those chemicals and the oil had formed a lethal union fatal to humans and other organisms alike up the food chain, all commercial fishing was banned for the foreseeable future in some designated areas.

We have extended the ban so that none will be permitted at any time in any area. That includes waters more than fifty miles off the Florida Panhandle, Alabama, and Louisiana coasts. These waters must be allowed to recover and produce viable and edible life forms."

"That means another war front with the East, right?" he asked.

"I hope they will respect our wishes. If not... well, we'll see to it that they comply. At the moment, I doubt there will be many

281

attempts to violate the law, since most of their waters are still unsafe for any fishing.

The only catches allowed will be for locals feeding their own towns and people, and then only where it is safe to do so.

To secure this, we have several former Coast Guard ships patrolling constantly and a destroyer on notice for any major reactions or resistance.

Here is the main warning I have for others in your audience, especially corporations and governments to which this applies. Since the food production value of the Gulf is basically nil for now, we have to protect the three areas that can help feed us.

The Grand Banks is now off limits to commercial fishing other than from Canada, or members of our Alliance. These ships must meet our standards and limits. This area will be mainly guarded by the Canadians; however, The Republic of Texas is also sending several former Coast Guard Cutters to aide in that area as well."

"Where in the heck did you get the ships? How many of them do you have?" he asked obviously stunned.

"For now I can't answer that for security reasons. Suffice it to say we are well armed in many ways.

The second area is the Ross Sea off the coast of Antarctica, and the coasts surrounding South America. For now it is being guarded by the Chilean and Argentine Navies with the help of many other Latin American countries. We may have to depend on them for a large portion of our marine food supplies.

We discovered that Asian and European commercial fishing interests have been depleting the waters off Newfoundland, Greenland, and the North Pacific to a greater extent than previously reported.

There is now a moratorium in all of those waters of any commercial fishing from any country other than those in the ATO, and there will be adherence to strict limits within our group.

In addition we have extended our coastal waters to one hundred miles in this ban. Therefore, smaller areas such as the Sea of Cortez on the Pacific side of Mexico, is included. That area was brutalized by Asian fleets almost to the point of extinction of many species.

It will take several years to bring these areas back to full production as those foreign commercial fishing interests have all but depleted those grounds beyond anything reported by past governments."

"This is not going to sit well with the rest of the world," George stated.

"I'm sure it won't, but it absolutely essential for our future survival."

"Are you prepared to enforce it?" he asked.

"With everything we have," she answered forcefully. "The most important area is the North Pacific, and believe me when I say this, no one wants to violate our orders there. Pay attention, all of you who are listening. You will be given one warning. If you don't curtail your fishing activities immediately on notice, we will board your ships and confiscate any inventory. Any vessel not complying will be seized and sold, or sank. There will be no second warning."

George gave an audible gasp.

"This could mean…"

"Conflict," she finished his statement. "We are deadly serious."

"Thank you," he said, "Is there anything else?"

"We are involved in some other meetings and as we reconcile each situation, I will let your audience know."

"Thank you Madam President and God bless you," he stated sincerely.

"The same to you George," she said and she signed off.

"Wow," he said with a slow expulsion of breath, "as if there weren't enough problems, now this.

Before I bring on our next guest, I want to remind all of you that our brave troops are still fighting tooth and nail each day. President Willard didn't bring up the battles, but the word I get is that it is pretty much a stand-off, even though it is truly a bloody one.

If any of you can volunteer some time to help with the seriously wounded, it would truly be appreciated by all concerned. I am told

283

that most of the hospitals have incoming almost hourly. Remember they are all fighting for our very existence.

As I said that, it suddenly hit me again how strange all of this is. Here we are trying to get our lives back together from the havoc of the decayed ideology of the past hundred years leading to the Madison fiasco. Now we're fighting a war on two fronts, and we have to be concerned about foreign incursions into our fishing areas. I thought life was complicated in the old days. It was nothing compared to this.

Governor Leslie Philips has been waiting patiently for me to stop rambling on. Governor, are you there?" George asked.

"Yes George," he answered. "I was listening to everything you and the president had to say. Let me add a couple thoughts before we start. What she was referring to is vital to the survival of all of us, here in the Free States, Texas, and the rest of the Americas. The basic needs of food, shelter, and energy are a constant.

As Governor of the Great State of California, I have learned it all too well. And if you want to speak of change, it was not long ago that most politicians and especially the radical liberals were treating all of this so nonchalantly. Their attitudes and stupidity led us to our current situation, and if I may speak frankly, I damn them every day of my life."

"As you know I am a man who believes in repentance and second chances," George said, "but we will never know if any of them would have disavowed their arrogance. They were the first to be sacrificed in the New Order."

"It seems fitting to me," Philips responded. "Look George, I thought as you do for most of my life, but when I saw all of the good men and women who have died or been maimed and injured, making sacrifices they should never have had to do, well it has slowly taken away some of my humanity."

"I certainly hope not," George said softly. "I have had the opportunity to get to know you pretty well, and I don't believe that is the case. You are a very good man who has been chewed up and spit out by the wheel of life. You have to understand the sacrifice men and women like you have to make."

"Thanks," he said, "but one's humanity takes massive hits, and its survival is as precarious as our liberty and freedom."

He paused then continued.

"I have two main topics to discuss today. First, we lost a very good friend and a fantastic human being yesterday, Lieutenant Governor Howard Castle. He was only forty-eight. A massive heart attack took him in his sleep. He will be sorely missed.

The stress of what has happened to us weighed on him daily. He was intimately involved in all aspects of our state. When we started out, I don't think he was convinced of our situation, but the last couple years had made him a true believer. Would everyone please keep his family in their prayers?

"Absolutely," George responded.

"In conjunction with that, I want to announce that I have appointed Ramon Ramirez to replace him. The new Lt. Governor has been a steadfast supporter of the state and I know our recovery would not have been accomplished as quickly if not for him.

You and your listeners know I have spoken of him often. He came from the ganglands of south L.A. to rise above his situation and perform miracles. Right now many of his original recruits are fighting and dying for our freedom in Colorado. I just can't say enough about him. Also, I am so deeply proud that I can call him my friend."

"I've had him on the broadcast once, but certainly would like to hear more from him."

"You will," Philips said, "I am also appointing him our Official representative to ALOCS, and I can't emphasize how important ALOCS is, and will be. There are other clouds on the horizon, and we aren't the nation of people we were even three years ago. The truth is we can't go it alone."

"I don't trust that the Harrington Empire will be defeated very easily, and though they only appear to be waging a limited war for now. I know that can't last," George stated.

"You are absolutely correct. Whatever our successes or failures in these battles, they will not go away peacefully.

George, we were speaking of basics a minute ago. News and entertainment was considered a basic that would never change, until it did. Your broadcast has been the sole avenue for news for months.

When energy and electricity was rationed under Madison, and then almost disappeared under Harrington, most all of the broadcasters had to close. The only exceptions were a few low-wattage mom and pop stations that tried to remain on the air with generators. They were a blessing for the locals. Most of them, however, were destroyed by the NSF and later the HSF.

We still have to ration electricity, but I am making a special provision in that energy edict that the radio broadcasters may operate again. There are no advertisers, but the owners have promised to stay on the air as long as they have access to the power. One condition I made was that each of them has to carry your show every afternoon, and the world-wide updates that you have added."

"That's great. Thank you," he said.

"Hopefully as time goes by they can stay on the air more and can develop new programming."

"What about the newspapers and television?" he asked.

"I don't think we will ever see newspapers being published again, at lest not for the duration. And television is too expensive at this time."

"Governor, I don't mean to interrupt you, but we've just had an emergency status update?" he asked. George went silent for a moment.

When he returned he read a bulletin.

"Harrington forces made a bombing run on Toronto and Montreal. The Canadian Air Force shot some of them down, but most of the aircraft were able to retreat back to their own air space. The general feeling is that it was in retaliation for the help they have given us, but more than likely it was for the edict concerning Canadian citizens working for Harrington.

Governor, it looks as if the war has been raised to another new level."

12

General Higgins had finally received word from Mitchell Grayson that he was alive and well. He had asked for a meeting in Sacramento, and the General quickly responded in the affirmative.

He called Gloria Martin in and told her the news, and she immediately wanted to accompany him. Since the compound was so well guarded, she had no qualms leaving Jeff there.

With an escort of two soldiers, they traveled to their meeting early in the morning so they would arrive at dawn about three hours before it was scheduled. Since paranoia had saved their butts so many times before they wanted to scope out the area while they waited.

Two minutes before the time Grayson had indicated, he drove in alone, parked his car, and entered the small warehouse. The soldiers had inspected it earlier and found it totally vacant; however, the General and Gloria proceeded with extreme caution.

Upon entering the warehouse, they found him standing in the middle of the open space in the center of the building. Higgins waved the soldiers off, and they took a position outside, one in front and the other out back, out of sight. He and Gloria kept their weapons on Grayson.

"How are you doing my friend?" Mitchell asked.

"Fine no thanks to you," he answered.

"Sorry about that. I know you better than I know my own hands. I knew you would make it out alive."

"It was damn close," Higgins said. "How long have you been working for Harrington?"

"They recruited me just after I mustered out of the army," he responded.

"How's it feel to be a traitor?" Gloria asked.

"If I were, you would be dead by now. I've had a dozen chances to kill you two," he stated. "Could you lower your guns? I have a lot to tell you."

Higgins and Gloria slowly brought them down. She took a lot longer than he did, obviously not comfortable with the situation.

"In the beginning, I thought it was just a great well-paying job. After a few years, I was admitted into a higher security clearance. It was then I began to realize their ultimate goals.

There is a central planning committee known as the Inner Circle. Only they have knowledge of the entire workings of the company. To this day, I don't even know who 'they' are. It could even have been someone with whom I've worked."

He walked over to an old table and leaned against it.

"I tried to pass on information to the patriots, but I had to make damn sure it couldn't be traced back to me. A dead man is not much help.

I needed some more credibility to get closer to them, so I told them where you were broadcasting. I said a very reliable source gave me the intel. They know I have eyes and ears everywhere, and didn't question me. As I said, I knew you were going to be safe, you old fart. It would take more than a few would be ninjas to kill you off."

"What about my nephew? You knew he was there," Gloria chimed in.

"And he had you and the General. I didn't see a problem. Maybe I have more faith in you two than you do in yourselves," he told her.

At that point the front door opened.

Higgins and Gloria turned and raised their weapons again. They immediately lowered them.

John Enman stood there observing the trio.

"Am I late for the party?" he asked. "I would have thought you would have castrated him and hung his writhing body over a rafter by now. You want me to do it," he asked confidently. Enman had certainly changed since his days affiliated with the Obama and Madison administrations.

Higgins had contacted him for backup just in case. There were now over twenty men watching the building, mostly hidden.

They brought him up to date on the meeting thus far.

"Why break cover now?" Higgins asked.

"I was in DC last week. There is a lot you really need to know."

"How in god's name did you do that?" Gloria asked incredulously.

"I said I'm rather high up in the company. I can travel as much as I need to and not have to report a lot," he answered.

"What was it like? What's going on back east? We hear so many awful things, and don't know what to believe," Higgins said.

"What ever you heard is probably nothing compared to the truth," he said sadly.

Grayson filled them in and they stood there stunned. After a while they all found a seat and listened intently almost in tears.

From day one of the existence of The New Republic of North America, and Paul Curtis' presidency the changes started. The pogroms developed by the Harrington think tanks were put into service and implemented immediately.

After the announcement that new identification papers had to be issued, each person discovered the process was not an easy affair. Background checks were conducted and the results were compared to their answers on the interrogation forms. They had to list their names, addresses for the past twenty years, associations with groups and individuals, employment history, or the lack of it, party affiliations, major purchases, property owned, and on and on.

There was no way to lie, because Harrington had accumulated years of information culled from internet records, credit card and insurance companies including the national medical data base in Massachusetts, and of course the former United States records in all facets of the government. They knew more about most people than their own families did.

Assignments and adjustments began immediately. Medical personnel were placed wherever needed, and were more than likely uprooted and relocated to different areas; they were not to be working with people they knew. This was also the case for most of the professionals whose services were still needed.

Lawyers and accountants were not included in that group. They were reassigned to menial tasks, almost as a punishment for their former misbegotten lives. Since the only law was what the Inner Circle dictated, there was no need for courts or litigators. One was determined to be guilty as charged with no possible chance of a defense. Most of this work was conducted by the Department of Safety and Reasoning, an irony in nomenclature to be sure.

The company moved out the residents of the better sections of DC including the Potomac area, and the upper echelons of Harrington moved in. The only ranking recognized was that within the corporation.

Status was now as passé as fast food joints. Along with every other privately owned business, restaurants and eateries were history.

The New Republic owned the whole country, every nut, bolt, apple and orange. What you needed to survive and work productively was furnished by the state, and the fruits of your efforts belonged to the state. There was the catch of useful functional labor; hence, the demoting of a lot of professionals, in addition to legal and business people. What purpose did bankers, financiers, and the like have when there were no bonds, stocks, or mortgages to produce or service?

The same was to be said for IRS agents, and other non-productive government agencies which included most of the former bureaucrats.

There were many positions in the farming and maintenance departments, planting and harvesting crops, and cleaning streets.

Some adapted trying to survive, many committed suicide.

As the "Borg" used to say on "Star Trek The Next Generation", when there were television programs, "Resistance is futile". Any opposition was met with reeducation or eradication. The camps became very small very quickly, and many cemeteries were being filled to capacity.

As Grayson continued the other three were speechless.

"The one bright spot in this whole scenario, if it can be interpreted as such, is that with all of their efforts the South has not been totally subjugated, especially the backwaters and hills. Many of our original cells are still semi-functional in the Gulf Coast and Eastern Tennessee, Georgia, and North and South Carolina. It could be as many as twenty thousand, not counting their spouses and children.

It is impossible for those folks to move from where they live, and the members obviously won't leave their relatives to the HSF."

"Are they willing to fight?" Gloria asked.

"The short answer is yes, probably to the last member of each family, including the children. They simply do not want any of their people to be assimilated into the Harrington new order. Since the HSF will probably exterminate all of them as incorrigibles, they would prefer to do it themselves or go down fighting.

Most are the poor of those regions, white and black, that normally would make up a huge part of the military. Many are former soldiers, and they are well armed."

"Is there any way to use them in our efforts? I know this sounds callous, but if they are going to die..." Higgins couldn't or wouldn't finish.

"That is the reason I mention it," Grayson stated flatly. "They have indicated almost unanimously that they want their deaths to mean something. They want a well planned event so that they can die for a good cause. "

"Then they shall," Enman said with a tear in his voice, and a lump in his throat. "We will make damn sure of it!"

"There is one major problem that I haven't broached yet," Grayson said for the first time hesitantly.

"Harrington has always been into scientific research and finding profitable applications of it. Long before most of the governments banned cloning of humans, they had purchased or stolen most of the mammalian research and were making replications for wealthy individuals worldwide.

Some were for families that wanted a bloodline to continue; however, many were for selfish reasons such as spare parts as they aged. In those cases they never saw their offspring. The company simply raised them in a secret facility so that when the time came they could harvest the appropriate parts."

"Oh my god," Gloria put her hand to her mouth in an uncontrollable move.

"It was possible for longer than what you might have thought. Cloning of cattle, sheep, and other animals such as dogs were done legally long after the initial work on humans was complete."

He paused for a moment before he spoke again.

"I know this all sounds like sci-fi, but it isn't. Governments as well as Harrington have been working on developing biologic warfare for decades, and all of them have made considerable advances. The problems though were insurmountable in many ways. Most of the agents that worked well were also uncontrollable, uncontainable and therefore of little use because they would attack both sides. Many were also indestructible.

After the human genome projects of the nineties were able to finally sequence the entire chain, things took a disastrous turn.

Re-sequencing of DNA chains in plants and lower life forms to reduce spoilage, increase viability or productivity, and develop drug fabricating life forms followed soon thereafter. These applications were quickly attained and used for more dangerous purposes.

The public knew of the "Frankencell" projects that were trying to create new life forms. Success was fast and extensive; however, only the innocuous results were ever publicized.

Harrington, in many cases in conjunction with the government, worked on remodeling the biological agents that were effective. Sadly they were successful in at least two instances that I know.

One is a battlefield virus that kills within ten minutes and only is viable for four hours. It can be spread over a contained area, kill and disappear. It has to have very special circumstances, such as favorable weather patterns as there is no defense. It penetrates every fabric known, even gas masks and HazMat suits, and it is deliverable in explosive form.

I found out about it just a few months ago. There were still a number of initial containment problems, but I'm sure they are well on their way in solving that.

My worry is if a desperate situation would present itself, they may deploy it and not deem the collateral damage as a problem."

The eyes of his listeners broadened, tears formed again, and then they glazed over as the turmoil of emotions ran through their very beings.

"The other life form is even more diabolical, an altered bacteria that can be programmed for specific genetic applications. Theoretically it could be designed to kill only green eyed people with red hair, but obviously it would have more practical applications in their minds for racial selection. It could be targeted against blacks, Asians, Native Americans, and so on, very easily."

"At what stage is the development on this one?" Enman asked.

Grayson gazed into the distance to an unseen place.

"It has been complete for over two years, and is being held in reserves for future applications."

"What in the hell would they be?" Higgins asked.

"After they finalize the takeover of this country, my guess is world domination, without undesirables… such as myself," he answered solemnly.

"But most of the HSF forces are nonwhite, or at least Hispanic?" Gloria asked.

"That is why is being kept back. They need many of us to accomplish their goals. When that is completed, they will have an apocalyptic final solution."

The building was deadly silent.

"How can we fight back? What if we simply announce it to the world?" Gloria asked.

"Not a good idea. Even if you were believed, they would probably start using any and all of the agents to try and sustain their own survival.

I know where most of it is being developed and stored; at least my sources are convinced of it. They have been zealously guarding Iowa and Nebraska for all intents because of the food production capabilities. Two of those facilities are there. The other is in Massachusetts."

"Can we bomb them? Are they at all vulnerable?" Higgins asked.

"Obviously they are underground and impenetrable to conventional weapons, and direct attack is totally impossible," he replied.

"A nuclear option?" Enman asked.

Grayson nodded slowly.

"A series of tactical field strikes would at least cripple them and hopefully destroy or contain the agents until we could work out something else. I'm afraid that is the only viable alternative."

Again he paused.

"Each of you has probably already realized the potential repercussions of using nuclear bombs on our own people, especially in a heavily occupied area such as Massachusetts. Each of the facilities was built near large populations for that very reason. I'm sure they have begun building duplicate projects out of country so time is of the essence. And, all of the strikes would have to be simultaneous."

"Damn," was all Higgins could say.

13

May 22nd

Harrington had agents in place in Moscow for years. When they officially took over, it was a simple procedure to negotiate some useful contracts and treaties.

In exchange for a guarantee to purchase oil, industrial diamonds, armaments, and other goods, they would have the rights to establish bases on Russian soil to prepare for future attacks on other countries.

Neither party trusted the other, but it was a mutually beneficial arrangement even if it proved to be only temporary. Harrington needed them and they were not fairing too well in the economic arena.

Many of their previous clients such as Iran were not in any condition to be trading partners. Russia had no love for the Chinese and feared an attack if the opportunity presented itself.

The first base they needed was on the Pacific coast of Siberia. The Russians felt that when their presence was made known it might be a deterrent to China.

Obviously, the base was to aid in the control of Alaska, and the retaking of the Western States. Troops had started amassing there from the day the base was begun, but when Alaska closed the oil pipelines from ANWAR and other fields in response to the attack on the Western States, the gauntlet had been thrown down, and they went into high speed.

The Inner Circle figured that if Alaska could be subjugated and Harrington bases established there, it would be much easier to take the Northwest Alliance, and then the others. It was their version of the old domino theory.

They quietly transferred troops out of the Mid-Atlantic and Northeast states, plus added some newly trained recruits. They felt these zones were completely dominated, so by May they had amassed almost twenty thousand men, two destroyers, and a small aircraft carrier which they had purchased the year before.

Since very little of the U.S. military returned to Madison, they were starting from scratch. This had been factored in from the beginning; therefore, they had made contingencies by purchasing, renting, and hiring ships, machinery, and armaments from militaries worldwide. When the economies went to hell, much of it was attained at bargain basement prices.

Enman had hired several topnotch computer hackers from outside the U.S., mostly from Beijing, Eastern Europe, and Croatia, when he initially set up his group in Fargo. Though there wasn't much for them to do in the beginning except check his own people's work, he eventually had them develop ways to get into the federal system and then later Harrington's. The later was much more difficult and in some areas impossible.

When the Fishing Limits pronouncement was made, he had already disabled the security satellites that were still functioning, and most of the enemy radar units covering those areas. This meant that they were operating blind as was the company.

President Willard had stated in her announcement that she had sent a couple ships to help patrol these fishing grounds. For obvious security reasons, she understated the coverage. There was a large aircraft carrier sitting quietly in the Aleutian Islands and another off the coast of Labrador, as well as two in the gulf. Repairs were almost complete on a fifth. When they were finished, it would be deployed in the South Atlantic near Antarctica.

Several other destroyers were sent to each of these areas as well as other ships. Under the guise of these assignments, protection was in place for the Western Alliances, Canada, and Latin America.

Alaska had a lot of short and long range radar installations from the previous days of the cold war, and they were made fully operational so that most of the North Pacific was covered. There were a few blind spots, but it was better than nothing.

Unless Harrington agents had penetrated this system, the company probably didn't know it existed. There were very few people that were aware of it, and it was kept as closely classified as was possible.

The Alaskan Guard was on constant alert, not only because of Harrington, but also the distrust of Russia and the possibility of Asian confrontations over Fishing Rights. These units were mostly deployed in the Juneau and Fairbanks areas.

George Ferrell had built his Alaskan Homeland Militia into a twenty thousand troop unit of volunteers and was recognized by the state. They were asked to work in the Inland Passage sections, south of Juneau.

They were basically unemployed hunters and fishermen that were thoroughly pissed off, and ready to fight for any reason, especially for freedom and their own rights to exist.

There were always rumblings, especially in their ranks, to create a sovereign nation, but they were satisfied at the moment to be part of the Northwest Alliance.

On May 22nd the HSF started maneuvering into position for an assault on the state. Initial attacks would begin as an armada of smaller ships took troops into the Inland Passage and attacked Ketchikan. The reasoning was to attempt to draw Guard units from the North exposing Fairbanks and Juneau for air strikes and later ground troops.

They couldn't have miscalculated more if it had been intentional. Every last man invading through the south of the passage was sacrificed for absolutely nothing. The Militia finished them off and took no prisoners, because as President Willard had said, they were terrorists and should be shot on sight.

The fast acting response of the Washington State Guard captured every ship that had entered the passage, and eliminated every crew member.

Before the aircraft carrier could get within range of the capital, it was torpedoed by one of the destroyers and sank along with all of the aircraft, pilots, and the entire crew.

The ships carrying the troops into the passage were either boarded and captured, or sunk. Over ninety percent of the soldiers from the Siberian base were lost.

It was an enormous but certainly not fatal blow to the New Republic. However, there were to be some major repercussions in the very near future.

14

May 23rd

John Jefferson Custis stood on the knoll of a hill behind his house near Chatsworth, Georgia. He fought the tears that kept welling up in his dark brown eyes as he remembered many of the stories his parents and grandparents had told him of his family's past.

The first of his relatives were brought into Annapolis, MD about 1765 and sold to a rich land owner in Virginia. A man slave, who was to become known as Jonas, and the woman Martha, were sold to the Custis family when the original master died. They were allowed to marry and had a son.

The Custis family's daughter was destined to become the wife of a man named George Washington, himself a wealthy farmer. When Martha Washington nee Custis freed her slaves, this boy took the name of John Jefferson Custis. The John was for John Adams, Jefferson for Thomas Jefferson, and the family name. He was the first of eight of the family men to have that same name.

They were never referred to as John Jefferson Custis the I, II, or Third or as Junior for that would have been going too far in adopting the white cultural nomenclature. As they aged most took their turn as Grandpa John, Daddy John, or John (the son). Some of the men did not carry that naming, and they were mostly Abraham Jackson Custis.

After they attained their freedom, they became share croppers in Georgia, and were the first to live on this land. Subsequent to the first Civil War, each family member received their forty acres and a mule. Somehow they were able to get the parcels located together incorporating their properties into one cohesive farm. They began working the land on their own and had done so for over one hundred and sixty years.

As they were able, additional acres were added until the joint venture was over fifteen hundred acres. In all of that time, it remained entirely in the family. There were now sixteen homes on the land, full of their kin.

One son after another took over the farming as the elders aged. Not all of them went directly into it. Like his father, John had gone into the military for eight years. His Daddy John spent three tours in Viet Nam, came home, and never had a decent night's sleep afterwards. Through it all he was still able to be an absolutely wonderful father, and immediately agreed with John when he decided to enlist.

He spent six years in the Middle East and saw dozens of his military brothers die in front of him, all with honor. To a man (or woman) they all felt they were sacrificing everything for the good of the country. When ordered home with their tails between their legs, they never understood or forgave the politicians who had wasted all of those lives.

The man who was to become his best friend was born and raised just a short distance away, but they didn't meet until they were in Baghdad together. If they had, they would never have been close because of the racial difference. Eddie Mayes was as white as any Caucasian ever was.

They each in turn had saved the other's ass more times than could be recalled. That kind of experience changes things. In their case, it altered everything, and upon returning they remained close.

He and Eddie were leaders of two cells of the Patriots. When the New Republic was formed, they knew it was only a matter of time before they all would be hunted down.

A lot of the rural folks were abandoned under the Madison regime, especially after the two hurricanes hit the East Coast, and the new order never really saw them as a threat or an urgent problem.

Throughout the south there were close to a hundred thousand of them who had been left alone, but that was changing.

For the most part they were self sufficient. Some had gotten really good at smuggling and trading on the black market. A few had been arrested, but most were extremely careful. Those that were caught never gave up any information and were summarily shot by both governments.

For the past four months the reach of the "revenuers" as they jokingly called them had begun to spread out from the larger towns in all of the Gulf and Atlantic Coastal States as well as Southern and Western Tennessee.

The groups had taken a chance and held a meeting at a secret location near Murphy, NC in what was once known as the Great Smokey National Park, a range of mountains at the southern end of the Appalachians. They had decided on their plan of action and took it back to the membership who then presented it to their families.

It was unanimous. To a man, the black folk said there was no way in hell after almost two centuries they would allow themselves, and most especially their kids, to become slaves again. Although it was never mentioned, most felt certain, it would never come to that, because they had very little value to give to the state.

It was made evident to them when the new Health Care Boards deemed them as not worthy of any more than cursory medical care. Soon after his election Madison had therefore removed most availability of the few clinics still operating.

Yes sir, they knew exactly where they stood, right behind the shit pile.

At last estimate there were over twenty thousand of them in their groups, all ready to die. Including family members too old, too young or too sick, the number was closer to fifty thousand. They all knew it was a losing situation, but there would be a great deal of hell to pay first.

John Jefferson Custis was late for a planning session with Eddie Mayes. In his heart he knew he may never have another moment to enjoy the natural beauty of this land. That did make the tears flow, and he wiped his eyes unashamedly.

15

May 25th

Even for a spring day, the weather in the water off the Aleutians was rather nasty. The few trawlers working the area between there and Fairbanks had been moored at one of the coastal ports. No captain in his right mind would be working out on the waters at this time.

One of the ships from the Texas Navy that had been normally operating in its assigned zone was in the midst of having a shift change when a distress call came in to the tower. The message was from a fishing vessel that was taking on water about twenty nautical miles to the southeast. Without a second thought, the captain set a direct course to it. The next closest vessel was a half day to the south, so he had little choice.

After the Fishing Declarations Edict had been announced, very little action had taken place in the Northwest Alliance waters. A couple small incidents had occurred off the coast of Newfoundland, and several Japanese factory ships had been run out of the Ross Sea. Few if any confrontations had occurred and no weapons were fired.

The Harrington attack two days before had put all ships and ports on notice, but the moods had calmed after the bad weather had moved in to take everyone's attention away from those battles.

It was slow going. What would have been about a two hour run, turned into a six hour rough rollercoaster ride. Most of the crew had little doubt what they would find when they arrived.

From the beginning there was concern over the actual message, since no vessel name or country of origin was given. Only bits and pieces of it were audible.

All hands were armed and ready for anything. The ethics and laws of the sea dictated they check it out post haste, but nothing said they couldn't be careful doing it.

When their approach finally took place, they were surprised at what they found. It was one of the largest factory ships anyone had ever seen. Even in the stormy night, it was immediately determined by all who saw the giant that it was worth hundreds of millions of old dollars. God knew what it was worth in the present inflated world currencies.

It flew a Japanese flag, and all knew instantly there was going to be trouble.

The captain hailed the ship and finally got partial segments of further messages. When they were compiled, it was determined that the monster had developed a massive power surge and fried most all of the guidance and operational infrastructure wiring. They were using generator backups to try and broadcast their distress calls; other than that, they were dead in the water.

Since the engines had stopped and there were no hydraulics functioning, the control of the ballast systems was impeded and the entire crew was concerned that the ship would flounder.

The captain did not understand their apprehension, but it was a grand opportunity to take another one of these factories out of commission, and an impressive one at that.

It was eventually discovered that this was their maiden voyage, and even though the officers and crew were well seasoned, none had worked such a massive and complicated ship before.

The fear present was as much for the loss of the ship as to any loss of life. Little did they know that the first was an absolute certainty at present, or those officers in charge would probably have jumped into the ocean. Losing the ship would be a massive loss of face back in their homeland.

After a conference with his first mate, the captain decided that his initial perception was correct. He would watch and wait until the storm subsided but be prepared to rescue the crew if needed.

For twenty-four hours, the Texan ship observed and the other ship's crew waited terrified. They were as much afraid of what was to come as their physical predicament. Seasoned sailors were sick as the ship had no control and simply bobbed its enormous mass in the water.

It was jokingly referred to as the second Titanic.

When the skies finally cleared, a boarding party made their way onto the floating fish processing plant to find most of its crew in exceptionally bad shape. There were several injuries that needed care, and they were moved to the naval vessel.

Communication with the Alaskan governor in Juneau and the base commander in Fairbanks was finally established and repair crews were to be flown in as soon as the damage was assessed. It took over two weeks to get it overhauled enough to limp to a port near Fairbanks. When it arrived it had to be moored about two miles out as it was too large to dock.

At the time of the initial boarding, it was discovered that the behemoth had been working the North Pacific waters for over a month and had hundreds of thousands of pounds of contraband fish processed and frozen.

It was determined from the officers who had asked for asylum that it had been put into service several months prematurely because of the famine that was beginning in their homeland. There had not been enough financing to finish the checkouts and even some of the detailed construction. This was an historic hail-Mary pass if there ever was one.

Even though orders had been given after the announcement to throw overboard any crew found manning one of these ships, no one including President Willard had any intention of doing that.

Thought was given to granting refugee status to part of the crew, but not the officers. Eventually, it was decided to send them all back. If they were dispatched by their own people, that was too bad.

Of course the ship and cargo were another story. They were confiscated. It would be determined later if it would be sold or used, but it certainly was not going to be scuttled. It would probably be moth-balled until the moratoriums were over.

Some wondered if something this huge would ever be feasible. It would not take many runs to put a hurt on the affected populations of marine life in any given region.

When it was boarded the first repairs were to the refrigeration units. More generators were sent to keep it functioning until the remaining corrections could be made. The recovered cargo was divided among the states of the Northern and Southern Alliances and Texas.

A major question and to a degree a concern was because of its huge value, why had it not been guarded by aircraft or naval vessels?

Deep inside many in the involved governments was a nagging thought that this was a harbinger of a bleak and awful future. Again, fraught people do desperate and dangerous things.

16

June 5th

Jeremy Hancock and his family were your typical rural folk straight out of a nineteen-fifties movie. Their homespun manner and attitude was the genuine article. He was a good father, and she a caring mother to three boys and two girls, ranging in age from eight to sixteen. The family resemblance of all of the children to their parents was unmistakable and undeniable.

They were as close as any family could ever want to be. Of course the kids were trying at times, since that was the way God made them. At least that was what his father had said about him and his sisters when he was alive.

Everyday Jeremy was grateful his parents hadn't remained on this earth to see the sorry state of affairs into which their beloved country and his family had been thrust.

He had worked for years in a car dealership in East Cleveland, North Carolina. Driving there each day from his small but adequate home outside of Benton was a real pleasure. The trip was a little long, but he didn't mind at all. The scenery was nice and it allowed him to live near his mountains and muse of his many excursions into them.

Being born and raised in those forests he could not imagine a life without them. His mind just could not comprehend how "flatlanders" existed especially in the cities.

His job had disappeared overnight in Madison's big takeover, and he was forced to feed his family anyway he could. The two oldest boys and he had spent many days hunting deer and other animals to put meals on the table. Though they were not the only folks doing this, the abundance of game was still holding. When the electricity had stopped, they dried it instead of freezing. Somehow there was always a way.

A family friend had long been a moon-shiner, and Jeremy helped transport the alcohol to various locations in trade for staples he couldn't find or kill. He had converted one of his best trucks to run on the very booze he was carrying. It all worked out.

There weren't a lot of luxuries as before. Without the internet, a computer was of little use to them, as were video games and television.

He had also changed over a generator to use the clear liquid that kept his family going. Its power use was limited to such things as a washing machine and the cooking stove.

Never being a drinker himself was a wonderful blessing as he had seen what had happened to many folks. Their lives weren't bad because they knew how to fend for themselves. However, many people had lost the survival instincts that the hills had nurtured in the past. Some of them crawled into the bottles of booze that they consumed or did stupid and despicable things to their families, neighbors and themselves.

He felt guilty that some of that came from the merchandise he carried, but he had to take care of his family. There really wasn't a choice; at least that was what got him through the day.

Cleveland is the largest town in Southwest North Carolina, just down Route 75 from Knoxville. The HSF had a field office there, but they had spent most of their time and effort subduing the folks in and around the city. Having limited manpower, they had taken their time, and the surrounding areas were left alone. Without utilities, it was figured there was little real trouble the people living there could generate.

That was the approach which had been decided by the Inner Circle to be used throughout the south. It was a good plan simply because most of those folks outside the cities and big towns kept to themselves and just tried to stay alive.

These inhabitants were never considered an asset to the new regime, and it had always been intended that they would be handled at a later date.

That day arrived. The northern cities were well under control and slowly HSF staff and officers filtered into the southern towns. Cleveland reached a critical capacity of insurgents in May.

The need to justify their existence coupled with the pressure to bring the completion of the plan forced changes. Every day the arena of that action moved further into the countryside.

If they thought conquering and regulating the southern towns was difficult, they had no idea what was in store for them as the regime spread its tentacles towards the mountains.

Each day brought more bloodshed. These folks were not going to go quietly into the night. Most were subdued by shear force through beatings and separating neighborhoods and families. As in the north, buses ran daily moving people to where they were needed, to do whatever work was necessary for the Republic. Some were sent to reeducation camps, others to extermination facilities.

If resistance was met, they simply shot the man of the house, the mother, or an eldest son, and the rest would capitulate.

It was open season on the clergy since religion had been banned as soon as Harrington had taken charge. Being a man of God was now a capital offense. As they moved through the area any remaining churches suitable for it were converted to office or storage space, or if not needed, burned to the ground.

Their rationale was that religion gave the people hope, and by eliminating that source they demoralized them more quickly. It was right on the mark, and was one of their most effective tools.

In the beginning of June, a force of about one hundred HSF started working its way out Benton Pike NE from Cleveland to Benton. One after another smaller towns and groups of families were absorbed into the system. Casualties ran normally about twenty to fifty a day.

With all of it, the forces were getting weary of the repetition of the grizzly scenes though none would admit it, and their leaders didn't want to hear it. They were foreigners in a strange land who were once fairly stable men and women that were being asked to continuously perform those heinous acts until their humanity began to wane.

By the time they had reached Route 314 and the Hancock home, most of the force had been at it for weeks, some for months. The southern mission was more nerve-wracking and brutal than anything experienced in the north. Many of them that turned onto the road on the morning of June 5 were empty shells ready for most anything.

Jeremy had considered running, but he had no idea how to do it with all seven of them. He and his wife Beth discussed it and decided that they would simply give in and try to survive whatever was coming. They had heard stories of what had happened to others who had resisted, and figured as long as they were all alive there would be hope.

Two vans of uniformed men and an empty bus worked their way up the dirt road to the Hancock house.

As soon as they saw them, Jeremy and Beth came out onto the front lawn and waited. They stood there with four of their children not uttering a word.

Mark, the oldest boy had gone hunting in the morning as he had always done, not knowing that the troops would be there that day. When he returned his family was being ordered around by the HSF.

One of the men saw him coming into the lawn carrying his hunting rifle and shot him dead. Jeremy and Beth reacted by immediately running to him and were shot in the back. The second oldest ran to them and was also gunned down. When the girls and the youngest boy screamed, their bodies were added to the pile. Firing did not cease until the whole family had been annihilated.

The entire gory scene had been observed by a neighbor about three hundred yards away. He turned and ran to his home. In a few minutes he and his son saddled two horses that they had in their barn, and rode off into the hills.

With them went the story of what had happened, and the Hancock Massacre spread like a wildfire throughout the south, and became legend.

The fact that the overzealous men who had killed the girls and the two youngest boys were executed in public by firing squads did nothing to curtail the tide of resentment and fear the act had generated.

This confirmed the deepest fears of the thousands of southern Patriots, and moved them into their next state of mind.

17

June 7th

George Barnes faithfully worked at his unpaid job as if he were earning millions of dollars. His passion increased by the day. Some might have said it was manic. Whatever his power source, he was effective and he kept the world alert to everything that was available to him.

The changes Enman brought about with the additional journalists proved to be almost as successful. Hundreds of millions of people were listening at any minute. In the old days there were those who would have killed for those ratings.

He had opened the broadcast with the news of the Hancock Massacre. Obviously it was compared to Ruby Ridge and the Branch Davidian fiascos of end of the last century. It was the continuation of the same actions on a daily basis that set them apart.

The story of the giant fishing trawler had just been released in Alaska and forwarded to him. He used it to make light after the heaviness of the initial news. He did speculate on the possible repercussions but nonetheless made it to be a matter of pride.

After hearing from each of the foreign correspondents, he made a few observations.

"Folks, we had better keep an eye on the middle east. I know we have our hands full here at home, but is it me or is the whole world becoming thoroughly unstable?

18

June 8th

The Harrington Inner Circle had anticipated the edicts concerning nationals working for their organization; however, they had not expected the formation of ALOCS and the subsequent fishing bans.

These limitations would not affect them in the near future, since most of the food production was covered in their allied pacts, territories, and of course homeland farms. African exports of table fish were more than adequate.

Their major apprehensions were that the alliances would solidify the Americas against them and increase the difficulty of incorporation of the remaining states and countries necessary for their overall plans.

Though many had speculated the raid on Canada was in retaliation for the repatriation edicts, it was really to test the resolve of their Northern neighbors.

The one natural resource that would prove to be a future problem was lumber. The continental Northwest and Canada were the closest major sources of this necessity. Shipments from other parts of the world were determined to be extremely unreliable in the future because many were from increasingly unstable governments.

Continuing advances in alternative building materials were expected, but most likely not soon enough.

The next nearest supply was in South America, and that too was at least temporary a problem. Many of their agents there had been discovered and eliminated, but not all of them. There was a degree of hope remaining in that region for compromise or coercion. It all depended on the resolve and future cooperation of the members of ATO. That was the avenue they would have to pursue, finding a method of disrupting that alliance.

There were other resources that the depletion of their stockpiles would present future shortages and efforts were constantly under way to plan for their acquisitions. Bribes, conquest, and forced purchases were all on the table.

Construction of military equipment and vessels for several years prior to the government takeover had been contracted. Many of these agreements were fulfilled, but for one reason or another, the majority of them were not. The main hitch was again the instable of the governments involved.

They had been able to purchase a great deal of what was needed on the open and underground markets and store them in other locations, mostly in Africa. These were being deployed as quickly as possible.

Every effort had been made to determine which areas would be fortified and the timetable to be used.

The military efforts in the west were mostly for containment, not conquest. The manpower necessary for a total occupation was more than could be spared at that time.

Most of the U.S. military has returned to Texas or the West Coast, in particular the naval personnel and ships. Very few army units even considered coming back to their bases. Those that did deserted and went west before Madison was eliminated.

The New Republic depended entirely on foreign recruits, exclusively mercenaries of varying capabilities. This was planned from the beginning because regular troops might decide to go back to their native lands if there was trouble at home.

Any attempt at leaving the HSF or muttering about conditions was dealt with severely. This seldom occurred with the salaries that were received even by the regulars.

The Inner Circle had planned extensively and precisely, but as history has shown over and over again, shit can happen.

19

June 8th

George Barnes was almost ready to start broadcasting, but just couldn't quite get it together. He did not have to hit the hour mark exactly and his audience was used to him being a few minutes on either side of the time.

Typically he was still preparing a late breaking news event or wasn't entirely sure how to work in something that he felt should be included.

Given that he was still pretty much the only game in town, his normal method of attack was direct on, with very little segue from item to item. There really was no problem with any of it, but old habits die hard even when many of the memories are viewed with through drink fogged memories.

The battle lines in the west were fairly stationary and reduced to troops firing at each other continuously. If either side stopped the other would rush in so it went on and on ad nauseum.

Because of that the casualties declined considerably; however, those that occurred were usually gore fests as mortars did hit targets if fired often enough.

Aircraft had stayed out of it on both sides as neither wanted to lose the few they had for no foreseeable reward.

Barnes had visited some of the soldiers that were in hospitals from the front and he never quite got over it. It was easy to talk about things you don't see. After the experience first hand, it was a totally different situation. This was an enormous part of his problem initially on each broadcast.

The governor had wanted to send a close friend who was a therapist but it had been declined. He had said it was for security reasons, but deep inside he knew better. Many times he had wished there was an AA meeting available as he was the only known alcoholic on the base and had no one to relate to his situation. There was no way he could go off the wagon because for obvious reasons, no alcohol of any sort was allowed there.

Higgins had brought him some self help tapes which did no good. One of the other men was into yoga, meditation, and such and gave him a couple tapes of Tibetan monk health and chakra alignment chants. They seemed to help, and the dual note intoning was amazing.

He had just finished one a session of the chants an hour before he was due to begin. It hadn't helped this time. There was nothing specific, but his gut was giving him that foreboding feeling and he hated it.

In was fully fifteen minutes after the hour when he began. The studio tech and producer breathed a small sigh of relief as he started talking.

"My friends, I wish you well today. I am deeply sorry for the delay in opening the program, but it couldn't be avoided," he said, without going into detail which was absolutely bizarre for him.

"We have a lot of ground to cover including special reports from the other hosts on here. I asked them to join me so that we all could get a handle on what is happening elsewhere in the world and what effect that might have on us.

First, I have it on good authority that Ramon Ramirez is going to be a grandfather. Our congratulations go out to him and his lovely daughter."

319

"That was it," he thought, something light to begin. He couldn't believe he was talking to himself.

"Also, it looks like we are going to have bumper crops in the Alliance states this summer. We don't have the weather forecasting abilities of the past, but some educated guesses are that it will hold."

What he didn't tell them was the sun spot activity was increasing and Enman had told him that it was becoming more difficult to keep the signal perfectly clear. In addition, he had relayed that at any time it could harshly affect weather anywhere in the world.

The big unknown was in which direction the ensuing climate change would take, cooling or heating. Most scientists expected it would alter patterns even if it didn't alter the averages worldwide.

"I covered most of the Alliance and New Republic current events yesterday so let's go around the world in a few hours." He was trying to be cute and even he didn't get it.

"Now we are going to Guntars Wiesel in Europe. How are you today my friend," Barnes asked?

"I have mixed feelings. I am currently in my home country of Lithuania and I am saddened beyond belief. Most of the former East European states are being over run with refugees.

The numbers of Italians, Greeks, Turkish Christians, and others that are fleeing their homelands have been increasing monthly. Here in Vilnius we had over fifty citizens of Switzerland arrive today.

The Swiss have had neutrality from any conflicts for centuries, but at this time their whole society is being torn apart. They did not allow the unbridled immigration that other countries did over the past four decades, but there were some temporary Visas issued for employment as they have always hired outsiders for their menial tasks. Now, with Moslem insurgents from their neighbors, most especially Italy, the turmoil has arrived at their doorstep.

The Netherlands, Belgium and the Scandinavians have been successful in deporting most of them. They were roundly criticized in the beginning, but are now truly envied."

"Guntars, I want to get our co-correspondent Abdullah Ali Alazerha on here with us," Barnes interjected.

"Of course," he answered, "My friend Ali, how are you?"

"I am well thank you Guntars," Ali said. "I believe I may be able to shed some light on what you are reporting."

"That would be great Ali," Barnes said. "Where are you today?"

"I can not tell you dear friend for many reasons, and I do not want to even go into those reasons right now.

There has been a major development here in the Middle-East. A distant cousin of King Abdullah II of Jordan has risen out of nowhere to head a small army made up of members of several former groups from that region. He has stated his purpose is to reunite all of Islam and stop the infighting. He has met with a degree of success even though he has been declared a rogue by his homeland Jordan, Iraq, Egypt, and several other countries.

His new-found followers have been connecting with former cells that are still functioning in Europe. The insurgencies you spoke of are most likely of their doing and support. They are going to try and foment conflicts wherever they can.

I sincerely believe these are not good signs my friends. Hopefully, they will go by the wayside and disappear, but there is always the possibility the basic premise will take seed and grow.

Most all of moderate Islam kept quiet in past difficulties, but now many are trying to speak up and hold the line on this new cancer. They are now truly putting their lives in danger doing this.

I hope it is not too late now. Former President Madison exiled thousands of American Moslems last year which did not help.

The fact that the American Alliances did not follow his example, but instead have taken many thousands of refugees that had to flee to the Western states in and aided them, may soften the impact world-wide.

Again my friends, only time will tell." He stopped speaking.

"If this is the reason for the arising conflagrations Ali," Guntars added, "then we may be in extremely big trouble. All we would need is a major event and the entire continent could go up in flames. God help us."

321

"Indeed God help us," Barnes said. "When you think it can't get any worse…" He didn't finish his statement.

"Thank you both," he added.

They signed off and all was silent for a moment.

"Are you there George?" a beautiful female voice asked.

"Yes Soshi," Barnes replied softly. "I apologize but I had to compose myself."

"That is understandable," she replied kindly.

"I have been extremely troubled today," finally exposing his inner qualms. "I didn't know why, but I think I am having more and more trouble coping with this new world."

He hesitated again, and then said, "If I am feeling this angst, how in God's name is everyone else handling it?"

"You are just sensing your humanity and fearing for its loss, just as we all are. Please understand how important you are, and keep the love and respect from all of us as your anchor and strength."

"I will try and thank you dear Soshi," he said even more quietly.

When he was silent for too long, she began her report.

"George, I listened to my two colleagues just now, and I too am concerned. Here in Asia there may be even more problems arising.

China is making an amazing recovery, much faster than anyone could expect. Besides the economic improvements of the past two decades they have been doing extensive research and development in many areas. Agriculture, waste disposal, and health care to name just a few.

They have made fantastic advancements in new crops so much so that more of their harsher land can be used for growing their own food. They have a goal of being totally self sufficient. Though that is probably not going to happen in the near future, they have made enormous strides towards it.

After they had been the world's dumping site for hazardous waste all those years, they have also made huge advances in recycling and using these materials. I have heard unbelievable stories about some of it, and if true, it is earth shaking.

322

They have had some major breakthroughs in cancer research. So many, that I am thinking maybe all of those thoughts of American cancer research being stalled because the disease was such a giant business may have been true."

"I hope not," Barnes finally entered the conversation. "Soshi, how can they be stabilizing when most of us are just trying to survive?"

"For the past twenty years as the economics and their GNP raised, every person, business, and the government purchased gold. In the years 2009 to 2011, the quantities were staggering. That was one of the main reasons for the huge price rises of that time.

India also bought precious metals, including gold. They deemed the ownership a necessity if not a duty, especially silver. A huge portion of the world supply of that metal is owned there. Their economy wasn't as strong as China's, but it is recovering, only at a slower pace.

Herein bodes a potential problem."

"Are we going to hear anything other than latent crises today?" Barnes asked.

"I'm afraid not George.

Ali spoke before about the developments in the Middle-East, and as we all know Pakistan and India have always been mortal enemies. When the Kashmir province, which is mostly Moslem, finally separated last year, the intensity of the hatred increased exponentially.

India would have under normal circumstances never allowed this to happen, but with their unstable economy, internal political conflicts, and the possible threat from China; they had no choice but to stand back.

My friend this does not portend well for the future."

"I know Soshi. I know," he responded. "What of the rest of the area? I have heard nothing about Australia for quite a while."

"They are an island of hope in a sea of turmoil. Their major problem will be defending what they have. For the most part they are self-sufficient. Yes, their economy took a nose dive when natural resource exportation all but ceased, but they are more than surviving.

If they can hold on to their sovereignty, they will be a major player if a world recovery ever comes about.

The other nations of South-East Asia are in dire straits and the potential refugee problem for Australia may force them into an isolationist position. This could cause extreme difficulties with their neighbors. We have to watch this closely."

"More and more," he almost muttered.

"Take heart dear friend," she said. "Humanity has survived many dire situations in the past and I believe we will also get through this."

"I truly wish I could have your optimism," he told her. "Before you go, has there been any word about the crew of that huge factory ship that was sent back to Japan?"

"The Captain was allowed to commit suicide, the officers were sentenced to twenty years in prison, and the crew each got one year," she answered.

"What about the company that sent it out without finishing their work?" he asked.

"It had declared bankruptcy before this incident. However, the officers have all left the country. About half were foreign nationals and the rest were Japanese," she stated.

"No suicides there?" he queried.

"No," she laughed as she said it. "There is very little honor in business even in Japan."

She signed off.

"I am going to take a break now," he told his audience. "We will talk with Niels Hammond and Jose Verde later."

With that the broadcast went to music for a time, and then repeated the part of the show that had just aired. Barnes left the room shaking.

20

George Barnes' words echoed throughout the world, as the message, whether intended or not, was a resounding statement of failure. The very program that had given hope and promise unknowingly planted the seeds of despair. Though his inner conflicts were entirely reasonable, their exposure invaded all who listened like a virus. Whether any of it could be altered or salvaged was a matter for speculation.

Six of those who heard the broadcast were sitting in the back of a former convenience store just outside of Chatsworth, Georgia. John Jefferson Custis and Eddie Mayes were included. One of the others turned off the radio.

"Ain't that a kick in the ass?" he said.

"Maybe he was just depressed," Custis offered.

"Yeah, he was," the man shot back. "That's the whole point. If he is that way sitting out there in the Free States, what the shit is there for us here?"

No one offered any answers.

After a while, Eddie asked, "It looks like our original plans are all we have. After what happened to the Hancocks... I don't want that for any of my family. What are we going to do?"

"Kill every damn one of them Harringtons we can, before they get us," one of the others shouted.

"That goes without question Mike, but the real dilemma is how can we make our lives count for something? How can we maximize the damage to those bastards? And, most importantly how do we handle everything at the end?"

For a long while no one spoke, most of them were staring at the floor, and couldn't look each other in the face. One of them prayed silently.

Finally Eddie said, "There are about twenty thousand of us, maybe thirty thousand including the older boys and the more capable of the older guys."

"Add another ten thousand if you include the women who will want to go. Hell, many of them can shoot as well as us or maybe better. Besides, hell hath no fury like a pissed-off woman," another one spoke rather quietly, probably out of respect for his own words.

Of course each and every man and woman in their loose-knit group had discussed the situation many times, and most had made their decisions. After that, the subject was never brought up again.

The general consensus was that there was no way their kids were going to be enslaved or massacred by the damn HSF.

Everyone who had been able to do so, had gotten as much of their family to relatives in the west, but that was a small part of the total folks.

"I have word that there is something big going to happen, and that it is vital for the survival of the Free States and possibly the rest of the world. I want all of our lives and deaths to mean something if at all possible," Custis said.

"Amens" spread through the room.

"I still want to put a real hurt on them before we go. I swear to God I do," the first restated his anger.

Another round of "amens" resounded through the room.

"We have to prepare," Eddie said. "Hank over in Easton said the word would get to us about a week before we are to start. We have to quietly form squads and plan our attacks. From what I gather it could come down any time."

"Those ass-wipes are beginning to come this way. I heard yesterday they were fanning out from most all of the towns that have larger HSF headquarters," the second man who spoke added.

"Yeah that's going on," Eddie agreed. "I think our best plan of creating a real commotion is attack them in those central places, and try to strand the others on the outside. Then chew their asses up."

Heads shook everywhere, and they all realized it was time. They had to make some final preparations and plans.

"Eddie and I'll have a meeting day after tomorrow with some of the others," Custis said. "We'll get word at that time. You all had best get it out to all here, and say your good-byes."

Tears should have poured from their eyes at the thought of what that meant, but to a man they were too damn angry and filled with righteous hate to allow it.

21

June 8th

George Barnes came back on the air about an hour after he had signed off. He had sipped a glass of hot milk and honey with extra added sugar. He didn't smoke or drink coffee or it would have felt like an AA meeting as he remembered them.

He had prayed so hard that he was extremely tired, but feeling better. His main hope was that he could improve his on air persona. God only knows what his earlier angst had caused out there.

"I'm back my friends and with God's help we'll try to bring more hope to this program," he began, not knowing if he was gong to say. He knew his scheduled items but for one of the few times in his career he was winging it.

"I am going to bring both Niels Hammond and Jose Verde on now, if for no other reason than they are reporting from the southern hemisphere," he said, wondering how lame that was.

"My friends, how are you?"

"Grateful to be alive," Niels said.

"Feeling blessed, George," Jose added.

Their words helped him.

"Niels, please explain," Barnes asked.

"Well George, I have had to stay on the run here in Africa. It is not at all safe to stay in the north. I hear all non-Moslems are trying to leave those countries where the governments are controlled by Islam.

The problem is that everything south of these places is controlled by or under the influence of the Harrington Empire.

Since I began reporting on here I am persona non grata everywhere," Niels started.

"I'm not going to ask where you are or how you are contacting us," Barnes interjected.

"And my friend I am not going to tell you, with apologies," he said. "I have many dear friends on this continent or I would have been dead weeks ago, and I will protect them at all costs.

What I have discovered is that Harrington has been backing businesses such as mining operations and governments for decades, always behind the scenes. The dictators that have come and gone were placed here and supported with their money and influence. Of course they owe all of their status and positions to the company.

If any had ideas of independent thinking they were either overthrown or eliminated. Fear has ruled this continent and will continue to do so for the foreseeable future.

You have to understand the significance of all this. So many natural resources that are absolutely necessary for military defense, manufacturing, and the general wellbeing of the rest of the world are found here. For many of them, the only substantial quantities known on this earth are here. The company now has the rest of the world in a real bind if not now, in a very short period of time.

I have never understood why the American government gave such little thought to Africa, especially the so-called caring liberals. Maybe it was because most of the population is just poor blacks. Who cares if they are enslaved, kept under educated, or left to die of malaria and AIDS."

There was a moment of silence.

"I truly understand your frustration Niels," George said. "Your home country was South Africa, right?"

"Yes it was," he said. "I never was one to agree with Apartheid, but instead of correcting all those years of neglect and bigotry, a hideous form of reverse discrimination evolved. Not only were whites persecuted, but the black population was split into have and have-nots. In reality very little changed. Of course Harrington was in the background the whole time.

The bottom line is the whole continent is enslaved and with little hope of change.

Jose, I would like to stay on here and talk with you, but I have to move to another location immediately. I will talk with you as soon as I can George."

His signal was gone.

"God bless you and protect you Niels," Barnes said.

"George," Jose said.

"Yes," he answered.

"After that I am almost reluctant to give you my report," he began.

"If it has good news, for all that is holy, please do," he urged.

"Here in Latin America, it appears we have the most stable of situations. After centuries of internal conflicts we are working closely together. Because of the increasing power of the OLACS we have rid most of our countries of at least the overt influence of Harrington. Only Cuba and Venezuela are holdouts, and both appear to be headed to civil war within their borders.

The leadership in Cuba is in total disarray with the passage of the final Castro brother last month, and Chavez still has his country in a perpetual state of martial law but he may not be able to hold on much longer. All of his friends are either dead or near collapse, such as I said for Cuba.

Because of our freedom, business is recovering more quickly than anticipated, and our agriculture appears to be headed for a bumper year. Between our efforts and those in California we are going pull it all together."

"How is the A.T.O. working out?" Barnes asked.

"Fantastic George, with our combined endeavors, the borders appear to be safe at least down here, and the fishing bans are holding.

I have two concerns right now. One is that we may be developing into a target for the rest of the world. It is my understanding that there could be a worsening famine in the Far East. Also, with the devastating heat and conflict in Europe the specter of starvation could be advancing there.

Our good fortune could spell trouble soon.

The second anxiety we have is with your Free States George. For humanitarian reasons, as well as political, we fear for your ability to hold back the Harrington forces."

"Yes that is absolutely on all of our minds Jose, every second of every day," Barnes said.

"We will keep you in our prayers mi amigo," Jose said softly.

"Thank you, we appreciate that," he answered thinking, "That's great, but we will need a whole lot more than that."

22

June 15th

President Willard walked out of her office to a large meeting room a few doors away. It was obvious by her extremely serious demeanor that something major was about to happen.

When she entered all of the people seated at an enormous long table stood in respect.

"Please sit down," she said, "and thank you all for coming here on such short notice. I hope your travel was, let's say interesting." She smiled.

"Yes indeed, Madam President," said a respectable looking gentleman at the far right side. All of those in attendance nodded their heads in agreement with him.

"Thank you Secretary Ramirez," she said smiling.

President Willard had sent military jets to pick them up and deliver them to Austin, one for each of them, and two to ride shotgun on either side. She was not in the mood to take any chances. The whole thing had to have been an adventure and strictly classified. Most of their own governments didn't know they were there.

"I have called you here for an extremely important, dare I say earth shaking, event." She still stood at the end of the table as she continued to speak.

"I am going to introduce each of you so that you all understand who you are dealing with here today. Some of you might know each other, some may not.

On my left is John Enman. If you only know him from the Obama and Madison days, you are in for a surprise. Without his efforts, and those of my father Joe Boudreaux, we would probably not be sitting here as free citizens.

After he saw the light, the error of his former misguided life, he changed as no other man has in modern times. His hard work in communications and intelligence are the very backbone of our abilities to confront the heinous elements loose in our world.

I want us all to thank him profusely," she began to applaud in a very vigorous manner, as did all of the others.

"Thank you. You are all too kind," he said, doing something he could never remember doing before, he blushed.

"Next to him," she continued, "are retired Four Star General Carl Higgins and his associate Gloria Martin. Later you will come to appreciate the sacrifices they have made over the past few years."

She nodded to them, and they returned the gesture.

At that time she turned to her right and indicated the light-skinned black woman next to her. She was very formal in attitude and appearance, but as often is the case, looks can be extremely deceiving. She was a hard-headed hell cat that fought her very way into the position she now held, literally.

"This marvelous woman is Harriet Bailey from Jamaica who is now the Secretary General of the American Treaty Organization.

She and her colleagues overthrew the Harrington led government of Jamaica and in less than two months. They rid the whole island of drug dealers and other odious felons.

Her nomination and election was unanimous. This too is almost unparalleled in recent history. I am indeed honored to have met her, worked with her these past months, and delighted to call her my friend."

Everyone at the table stood and applauded her with the deepest respect possible. She smiled in return with a degree of appreciation that only she could have produced.

It went without saying that she now represented every government and citizen south of the Rio Grande. Their lives and votes in this meeting would be backed and honored without question.

"Next to her is Carl Mason, the current Premier of Canada. He and his fellow countrymen have saved untold numbers of American lives for which we are so grateful.

It was with a good deal of labor that not only did they come to our people's rescue with food and medical supplies, but opened up their wonderful country to thousands of refugees. Madison died without ever knowing to what extent they worked against him.

Mr. Prime Minister, we are not only appreciative of you and your fellow Canadians, we are so honored to have you as allies."

She and the others gave him a round of applause.

The next person seemed a bit uncomfortable in the midst of these amazing figures. She appeared to almost hold her breath as her turn came.

"Then we have another truly incredible leader, Governor Alicia Fairchild, the President of the Northwest Alliance of Free States. Cast into this role by happenstance, she has grown into a truly intelligent and knowledgeable head of state with the undying trust of her electorate. In last week's election she received over ninety percent of the votes cast. A compelling referendum if there ever was one."

Again they all gave her a loud round of applause.

"I don't think there is a person at this table who doesn't know or recognize the gentleman at my far right. From the streets of South Los Angeles to the state capital of California in Sacramento as the current Lt. Governor, and as of yesterday the Secretary of Defense for the A.T.O., Ramon Ramirez."

Again they all stood and gave him an amazing round of applause. Never in his wildest dreams a couple years ago did he ever think this would happen. He was still astounded. Standing, he applauded them and bowed.

They all settled down and took their seats.

"That may be the last time we have the opportunity to be this uplifted, and I felt it was essential to begin this meeting in such a manner.

My friends to my left are the only three people in this room that know exactly why we are here. Indeed there is only one person other than myself who knows."

The folks on her right looked at each other incredulous.

"I did not mean to bring you here on false pretenses and when you hear everything you will totally understand," she continued.

"All of the planning that each of you has made over the past weeks, and the preparations of your governments will be absolutely vital for the events of the forthcoming incredulous days.

We have a dire... no that is too feeble a term... a monstrous dilemma presented to us. If we survive, the results of this meeting could go down in history in the same category of events as the Magna Carta, the Fall of Rome, the shooting Archduke Franz Ferdinand, and... you get the picture. The other possibility is we could become pariahs of humanity for all eternity, the alternative of that could be total annihilation."

Faces fell, breaths abated; stares of disbelief were all around the table as she began to spell out the predicament that had been presented to them by Mitchell Grayson. In the end there were no longer smiles and hearts of joy, but tears and sorrow with no bounds. The pain on their faces was only exceeded by that in their guts.

The live and death decisions that they were about to make would haunt them for the rest of their lives.

PART 4:

Atonement

1

In was six-thirty in the morning and a bright yellow school bus drove over Upper River Road outside of Macon, Georgia. Everything about the scene would have been normal except for a military vehicle following it at a distance of about a half mile with three HSF soldiers on board.

If the bus slowed the jeep slowed, and vise versa. It mimicked the first transport exactly.

Forty-six passengers were crowded on the bus, locals being carried to the country seat and HSF headquarters. Not a word was allowed to be spoken, though no one on it was inclined to be very talkative. Most had seen one or more of their family killed just a short time before. The crews were out early and being very productive.

Some of the passengers were crying silently anticipating the worst, and they were most likely correct in their concern. Some had that dead look in their eyes. Others were basically catatonic.

As the bus slowed and made a sharp turn, the jeep did likewise. Simultaneously the bus stopped for a woman on her knees in the middle of the road crying over a man lying in a pool of blood, and an

338

old wagon loaded with tree branches rolled out from behind some bushes to crash in front of the jeep.

The soldiers were at first a little stunned then reached for their rifles and stood. They looked around and immediately lowered their weapons. Surrounding them were twenty plus men and women ready to blow them to hell.

They motioned the men from the vehicle and marched them down the road. When they cleared the curve, they saw the bus and their comrades and the crowd beside it.

When it had stopped, two of the HSF had gotten off the bus to get the woman and throw the man into the ditch. To their surprise he rolled over and pointed a revolver at them. At the same time she also pulled one out from under her waistband and blouse.

The men were considering a fight until they realized another group of people were surrounding them and the bus, locked and loaded. They tossed their weapons on the ground.

A rather belligerent looking woman motioned the driver out with a threat to blow him apart with her shotgun. The remaining soldier tossed his weapon out of a window without even the slightest indication of a struggle.

All eight of the captives were led to area behind a large boulder and were forced to remove all of their uniforms except their t-shirts and underwear. Three of the rebels carried the clothes to a group of their people so they could dress in them.

One of the men had gotten on the bus and told the passengers to get off. The woman just outside of the door had them gather in a group. She was a tall woman in her thirties with long brown hair. Her whole attitude was simply no nonsense, and was displayed in every move she made. The internal emotions of hate, angry, and grief ruled her very being.

"Ok folks. Here is how it is. Just over there," she pointed to a cluster of bushes, "is some food and water, probably enough for a day or so. From here on you are on your own. I suggest you run for it, maybe to the hills and hide. They will probably track you down and kill you, but you have a shot at it."

"What the hell have you done?" one of the passengers screamed. "They will kill us!"

"Look lady," one of the men said bluntly, "that was what they were aiming to do anyway. They had no intention of rehabilitating you."

"They're simply taking you to somewhere else to do it, so as not to rile any of your neighbors before they get them," the woman said, backing him.

"I don't believe you," the yelling woman continued.

"Oh for god's sake Wanda, you know damn well she's right. They ain't gonna do shit for us," the old lady standing next to her blurted out.

The first one shut her mouth, and then grabbed her two kids and began crying hysterically.

Finally they all began to walk toward the supplies that had been provided for them. Some were weeping like her, but most were simply morose.

One of the men fixed a silencer on his 9mm automatic and when finished began to walk to where the soldiers were kneeling on the ground with their hands tied behind their backs.

The woman who had riled up the crying woman walked up to him and reached out her hand. He looked at her and hesitated.

"Give me the damn gun," she said forcefully.

He handed it to her. She pulled back the slide and chambered a shell and walked behind the boulder. All that was heard were muffled pops as all fourteen bullets found their mark with deadly accuracy.

She simply strode back to him and placed the hot weapon into his hands. He immediately grabbed it by the grip and waited for it to cool, so that he could remove the silencer.

As the rebels were getting onto the bus to replace the others, three of the original riders came to them. They were the older woman, another younger one, and a boy probably in his late teens.

"You need some help?" she asked with a strong voice.

"We're probably going to be dead within a couple days ourselves,' the man told her.

"So what," she said, "I'm already dead. They killed my boys this morning and I don't give a shit about anything other than paying them bastards back as best I can. Believe you me I can outshoot anyone of you."

They believed her.

"I can vouch for these two," she pointed at her friends.

The three of them got onto the bus without another word, not waiting for an invitation.

As the old group looked on, the bus and jeep continued down the road with their new load.

2

June 18th

John Enman returned to his temporary headquarters in Canada. The despondency of the meeting weighed heavy on his soul. They had made the only choices they could have for the survival of humanity and the continuance of its freedom and liberty. It was the burden that would be on their shoulders until they were laid in their individual graves.

The preparations were almost as formidable as the final solution. Each representative was given a plan of action for his or her respective country or region. Enman's crews worked out everything for the logistics of the operation.

A signal had been sent to the people in the south eastern states. Just the simply realization of what they were about to do, the vital importance of their actions, and the unbelievable sacrifices they had made and were going to make for a world full of people they never knew, brought absolute respect and abysmal sorrow to each of the those who had participated in giving the order.

Never before had a nation or the world been this close to complete and utter annihilation, the future of over six billion people depended on less than one hundred thousand angry and desperate souls.

The few who knew prayed constantly for them.

3

Custis, Mayes, and their group made their way into Macon from the west on Thomaston Road after they had commandeered their bus and took care of the accompanying HSF. One of them had gotten off a round and killed one of the rebels. He was shot immediately and the others surrendered.

They could not use the uniform of the dead man because of the blood soaked appearance of it, so there was only one soldier in the bus. It was hoped that it would not be noticed until it was too late.

Four more busloads were converging on the town that once had a population of almost one hundred thousand people. After Madison's term it was down below ninety thousand, and in the past few months had been further reduced to less than seventy thousand.

Poor medical care, suicides, fleeing refugees, and of course the exterminators from Harrington had taken their toll.

The HSF had taken over Mercer University and used the dorms for billeting their men, the other buildings for headquarters, the field houses for temporary detention, and buildings near Tattnall Square Park for processing the captives. Normally the buses stopped in the park and the people were led across the street into Willingham Hall.

The plan was to coordinate their arrival so that two groups could go through the usual entrance procedures and hopefully take over that building, and proceed from there.

Two more would get there about twenty minutes later and surround the Godfrey Administration Building. That was where the main offices were located. At this time of the day the majority of the HSF were scattered all through the town and from one end of the county to another. The remaining troops were sleeping in preparation for their shifts.

The fifth busload would arrive an additional ten minutes later and take on Knight Hall which was northeast of the Admin Building. Custis, Mayes, and a small squad of other veterans had reconnoitered the area and discovered that the Amory was located in its basement. Two of them spoke Spanish and had no trouble eliciting that information and more from one of the grunts they had captured.

Their further plans were contingent upon these going smoothly. No one was under any delusion that it would proceed totally as intended.

They had a limited supply of silencers, factory and hand made. They did not want to sound any alarms or draw attention, if possible.

Protocol was that each captive was allowed a bundle of clothing which had been inspected several times before entering the buses; therefore, no contraband would be anticipated in them. That was where the weapons would be hidden.

Any success would be derived from the element of surprise.

At eight-thirty-five the first two buses arrived. The passengers disembarked and were led single file across Coleman Avenue. During their scouting in the area, they had noticed that the buses had pulled in shortly after each other but not at the same time. It was hoped that this plan would be readily accepted.

At least one person in an HSF uniform from each bus spoke Spanish and was prepared to interact with anyone with questions.

As the first group entered the building the guards at the front used hand signals and never spoke a word in any language. All of them were armed and at the ready.

Everything went well until they were instructed to throw their clothing in a bin at the end of a large hall. They had been paraded through a series of rooms which would end in them being stripped naked, searched, and given orange prison uniforms.

This was particularly unappealing as there were no women HSF in the processing area. Each of them could only imagine what else had gone on before this. Their initial anger increased exponentially as they figured out the obvious outcome.

They proceeded along with three of the uniformed rebels leading each group. Enough of them complied until they were strung along the entire length of the processing area.

By a preordained signal the action began. When she had been instructed by hand movements to commence, a woman in the middle grabbed her belly and screamed, falling to the floor.

Immediately when their interest was drawn to this noise those with the silenced weapons shot and killed every HSF in sight in less than ten seconds. Their guns and ammunition were taken from their dead bodies. They distributed to the unarmed and newcomers in each group.

When the scream had been heard by others on that floor of the building, a few more people ran in to see what the trouble was and instantly died for their efforts.

The rebels then broke up into squads of eight and searched the building from bottom to top. All totaled, forty-six HSF died in under twenty minutes. The building was theirs.

One of them had been stationed at a front window and signaled that the next two buses were arriving. He also indicated that three more HSF were entering the building.

The door had no sooner closed behind them than they were dropped by clean shots to the head so that their uniforms were usable. Three of the rebels immediately changed into them.

Groups of four were stationed at the front and back main entrances and all other doors were locked or barricaded.

When the next passengers began to leave their buses, seven of the uniformed men left Willingham Hall and went to the Admin Building. They entered as if everything was normal.

The lines filed past the landscaped front but instead of entering the processing center, they immediately began circling around to the back of the headquarters.

Those not deployed as sentries in the processing center left their areas and joined the rebels next door. The remaining uniforms hurried to the front of the lines so they would be available to enter the building first.

When they opened the door, four more HSF were exiting the building. They held the door for them. As the soldiers lifted a hand in thank you, and they were immediately dispatched. Their bodies were tossed behind some shrubbery.

All but four of the rebels in back went into the building. About twenty had stopped at a side entrance and another twenty continued on to a door on the far side. Those on the sides were waiting for a signal to enter.

Encountering no resistance, the first seven uniforms in no time at all had killed everyone in the front lobby, including the civilians working at the desks.

They had discussed beforehand how the non-uniformed HSF would be handled and it was decided that if they took the time to determine who was who, it would spell almost certain failure.

The ultimate factors making that choice were that anyone there either was working of their own accord or had been reeducated and were therefore most likely hopeless. Also, for what they had done to prepare for this day, none of them truly gave a shit about anything other than eliminating as many of the scum as they could before they died.

There was an old quote that the military had updated and used for decades.

In 1208 Pope Innocent III declared war against the Cathars in the south of France, felt to be heretics. They were actually another branch of Christianity known as Gnostics who believed one had control of his own salvation and did not need an organization like the church to do so. Not a healthy concept to hold at any time, let alone then.

When the battles began, it was said that Arnaud Armaury, Abbot of Citeaux, who when asked how to distinguish which citizens of the town of Beziers were Catholics and which were Cathars, reportedly replied, "Kill them all, God will know his own."

That fit this situation to a tee.

Maneuvering through the building, the combined efforts and quick action of the rebels brought the headquarters under their control in less than twenty-five minutes. All of them had come in through the assigned entries and had worked their way door to door, room to room, mostly using knives and the occasional silenced gun so as not to attract more attention, until it was unavoidable.

Two hundred and thirty-five workers were executed including fifteen more uniformed HSF. Those, added to the four from outside which had been brought in, outfitted more of them as regulars in the HSF.

There was the frequent stress titter loudly echoing through the halls, since a lot of the military clothes were small and tight-fitting on these rather large country boys. This tiny bit of levity helped some of their taut nerves calm down.

Again they were signaled that the last bus had arrived. They indicated to its passengers to go into Willingham Hall instead of Knight Hall. Now that they had a large group in uniforms, it was decided that a squad of them should go to the Armory.

Custis, Mayes, and six others volunteered to take that building. Previously they had drawn straws to see who would be leaders on this mission and none of them had won, if that was winning. It was decided that a small unit would be able to proceed more readily than a large one.

They each had automatic military rifles captured from the HSF, and partially hidden 9mm handguns with silencers. They left in two groups of four and casually walked toward Knight Hall. One group stopped and chatted for a few minutes and then proceeded onward.

There was no way to know if anyone was watching or noticing what was happening. Extreme luck had been with them so far, and each of them felt it would not last forever.

The first four went into the building where they met three men guarding the front. Raising his hand the main sentry stopped them. All three died quietly and were hidden behind a desk and two dead plants that obviously indicated appearance was not a priority in this regime.

Custis motioned for two of them to wait and guard the door as the next four came in and joined their comrades. Then those six started down the stairs to the basement. They wanted to have command of the Armory before they canvassed the remainder of the building.

Upon entering the basement they discovered four more men playing cards. They waved at them and at first they smiled back. It was probably noticed that they were not in the right size of uniforms or that maybe they were too black or white. Either way they died instantly.

One of the men found a set of keys on a guard. The others had made their way to the locked door that was guessed to be the arsenal.

As the rebel with the keys started to open it, Mayes said commanded, "Stop!" which he did immediately.

Eddie walked over and felt around the door frame and looked at every inch of it closely.

"I can't believe an advanced company like this would simply have a lock on as an important door as this is," he said.

The he found what he was looking for, a small sliding panel that hid a screen and camera lens.

"Bring me the guy that had the keys," he ordered. "The key lock is probably booby-trapped."

Two of them dragged him over to the door, and held up the body. Mayes placed his hand on the screen and his eye in front of the lens. They were scanned and the door unlocked.

When it was opened, they smiled with joy. There were enough weapons for a small army, including several full cases of silencers

349

and the automatics that used them. There were more than two hundred assault rifles, and a large number of SAM's, plus a big assortment of mortars, and more.

It would take them several hours to load everything, and they had to find the trucks necessary to carry it all.

Time was of the essence. After leaving four of the men to guard the front, and sending one to go get reinforcements, they began to canvas the building.

It was discovered that only a few more HSF and staff were there. After taking care of them, they sent sixteen from Willingham Hall to the building that was determined to be the laundry to acquire more uniforms.

That shop was taken very quickly and within another hour everyone was fitted with proper attire.

The remaining rebels were given silenced weapons and they proceeded to the dorms. It took almost two hours but every last sleeping HSF was killed. Only one had been awake and was in the bathroom taking a piss when he heard the soft noises the exterminators were making.

He waited until he had the opportunity to reach his weapon which was always kept near the bed. After firing a single shot, he died from the hail of bullets of four guns.

Everyone held their breath waiting for the response from the loud noise of the weapon's discharge.

Thankfully they were near the end of the last dorm. A few others had been awakened, only to find death next to them. They never had a chance to join in any reaction.

One other group of HSF stopped in their tracks and began to run toward the dorms, but they were dispatched before they got there, by the now fully equipped rebels.

Someone had found a can of white paint and had the brilliant idea of just touching a spot of the paint on the left shoulder of each their uniforms. It was hoped that this would help avoid the problem of friendly fire killing some of their own. You could not really notice it unless you were looking for it.

By noon the campus was completely in rebel control. Units were stationed at the first three buildings, the dorms, and the mess hall.

For the remainder of the day as HSF returned from one activity or another, usually a few at a time, they constantly walked into seemingly normally functioning buildings only to find their demise.

At the end of it all, six truckloads of supplies and uniforms, and four trucks full of weapons had been filled. They left the area in a convoy with six jeeps guarding them.

By midnight the supplies were hidden miles away waiting to be used as needed.

The remaining troops stayed until midnight and finished their grizzly work of eliminating the enemy.

When they finally grew tired and wary of possible mistakes from the exhaustion, and well aware and proud of what they had accomplished, they too disappeared into the mountains.

The next morning the results of their efforts were discovered and forwarded to Washington. Nearly all of the three thousand plus troops, officers, and staff had been killed and thrown into trash bins as a message.

This was repeated over two hundred times in as many locations at centers large and small throughout the south. Of course there were varying results mostly successful, to one degree or another. One in Biloxi, Mississippi was a total failure with every last rebel killed.

There was just cause to celebrate as they had truly put a hurt on the Harrington Empire, but as with most things in life the success would surely be short-lived.

4

The vacuum created by the catastrophic loss of over two hundred thousand HSF troops and staff forced the New Republic to react immediately and in a sense rashly.

This was exactly what the Alliances had hoped.

Thousands of units were pulled from every area of the country to quell this upstart rebellion. The largest percentages were from New England as it was deemed the least likely to cause future problems. This gave the Alliance operation a big advantage.

The subjugated populations of the Mid-Atlantic and North did not join the battle as none had an idea any of this was occurring. They were constantly kept in the dark. No information dispersal was permitted in their new societal order.

A decision was made to move troops from the Northwest and West. New personnel were arriving continually and could soon replace them. In fact the twenty thousand that entered the country the previous week in St. Petersburg, FL immediately began a drive into South Carolina.

Although they had no choice but to take these actions, it left them weakened in many areas. Every effort was made to maneuver the units in a safe manner; however, for the first time they were operating on the trickiest of commodities, hope. As is usually the case, it is a frail defense indeed, and destined to failure.

When the forces in the Northwest were reduced, the Alliance sent in everything they had, and for the first time Canadian troops joined them.

With the additional manpower, the front lines were pushed back within days until HSF control of North and South Dakota was ceded to the native forces. For the first time in months Wyoming and Montana were completely free.

The New Republic lost all of Colorado and any influence they had in the far West. What remaining control exerted west of the Mississippi River was over Iowa, Kansas, Arkansas, and some of Oklahoma.

A good portion of that state was freed by the Texas forces with the aid of a battalion of Mexican troops. This was one of the bloodiest battles of the entire war because the HSF had orders to defend that area at all costs.

The war for dominance of North America catapulted into myriad battles. Chaos was the order of the day, which was exactly what the ATO wanted and had planned.

It was entirely the result of the actions, valor, and self-sacrifice of the thousands of brave souls in the South who gave up everything to fight back.

Over the next days Custis, Mayes and their comrades were eliminated until the last one died in Greenville, NC.

That they lost their lives for the betterment of humanity was a certainty, and it would be centuries before anything of that magnitude would be repeated on North American soil.

With the help of her fellow rebels, the woman that swore there would be legions of HSF and New Republic people joining her in hell kept her word. When the dust settled, over three hundred thousand made that journey.

5

July 4th

The significance of the date escaped no one; however, after the events that would hopefully unfold this day, it would hold a much blacker meaning in the future.

Enman's crews had established audio links with each of the countries and regions represented at the meeting in Austin. They were state of the art, but with the ever increasing sunspot activity, the sound blared from the speakers statically like a space launch in the early sixties. To keep security as strong as possible, there was no attempt at using video.

They worked with a satellite over Canada and a similar one over Mexico so that he was able to join all concerned in real time. His hackers from China had come through with extremely secure encryption algorithms that even Harrington's people couldn't penetrate.

The basic plan was for Special Forces units dressed as HSF troops to infiltrate the three sites they believed to be Harrington biological research centers.

Their justified fears were that in this current situation the New Republic would be desperate enough to utilize their terrible

354

discoveries randomly. Therefore, an attack on them was essential and needed to be immediate and timed perfectly.

Three units were in route to each installation for redundancy as they knew that there was only one shot at making the operation succeed. Their mission was to pinpoint the strikes as accurately as possible and to hopefully reduce collateral loss of lives.

They were equipped with the best laser guidance equipment that could be found, targeting the exact areas Grayson had indicated, praying that his information was correct. Even though the idea was to do so within a two to three mile range, anything could happen. In that case alternative close range equipment was being taken with to do the job. If that happened, it would end up being a suicide mission for all deployed, and to their credit each man of them had volunteered readily.

There were many more offered to go than were sent on these operations, such was the valor of those troops. They knew if their families or friends were to have a fighting chance, it had to be done.

At least three jets were also dispatched to each site. Each was equipped with a tactical field nuclear bomb. Knowing that they were not all expected to complete their mission, the multiple efforts would help to secure a success.

"I've just been told that ground units are approaching each of their respective targets," General Higgins announced to all listening from Yosemite.

"It's too bad all of that great technology we had a few years ago isn't available. We could have watched them as if we were there," President Willard said. She was in her strategic activities room with two of her trusted advisors. No one else was in attendance, or for that matter even knew anything was happening.

It was the same at the other locations.

Secretary Bailey was with her Security Advisor, who was also her son. They were keeping it all in the family as well as highly classified. She thoroughly understood that she had the utter confidence of everyone in the organization, but deep inside, she had some trepidation that this mission could weaken that trust, maybe disastrously.

"Squad Alpha Three checking in. No enemy contact," a barely audible voice was heard.

"Alpha Two. No contact," another group reported. "Within two miles of target location."

"Can we speak?" Ramon Ramirez asked from his California bunker.

"Yes," replied John Enman in Fargo. "They can only hear President Willard, and then only when she wants them to."

"Those two squads are in…" Ramon hesitated double checking his code list afraid he might say the wrong word, "Sector One?"

"Yes," Enman answered him.

Sector One was the indicator for Des Moines, Iowa. The current population was still almost 200,000. The facility was believed to be under an old municipal building in the Northwest section of the city. It was constructed in 1972 by none other than Harrington Construction Company. This alone gave some credence to the idea of a laboratory existing beneath it. The original development could easily have been hidden in the building process.

Sector Two was at the center of Lincoln, Nebraska, population over 300,000. Here too, Harrington built the structure over the suspected lab in 1979.

The worst of all situations was Sector Three in Worcester, Massachusetts. The immediate population was close to 800,000. The target was dead center in the heart of the city. Taking no chances, it had been agreed just three days before five planes were loaded for extra surety.

Even though the bombs were close range tactical nukes, with the surrounding areas the possible exposure was almost 2 million people. The immediate loss of life would almost assuredly be a quarter of a million. These estimates were the cause for the sleep depravation of all concerned.

"Has the first group checked in yet?" Prime Minister Mason asked. He had joined the linked meeting from Toronto. His aircraft were supplying cover for the three jets coming from the Texas Aircraft Carrier, the Sam Houston, situated off the coast of Newfoundland, and the two that were leaving from Montreal.

"No," said Ramon.

The group remained quiet for several minutes.

"Alpha Four in position," a new voice stated. They were calling in from Sector Two.

Shortly thereafter another announced "Alpha Five in position"

Then Alpha Six reported.

There was still nothing from Alpha Three.

"Alpha Eight here, we're taking considerable fire. I and one other are all that's left." Muffled sounds of gunfire and an explosion were heard then nothing further was broadcast.

No one spoke for a long time, then Governor Fairchild asked, "What are we going to do if..." She didn't have time to finish.

"Alpha Nine, we've made it to targeting point, but we are surrounded. There must be security all through this area. We hear fire from everywhere. Signal set. Position will have to be defended." The voice stopped.

"I hope they can do it," Higgins said. We haven't heard from Alpha Seven. We knew this would be the most difficult and our information that this was the most important target seems to have been accurate."

"How long before the planes will be moving in on the objectives?" President Willard asked.

"Approximately fifteen minutes," Enman told her.

"Why haven't we heard from them?" Ramon questioned.

"They are to keep radio silence until seconds before the drop," Enman answered. "It is vital that as many of them possible reach their targets. We are still unsure how effective the bombs will be. We can only speculate how far below the surface the labs are. Most likely the materials in questions are in vaults too. Our best hope is that if we can't destroy the agents we can at least seal them off and make it more difficult if not impossible to reach or use for a protracted period of time."

Every effort had been made to have the bombings coordinated to within a few seconds of each other, but there were no guarantees that would occur.

Alpha One still had not checked in, and as time passed everyone accepted the fact that they never would.

No one spoke as sporadic reports came through.

"Alpha Three in position."

"Alpha Two here, we are just about, yes we have a go on our positioning."

"Alpha Six...," the report began but was interrupted by another.

" Beta Two, Sector One. We are under pursuit and need a go, now." The voice was strong but urgent.

"Beta One, Sector One. That's an affirmative here also."

The Alpha Squads in position responded immediately by lighting their targets.

"There," shouted Beta One.

"Locked on," called out Beta Two.

"Beta Three here. I'm hit go get them," another voice rang in.

"Target locked."

"Target locked," said another one.

"Firing," they both said simultaneously.

"Two direct hits. We're out of..." he never finished.

"Beta Two is down, and I just got it," Beta One stoically gave his last report.

Two small but deadly mushroom clouds arose over Des Moines, Iowa. The mission was accomplished, but the casualties were horrendous, much more than anticipated. Fifty thousand were killed immediately, and another hundred thousand died within three years.

Most of the leaders listening were in tears, and one of President Willard's people could be heard retching in the background.

They had little time to recover before Betas Four, Five, and Six checked in and asked for targeting.

"Beta Four and Five only. Beta Six stand by in reserve," President Willard instructed.

"Beta Six, roger that," Six responded.

"Target lit, locked on, and firing," Beta Five called out.

"Firing," Beta Four added.

Again, the night lit up over Lincoln and death busily claimed thousands more. Casualties were reduced significantly by President Willard's last minute call. She determined that with no intervention, the possibilities of the lab being less significant than the others was correct and tens of thousand were saved from a third bomb hitting.

"Alpha Nine reporting. Target is lit, but there are only three of us left to defend position."

Multiple shoots were heard.

"Damn. Everyone's out but me and I've been hit" More shoots rang out. "Get those planes here, now!" he shouted.

"Take that," he yelled over more shooting, probably his own weapon.

"Where are those planes?"

An explosion was heard and then there was silence.

"Beta Seven, here. Breaking silence." There was a tiny pause. "There are only three of us left. Beta Ten and Eleven killed minutes ago. Target was lit but now gone."

"This is Beta Eight, can't see target."

"Me either. Beta Nine here. What the hell are we going to do? They're firing all around us. I've taken a couple small hits."

Everyone listening found themselves holding their breath.

"Beta Seven. I have about thirty seconds. May have to crash, losing altitude. I need to know where. Get me a light."

Since all of the war heads were armed at the initial reporting from the Beta squadrons, any crash outside of the target would mean loss of life for no reason. Without control of the plane he couldn't ditch it away from the city. Their frayed nerves were about to shatter.

"I'm hit. Damn it," the voice of Beta Nine rang out.

"There. Over there," shouted Beta Eight. "The target it is lit."

"See it," shouted Beta Seven.

"Me too," added Beta Nine.

There was silence for many seconds, and all of them gasped for their breath as two of the signals vanished.

"Two hits." Beta Eight shouted. "Now mine. Eat shit Harrington." His signaled also stopped and all was quiet.

No one was brave enough to ask if it all had succeeded.

"Watchers in New Hampshire reports three bright explosions from their vantage point. They are in the right direction but no idea as to target destruction or affect," Enman announced.

It was a considerable time later before the results were established.

At the last second the remaining member of Alpha Seven was able to light up the target for the few seconds needed for the planes to establish its location. His squad's distant laser guidance equipment had failed and he had to go to the target and light it up standing right next to it.

Beta Seven and Nine crashed their jets into it with their armed warheads sending two simultaneous blasts into the sky. Beta Eight added his load on top of theirs.

He was the only one to escape from the area, but damage caused him to crash into the ocean on his way back to the ship. He ejected and was picked up almost immediately. For days, his was the only report available.

From the information forthcoming over the next two weeks, it appeared their goal had been reached. Whether the lab was totally destroyed or not would not be discovered for months.

Harrington was not able to use their biological weapons as was anticipated. They did however begin to retaliate in earnest and Canada was now at war with them. The fighting eased after a week of air raids from both sides.

Strikes were made into the Northwest Alliance and Texas. By their actions the New Republic declared they would not stand by and allow other interests to do what they pleased.

When the mushroom clouds formed over these three states, another era of humanity's existence came to an end. This type of warfare had never been used on one's own people, even against a renegade regime.

The world gave a collective gasp.

Even after the reason for the bombings was revealed, there were those who questioned the wisdom of the decision to take that action. The deniers of the existence of the biological weapons would proliferate as did those of the Holocausts in the previous century.

As is often the case, life and death decisions are made by true leaders without regard for their own lives and fortunes. No matter how important or dire the circumstances, those making them then must live with their actions.

Those brave souls sitting at that wooden conference table in Austin, Texas would never get a moment's peace or a restful night's sleep again.

6

July 6th

George Barnes began his show as he always had just a little more melancholy.

"Good day, my friends," he said. "I must admit that I have not had a moment's sleep these past three days as most of that time was spent on my knees praying.

I have asked God to bless all of those souls innocent and guilty involved last week, and grant them a place in heaven.

My heart goes out to those who gave their lives to try and stop the madness of the New Republic, and to their families who must live with their losses. I have to tell them that a grateful people, who are at least temporarily free, thank them all profusely.

Also, to those great leaders that had to make the decisions, set the operations into effect, and give the orders, thank you and bless you.

I know this will be difficult to accept, but please live in the knowledge of what you have accomplished for humanity. Don't give a second's heed to the naysayers that will come out of every nook and cranny. You believed what you had to do was correct, and from what I know, you were absolutely right.

The Bible says there will always be wars and rumors of wars, but it also tells you there is salvation at the end of your days. You all must believe this and strive for a better tomorrow with the hope of a decent and fruitful life for your descendents. For isn't that the purpose for which most of us live, for our children and grandchildren. I..." he stopped for a moment.

"My friends... I have just been handed a report that arrived seconds ago in the studio. Oh My Dear God... No."

There were a few minutes of silence as he collected himself. Every ear that listened did so in anticipation.

"My friends... just when we thought it couldn't get worse. The military government of Pakistan just dropped a tactical nuclear bomb on the Indian Army guarding that northern border.

India has declared war and immediately retaliated."

Epilogue

Throughout history and pre-history, human beings have had their moments of glory and time of destruction. Empires, ideologies, countries, races, and species have come along, developed to one degree or another, and then devolved or vanished: a few examples are the dinosaurs, the Neanderthals, the Roman Empire, the Kingdom of Alexander the Great, the Mongol and Ottoman Empires.

Most do so from the efforts and strength of continuing evolution, a specific man or family, or the development of a major ideology or religion.

Two hundred and forty years before Madison took office, a new type of nation was conceived with multiple parents, with varied backgrounds and ideas. When the United States of America was born, the world had no idea what it would grow to be; however, it was still an infant when forces tried to corrupt it and make it something other than was initially desired.

The founding fathers knew it would be extremely difficult to establish and hold a representative republic, a nation under the control of its own people.

It was a grand effort, and before reaching adulthood, it had truly accomplished miracles. Not only did "Life, Liberty, and the Pursuit of Happiness" flourish and grow beyond words on a paper, the idea allowed for the development of industry, technology, and all those circumstances providing for the expansion to the west and beyond this earth.

The dark clouds of pessimism were always there threatening to leave the horizon and fill the sky. With the effort of many hardy, far-thinking individuals, those attempts were foiled or delayed.

But when does a nation lose its soul? There are always those who would sell or steal it, but I think that more than likely it is a gradual process of giving it away.

Years ago I came upon a building that was used as a library, back when people actually had the desire, time, ability, and safety to read. It was there I discovered many wonderful things and let my mind develop.

In one book, written by someone called T.S. Eliot, was a poem entitled "The Hollow Men". The last part read:

This is the way the world ends
This is the way the world ends
This is the way the world ends
Not with a bang but a whimper.

The once admired and beloved United States of America never survived its formative years. Was it any one catastrophe, maybe the bombs at the end of the Second Civil War?

I don't believe so. My judgment is that over the last third of its life, there were those, most likely with good intentions that had ignored the warnings of the forefathers, those brilliant men and women who certainly had lived with government corruption and tyranny in their day. They knew what could happen with their creation, and tried their best to warn the future generations.

These naïve and ill-informed individuals over the last hundred years of the country's life campaigned for more adherences to the old ways. They wanted a renewed effort to have a land where the politicians and leaders always knew best, and ruled accordingly. Possibly they believed they were ordained by God to watch over the despicable lives of their subjects. Their representatives certainly felt that way.

366

Just when our infant state was getting its walking legs, the industrial revolution came along and changed the world as it was then known. Coinciding with the end of the first Civil War it enabled the United States to grow as never before.

Yes there were those that made money, in some cases extraordinary amounts, and there were the folks that suffered, as is always the case. However, something else began during that era, a developing awareness of a general societal good that had never existed anywhere on the planet before.

Advances were furthered in women's suffrage, racial equality, worker's safety, health, and welfare. The hearts and souls of the descendents of all of those immigrants from the four hundred years since the Pilgrims made their fateful journey created a nation that was emotionally deeper and more aware. Their good works as a people soon far outweighed the mistakes made. No other nation in recorded history had the track record of beneficence that the old U.S.A. did.

Within a hundred years of its founding, America became the brightest beacon of light in a truly dark world. The French even gave them an enormous statue to celebrate its achievements in furthering the human condition. Sadly it no longer stands on its magnificent perch in New York harbor. The New Republic eliminated all such fantasies years ago. There could be no indications of hope displayed anywhere at any time.

I have tried desperately to study any information I could to determine what happened. When did it all begin to decay? What generated the desire and means to compromise such a marvelous concept? Why was the baby literally thrown out with the bath water? I read that in a book once. It brought a smile to my weathered face.

My conclusions are as follows.

The Corporate Act of 1898, which was patterned after a multitude of laws in the state of New Jersey, was passed establishing that a company could be born, live, go bankrupt, and die just as a human. I believe that this was the opening scene of the final act.

The concept of personal responsibility and accountability was no where to be found in such an idea. Every owner of a stock company is answerable for the actions of that business. Not so with a corporation. Its stockholders can just sell or simply throw the ownership papers away, merely losing their investment at the most.

The establishment of the Federal Reserve System took one of the main stays of a society, the ability to create and control money, from its owners, the citizenry, and gave it to a private company. With the stroke of Woodrow Wilson's pen, the banks were no longer beholding to anyone. The ability to print and lend currency, and charge interest on the fictitious funds was a potent tool for corruption and the wielding of power.

Through foreclosures and other such tactics, the financial system run by these nefarious people was able to steal money, businesses, farms, and lands from the citizenry from the time of the Great Depression until the collapse of the country. This was not only despicable but a plague on the nation.

I have read that many economists tried to get across that the concept of a private central banking system was inevitably a self-ruinous flawed scheme; however, no one listened. The forces of money and power were just too strong.

The attempt at the League of Nations, and the eventual founding of the United Nations served to deplete over time the sovereignty of the productive and responsible nations. This was for the benefit of the others who had no pronounced intentions other than what they could conjure and blackmail from them.

No matter what the reason, for a people to remain at liberty and free, they must have sovereign soil upon which to live.

The most destructive work had to be the bypassing of the Constitution and the negating of its influence and guiding hand in modern times. Using the Interstate Commerce Clause and the legal concept of precedence, the Anti-Constitutionalists were able to in effect relinquish the constitutionality of law, and centralize federal government control as no communist nation had been able to do.

By interfering in and regulating every aspect of human life and behavior through the three federal branches of government, the citizens were destined to lose those very ideas that gave them hope, the God-given rights of "Life, Liberty, and the Pursuit of Happiness."

I know I have repeated myself with that, but if anyone ever reads this and understands what happened, and what we lost, then I will be glad to write it a thousand times.

Another reference I read had many of the quotes of a former president by the name of Ronald Reagan. He said in 1964, "*If we lose freedom here, there is no place to escape to. This is the last stand on earth. And this idea that government is beholden to the people, that it has no other source of power except to sovereign people, is still the newest and most unique idea in the long history of man's relation to man.*"

Sometime before his first term in office as president he was quoted as saying, "*Freedom is a fragile thing and is never more than a generation away from extinction. It is not ours by inheritance; it must be fought for and defended by each generation, for it comes only once to a people. Those who have known freedom and then lost it have never known it again.*"

President Reagan was entirely right about the life expectancy of freedom. A spark of liberty remained in the Alliances, Texas, and most of the ATO, but that was basically all that existed in the entire world.

I would tell you what happened next, but that dear reader is a story for another time.

The End... of the Beginning

www.ingramcontent.com/pod-product-compliance
Lightning Source LLC
Chambersburg PA
CBHW070753280626

47162CB00016B/261